THE SELECTED WORKS OF
ABDULLAH THE COSSACK

THE SELECTED WORKS OF ABDULLAH THE COSSACK

H.M NAQVI

FOURTH ESTATE · *New Delhi*

First published in India in 2019 by Fourth Estate
An imprint of *HarperCollins* Publishers

Building 10, Tower A, 4th Floor, DLF Cyber City, Phase II,
Gurugram Haryana – 122002, India
www.harpercollins.co.in

2 4 6 8 10 9 7 5 3 1

P-ISBN: 978-93-5302-595-3
E-ISBN: 978-93-5302-616-5

Typeset in 11.5/15 Adobe Jenson Pro at
Manipal Digital Systems, Manipal

Printed and bound at
MicroPrints India, New Delhi

To Zafar Iqbal and Akbar Naqvi

NB: Dear reader, I'm not a writer or intellectual. I'm a doctor, a medical doctor, an ophthalmologist, not a PhD. But I'm not entirely unschooled in scholarly matters: I can distinguish between a nota bene and an afterword, as I was once a student of literature and intellectual history myself. I have to come clean about my qualifications because I'm the one who has compiled this volume. Some years ago, I received a hefty package in the post, but given my professional commitments and family responsibilities, the project has taken time. Organizing the texts into a cogent manuscript, glossary, table and all, has also taken some doing. I don't think I need to delve into the mechanics of the process here, but I would like to say that I've tried my best to honour the work and its author. The reader should understand that there is no manual for such an endeavour, and this is no ordinary opus, so please excuse any editorial errors or lapses of judgment.

—BB

FOREWORD
(AND BACKWARD?)

IT IS SAID THAT cities are founded by gods, kings, heroes, but Currachee[1] emerges from nothing, from stories. Indeed, one hears stories about Lord Ram's sojourn in the verdant cove known since as Aram Bagh, about the fag end of Alexander the Greek's bloody adventurism,[2] about that lad Moriro who saved the coast with steely ingenuity from a monstrous rampaging shark. But the fact of the matter is Currachee, like Calcutta, like Shanghai, was a modest entrepôt when the Britishers happened upon it a couple hundred years ago. Although expelled on several occasions by the hardy

1. This orthographic tic can be attributed to my affinity for the sonorous, indeed alliterative quality of the colonial appellation for the city—after all, I came of age during the Raj—but the long and short of it is that it's my city and I'll call it what I want. I can, however, mention other variations in passing: Karachal, Khor-e-Ali, Kalachi-Jo-Ghote, Crotchey, Kiranchi. A fisherman once told me that when his people were taking the Brits around the harbour, they kept asking 'What's this place?' viz., *Kroch hi tho?* but you can choose to call it what you like, disregard the fallibilist imperative or, for that matter, disregard all the postscripta on offer—it doesn't really matter to me.

2. I have it on good authority from a Poonjabi historian—they are a nation of historians, aren't they?—that the Greek was mortally wounded by a spear belonging to a mighty kinsman of yore who proclaimed, teeth-gritted, *Twadi aysi di taysee.* It's admittedly an apocryphal episode in the Annals of Recorded History. But you never know.

denizens, the blighters were intent on seizing the environs by hook or crook for the natural harbour promised great geopolitical potential. The community swelled from a few thousand souls in 1845 (when work began on St. Patrick's Cathedral) to millions today: you can fit the populations of Norway, New Zealand, Uruguay, Paraguay and the Republic of Congo (Brazzaville) into the city on a good day and have space left over. Due to the great demand for cotton during the American Civil War, a railway line was laid here and everyone knows that once you lay down tracks, the Train of Change barrels through. By the time our Empress Market became the second largest vegetable market in the world, my grandfather, a dry goods merchant, had set up shop there—tea, tobacco, coir, fibre, second-hand pantaloons—grafting our history on to that of the city.

But I am more phenomenologist than historian, less concerned with Who Did What & What Happened When than with the more discreet, indeed noble investigations—nary the chota chota but the mota mota.[3] For instance, the Mythopoetic Legacy of Abdullah Shah Ghazi (RA), the patron saint of my city, is one of the matters hitherto ignored by historians, pundits and punters alike, suggesting a variety of perversity that eclipses the newsworthy issues that vex the denizens of Our Broad Swath of the World. It is as if in this savage, insensible, this distracted age, we have become obsessed with anecdotal indicators, hermeneutic lint, ignoring What Makes Us What We Are, indeed, What Makes the World What It Is.

Consequently, I have been attempting to reify certain truths on the page, an endeavour that can keep me up from the onset of whisky twilight to the baleful call to morning prayer that animates the resident cock, the murder of crows, until my piles are damp and sore,

---

3. I have done some work on the Uses of Mother's Milk in Musalman Jurisprudence, for instance, the Zoroastrian Intellectual Traditions that Inform the Yazidis of Georgia, and the Leitmotif of Our Swath of the World in Hollywood (from *The Man Who Would Be King* to *Bhowani Junction*).

my extremities rosy with mosquito bites. When sleep eludes—my GP avers it has to do with the Circadian Rhythms—I observe the local nightlife from my perch, from the transvestite troubadours chanting vulgar odes on the street to the cockroaches pressed together like dried petals by my varicose foot. There have indeed been times when I have sensed daybreak only by the quality of light refracted through the dirty stained-glass windows, spring by the flutter of hummingbird wings, but I am afraid I have also been waylaid by anxiety, lassitude, contretemps and the intermittent shove of history, here in the bosom of the vast, cluttered, famously custard-yellow enclave known to all and sundry as the Sunset Lodge.[4]

---

4. The Lodge is situated en route to the zoo in the erstwhile genteel environs of Garden East. If you lose your way, you could end up in one of the largest urban necropolises in the world. There is a discrete, walled Jewish cemetery in the neighbourhood as well, a stone's throw from the site of the old synagogue. Only I can take you there now, but in the old days everyone knew: shuttling past, the bus conductor would holler, *Yahoodi Masjid! Yahoodi Masjid!* as if it were the most natural thing in the world. One of the best roadside joints is located down the street where they serve that thick haleem that burns your esophageal cavity if you wolf it down too quickly. The other landmark amongst the squat untidy flats that mar the topography is the sprawling police station mainly manned by gruff northern tribes. Once upon a time, Garden was populated by a decent breed: recall the Mehtanis off Pedro D'Souza Road, the Souvenir Tobacco people, the Royal House of Khayrpur. Eminent barrister A.K. Brohi took residence in the vicinity afterward, renowned crooner Habib Wali Mohammed & Begum Hamidullah, editor of the *Monthly Mirror*. Not long ago, I would come across the poet Rais Amrohvi taking his evening constitutional, but I do not get out often now.

VOLUME I

CRITICAL DIGRESSIONS
(OR THIS, THAT, THE OTHER)

MY HEAD IS LIKE a rubbish heap: you have to sift through the muck to find a working toaster. When I was eleven, I overheard one of my brothers telling another that I am a bastard. They say if you scale the bluff by Shah Noorani (RA), you happen upon the clenched mouth of a cave, and if you manage to crawl in, you are your father's son. I do not patronize Shah Noorani (RA)—if I am a bastard, I am a bastard—but you might find me at the seaside shrine of Abdullah Shah Ghazi (RA) on a Thursday night, inhaling hashish amongst the malcontents who congregate on the rocky southern slant of the hill. It's always a carnival, populated by fortune-tellers, bodybuilders, thugs, troubadours, transvestites, women & sweet, rowdy children. I am at home there.

When I enter the cool confines of Agha's Supermarket to purchase Smoked Gouda, however, shoppers part to give me way.[5] Those who once knew me turn to memorize the sodium content in shelved cans of French Onion Soup. The last time I was dragging myself through the aisles, I called out to this busty, sixty-six-year-old Persian cat who

5. Of course, in the old days, one frequented Ghulam Mohammed Brothers for bread and butter, and Bliss & Co. for tonics and balms. Long after the proprietors, Mr & Mrs Black, sold the business and moved to the UK, they wintered yearly at the Olympus. You still might be able to pick up a bottle of Bliss Carbonate or Calamine at pharmacies in the city, presumably even at Agha's.

had just celebrated her fifty-fifth birthday. Although married to a portly patrician now, she would be at the Olympus in the old days, making eyes at the young men with carnations fixed in their lapels. When I hooted *Sweety!* she paused for a moment, as if crossing off the loaf of bread on the list in her head, before disappearing around the corner from the shoe polish. Verily, decency is dead or dying.

I have been mulling a project, some permutation of the Mythopoetic Legacy of Abdullah Shah Ghazi (RA), since the fateful day my father asked me to punctuate the following sentence: *That that is that is that and that that is not that is not.* Naturally, I retorted, 'Comma after the sixth word, sir!' Papa could be difficult, but I knew then that he had in an indirect way communicated his aspiration for me to be a phenomenologist even if he would deny it vehemently afterward.

There is no doubt in my mind that my mother, an aristocrat hailing from an erstwhile martial state in the North, would have encouraged the project. When she entered a room, people squinted as if she were wrought of light. If I close my eyes I can recall hers: sunny and blue like the sea at Sonmiani. Married to a cousin at seventeen, the Khan of This or That Khanate, she ran away when she realized that he was only keen on hunting partridge. She met Papa at the Olympus in '29 when visiting an aunt twice removed for high tea. She had five sons with rhyming names: Hidayatullah, Bakaullah, Abdullah, Fazlullah a.k.a. Tony & Rahimullah a.k.a. Babu.[6]

When Mummy passed, the family, the House of K., became fundamentally unglued. After retiring from the army as a major, Hidayatullah moved to a palatial residence in the suburbs featuring a diamond-shaped pool whilst Bakaullah, once a card-carrying Communist, immigrated to some dusty corner of the Near East where

---

6. I once drew up a Sociocultural Genealogical Table that elucidates who we are, where we have been. I have it somewhere in my papers. You'll have to find it.

he reportedly runs a transportation & logistics concern. Tony,[7] my boon companion, left for university in the United States of America before squatting on our estate in Scinde where he cultivates dames & produces wine—our very own vinos de la tierra.

I am certain I was Mummy's favourite. She raised me to be myself. I am not a bad man but not good for much anymore. I am a fat man, and an anxious one. The insides of my thighs chafe when I climb down the stairs from my quarters; I avoid loitering below because my youngest brother, Babu, occupies the mezzanine with his twin boys and plain, moon-faced wife, Nargis—a lass with the charm of an opossum. The arrangement poses a bit of a problem because I love the children, those two crazy little Childoos.

When they manage to break free, they sneak up on me like those Ninja Warriors[8] and clamber atop my domed belly. We sing, cavort, creep up to the roof to observe the silently sundering clouds, the odd meteor. We startle the nesting crows and put the fear of God in their black hearts. When their rasping protests ring through the still of the evening, Nargis the Opossum comes bounding up the stairs. She does not approve and changes the rules all the time:

1. No Taking the Children to the Roof at Night (or During the Day, the Afternoon, or at Sunset)
2. No Feeding the Children Walnuts (or Custard Apples, Chilli Chips, Sugar Wafers)

---

7. I christened Tony *Tony* because as a child he could not pronounce his own name—like all our names, it is a mouthful—and because he resembled Tony Curtis circa *The Prince Who Was a Thief*.

8. You might recall that that Lee Van Cleef chap—a peer by age, perhaps, if not by distinction—played a Ninja Warrior in the serial in the early eighties. I am no Lee Van Cleef. I cannot scale walls or walk between raindrops. I would be happy if I could scratch my back without risking a herniated disk.

3. No Singing Tom Jones to the Children (or Cliff Richard,[9] Boney M., the Benjamin Sisters)

And even though I cradled him in my arms, carried him on my shoulders, even though I taught him how to whistle, how to say thank you—*thunku,* he said—the aforementioned Babu is not an ally. Many years ago, he laughed when told I was a bastard. Like many, like most, he quietly judged me then, quietly judges me now. I don't care. A fortune-teller named Sarbuland once told me, 'Tum lambi race kay ghoray ho,' viz., *You are the horse of the long race.*

But I am not the same man I was yesterday.

---

9. Who remembers today that Cliff Richard was a native of Our Swath of the World, a neighbour, a Lucknavi. Who remembers old Peter Sarstedt for that matter, a Delhi-wallah, who wrote, 'Where Do You Go To (My Lovely)?' And Pete Best, the Beatle from Madras? I ask you: why doesn't discourse acknowledge that we pioneered rock & roll?

ON NEGOTIATING ONTOLOGICAL PANIC

(OR DOWN & OUT)

I WAKE FEELING FRAUGHT and delicate like a soft-boiled egg for I have transformed into that dwindling subspecies *homo septuagenari* overnight, and there are few conjunctures that stupefy, that unsettle the soul more than the thought of a fallow life. Lying amid fading canvases, steamer trunks, rolled Turkish rugs, Mummy's cut-glass perfume bottle collection, Papa's clockwork gramophone, china and a brass candelabra from the Olympus, several dusty Betamax recorders and the cadaver of an exercise bicycle, I stare at the whirring fan with one open cataract-swept eye, dimly pitting reasons for & against remaining prone: *Nobody would care if you stayed in bed,* I tell myself. *You're a sad man, long in the tooth, an animal: you drool, soil your knickers.* It is a downpour of self-pity, a veritable monsoon of misery, but then the urge to relieve myself compels me to the commode. There is no doubt that there is reprieve if not respite in ritual, in diurnal bowel movements (even if the exercise has become trying on account of my piles) & the pages of *The New Golden Treasury of English Verse.*[10] Oh, that golden crowd! What jocund company!

---

10. A cursory survey of my lavatory library would reveal back issues of *She, Mag,* the *Civil & Military Gazette,* as well as *The Ornithologist's Field Guide, Justine, Not Without My Daughter, Freedom at Midnight.* The most entertaining of the lot, the lot that belongs in the loo, is Maulana Thanvi's *Heavenly Ornaments.* Did he not expire on the pot?

Slipping into Mummy's jungle-print robe de chambre after, I take tea and insulin on the balcony. The sky is cloudless and blue, the air smoky and trilling with crickets; an old crow perches on the ledge above, cawing hoarsely, damnably, like the Angel Israfil. I know I won't get any work done today—I have the feeling that it will be a very long day, or a very short one. Draining the acrid lees, I hoist myself from the cane armchair, dentures rattling in my pocket, and teeter purposefully towards the wrought-iron railing. As I consider the diagonally inclined potted cacti, the pansy bed below, I notice a pair of eyes peering at me over the horizon of the boundary wall as if I am on display, a primate shelling nuts. 'Stop, Kookaburra, stop,' I chunter, returning the gaze through the interstices of the evergreens, "That's not a monkey, it's me.' Then I apprehend the manifest drama: I am brandishing my member, flush and bulbous and overrun with wild reddish hair and, as usual, have nothing to show for myself.

Uncannily, the eyes, fantastic obsidian eyes, follow me as I collect my genitalia in the teacup & nearly trip down the stairs. It's not just my biscuit-box feet; no, I am curious, titillated, mortified—imagine a seraph, siren, a sphinx! But God knows mythology has long ceded to the mundane: I suspect a tarrying transvestite, or the maid's good-for-nothing locksmith husband, or that swine Chambu,[11] the manager of my piddling garment-dyeing operation who fleeces me every quarter and demands Other Sundry Expenses. Sundry, my foot!

By the time I fasten my robe and cross the lawn, the eyes vanish like fireflies taking flight. There is the wonted activity outside: lurching busses, rattling rickshaws, the odd donkey cart laden with galvanized steel pipes, and down the road, the street-side dentist sits on his haunches, administering what might be a root canal. Barefoot

11. I should note that the portmanteau was originally coined by Tony: Chutiya + Lambu = Chambu. I might add that he also coined the underexploited 'Khotiya' but will leave the import to other armchair philologists.

& breathless, I stand unsteadily on the toasty asphalt, considering the gaze that bored into my soul—*Who did it belong to? Why was I being watched? Why today?*—but then I hear the distinct voices of the Childoos over the clamour of traffic.

'Chachajaan!' they cry, 'Cha! Cha! Jaan!' they chant. They are single-pasli, suffer from unfortunate bowl cuts & wear white button-down half sleeves, navy blue knickers, white socks pulled up to their scratched knees. They waddle as they run, run as they waddle, backpacks flapping, maid straggling behind. I pick them up, peck them on the cheek, and break into song: 'There lived a certain man in Russia long ago!'

'He was bigs and strong,' they chime, 'and eyes flaming gold!'

And together we bellow: 'RA-RA-RASPUTIN / Lover of the Russian queen / There was a cat that really was gone / RA-RA-RASPUTIN / Russia's greatest love machine / It was a shame how he carried on!'

We make a spectacle of ourselves—several passers-by gather and gape—and why shouldn't we? We are loud and gay—the von Trapps of Currachee! We might have broken into 'Do-Re-Mi' next (an admittedly more apropos number) if it were not for the jaundiced attention of the authorities: I feel the quick teardrop eyes of my dear sister-in-law on my back. Not one for song and spectacle, Nargis the Opossum is undoubtedly leaning against the gate, wrist on hip, shaking her draped head from side to side like a broken doll. 'Chalo, chalain, bachon,' she bids. 'Lunchtime!'

Setting the children down, I surreptitiously fit my dentures into my mouth, then turn to greet Nargis, but she has already marched in, trailed by the Childoos. As they wave shyly, I wonder when I will see them again, wonder if they know it is my platinum jubilee. Not even my pal Tony has called. But then, who remembers sad old men? We die, rot, without acknowledgment, without ceremony.

I swear I could stand kerbside all day, watching the world go by, waiting for those haunting eyes to gaze upon my hairless, roly-poly, chicken-flesh chest—what else is there to do?—but the day has become hot and brackish like a belch. Shutting the gate behind me, I return unceremoniously to my perch and certain ontological panic. But as I consider launching myself over the balcony for the second time, my man mercifully shambles in with my daily jug of bitter gourd juice, sporting a red-and-white baseball cap and matching joggers.

Barbarossa, former major-domo, has been yanked from de facto retirement since the couple who cooked & cleaned for us failed to return from annual leave (because Nargis is a difficult customer), despite the fact that the old hand hears voices[12] & spends most of his time in the backyard rearing cockerels for the cockpits. Whilst he has become as weathered as a banyan, it was once said he possessed 'the jib of Clark Gable.'

'I will not abide this poison!' I protest. I have been protesting for a quarter century—bitter gourd tastes like vegetal diesel—but Barbarossa insists it mitigates blood sugar, and I am beholden to him; he oft saves me from myself.

'Juice especial,' he says in English. He is known to speak English on occasion—he picked it up buttling at the Olympus—but in recent history, he is only wont to mutter gibberish such as *Yessur, nossur, cocklediddledosur.*

'You garnished it with hemlock?'

Stroking his freshly hennaed beard, Barbarossa announces, 'Is the haypy-baday-juice!'

12. The story goes that Nargis' preacher instructed her to say *salam* before entering a room. When she entered the garret one afternoon, a voice replied & she yelled bloody murder & Barbarossa came to the rescue. He reported that the djinn bore no ill intent; he was just being polite. I don't mind; decorum is a lost virtue.

Kissing him on the head, I slip my man a note folded in the pocket of my robe, a tip for the wishes, the welcome watery wine, but since the old fox is not always compos mentis, I ask him how he remembered. 'You friend calling,' he replies.

'I have no friends!' I cry.

'Pinto phone.'

By Jove! Pinto, good old Felix Pinto, the Last Trumpeter of Currachee! When Barbarossa informs me that I have been summoned to the Goan Association, I doff my robe and proclaim, 'Prepare my bath! Dust off my smoking jacket! Iron my kerchief!'

In all the excitement, I forget the obsidian eyes and nearly tumble over the balcony yet again, not unlike Adam before the fall.

ON THE JAZZ AGE OF KARACHI

AN ANECDOTAL HISTORY

ACCORDING TO MY FRIEND and former colleague, B. Avari, proprietor of the world-famous Beach Luxury, jazz came to Currachee in '53. He told me that when his parents were away in Beirut or Mauritius or someplace like that, he 'booked this Dutch quartet, called several hundred people, many of them friends. They played all night. There was a traffic jam in the parking lot.' When jazz came to the city, it caused traffic jams.

Old Goan rockers, however, will tell you that they were grooving to jazz even earlier. They will tell you that their forefathers had started trickling into Bombay, Calcutta and Currachee by the middle of the nineteenth century to escape the Portuguese, a dashed scourge in the Annals of the Colonial Enterprise. They were D'Souzas, Fernandeses, Rodrigueses, Lobos, Nazareths, erecting St. Patrick's Cathedral[13] with the Irish Fusiliers and the Currachee Goan Association not long after, organizing choirs at the former, staging Gilbert and Sullivan operettas at the latter. Music, they will say, is in their blood.

Whilst the Anglos congregated at the Burt Institute and the gentry waltzed across the floors of the Gymkhana and Scinde Clubs, the Goans were doing the Lindy hop or cha-cha-cha to numbers

13. Who knows now or acknowledges the fact that the city as we know it is actually arranged around churches?

strummed by the Carvalho Trio or the Janu Vaz Band[14] at jam sessions at each other's houses, in the backyards of Cincinnatus Town: somebody would bring a guitar, somebody else the drums, and horns became de rigueur by and by. And of course, everyone would bring liquor—Murree, caju feni, or Goan hooch and, if they could afford it, the foreign sauce: Dimple, Black & White, Vat 69.[15] Before long, the legendary Eddie Carapiet began hosting the weekly radio show 'The Hit Parade,' injecting jazzy riffs into the bloodstream of the city. And one fine day Dizzy Gillespie rolled into town, cohort in tow, selling out the garden at the Metropole.

Although there was not much demand for what came to be known as Three Star Accommodation in the old days, there was the Killarney run by Mr Wyse, North Western, Marina, the Bristol on Sunny Side Lane,[16] and the Olympus. Then the Parsees, consummate visionaries, entered the frame: C. Framji Minwalla, for instance, transformed his guesthouse in Malir into the Hotel Grand, the only establishment that boasted a swimming pool. And when the city became the regional entrepôt—all flights, East to West, West to East, flew in & out of the city—the Dutch set up Midway House, and there was the

14. Lynette Dias-Gouveia reminds me that the band comprised Alex Rodrigues & Dominic Gonsalves on saxophone; John Fernandes on trumpet; double-bassist David William; and Basil and Rudy D'Souza on the drums.

15. Three Parsee brothers—technically speaking, two brothers and a cousin—had a virtual monopoly on distribution in the country by the middle of the century. They ran the Quetta Distillery Ltd. which, with the Murree Brewery, remains the premier producer of liquor in the country. One ought to avoid the former's Peach Vodka and also the whisky of the newer distillery in the Interior. It tastes like paint thinner.

16. The Bristol was built in 1910 by two Hindoo brothers & run by my drinking buddy, the honourable Mr Rizvi.

Hostellerie de France, and with the advent of cabarets, the Taj, Lido, the hospitality landscape began to change. We had to compete.

Run by my father, a Khoja,[17] the Shadow Lounge at the Olympus was naturally tamer than establishments such as the Excelsior where Gul Pari bared all, or Roma Shabana where you would attend cabarets featuring the likes of the Stambuli Sisters, or 'Carmen & Anita in French Cancan.' What you got at the Shadow Lounge were musicians who knew their Bird from their Beiderbecke. The stage was elevated and so spacious that you could fit a chamber orchestra on it. It faced a round, oak dance floor surrounded by tables draped with crimson tablecloths. There was a solid oak bar at the entrance and ferns everywhere, and on a good night, there would be close to a hundred aficionados, sipping cocktails, smoking 555s, nodding and snapping their fingers emphatically.

I knew all the musicians of the time because they were all regulars at the Olympus. They wore thin black ties and their black hair swept back: recall the Ay Jays, Bluebirds, Thunders, Keynotes. One night I came across this crazy, trumpet-playing cat, Felix Pinto, known to his audiences by his nom de tune: the Caliph of Cool. He possessed the shiniest trumpet this side of Saddar or, for that matter, the Suez.

It has been said that the Caliph had a hand in the composition of the National Anthem, though the stories were apocryphal even then.[18] When asked, Pinto would just grin mysteriously and raise a

17. For those not in the know, Khojas, known once upon a time as Lohanas, are a metropolitan mercantile community who revere the Mighty Ali (AS), cousin & right-hand man of the Prophet (PBUH). Although an intellectual, Ali (AS) could break you in two if you crossed him. Since the Prophet (PBUH) was a businessman, since business is Sunnah, we follow in his footsteps, pursuing commerce from Calcutta to Zanzibar to Canada. In fact, this country was fashioned by a Khoja. But I get ahead of myself.

18. The words, of course, were penned by the renowned poet, Hafiz Jalandhari, and the orchestra, reportedly a navy band, was conducted by one Ahmed Chagla.

toast to the well-being of the country—a woolly, wily strategy. Some attribute the commission to the Caliph's doppelgänger, old Dominic Gonsalves, but I believe that it belongs to Tollentine, or Tolly, Fonseca, the celebrated bandmaster known for original compositions that include the 'Barcelona Waltz,' 'Officer's March,' and 'Diwan-e-Khaas.' I never had the opportunity to meet the man—he expired soon after the anthem was completed[19]—but have come across his nieces at the Currachee Goan Association. Whatever the story, this much is certain: the Caliph of Cool was a legend in his time.

Although the Shadow Lounge was leafy, smoky and dim, you could always spot Felix Pinto: he sported a slick bouffant, a boxer's jaw and thick-rimmed, shaded glasses, whether it was three in the afternoon at Café Grand or three on a moonless morning at Clifton Beach. Verily, he was a dandy in a way that was only possible in Currachee in the Sixties. I would wager that he wore his glasses in the bath and to bed, sleeping or making love. Because they were glued to his nose, you would have never noticed his sunken blue vertiginous eyes. Ask me then: how do I know?

Pinto's trademark frames were knocked off his face once and only once, one night at Le Gourmet circa '59, when he was boffed in the face during a bar brawl with a young landowner known for his two-toned patent leather shoes. There was a dame involved, a sexy Anglo named Eleanor or something like that, and a spilt glass of wine. Although Pinto sported a black eye that night, he got his opponent in the bird's nest. When the arriviste crumpled, I whisked the Caliph out via the kitchen. Otherwise he would have had to contend with the landowner's thuggish entourage.

---

19. Although he was known to frequent the Olympus, I was not allowed into the bar before I was eighteen. Of course, I didn't drink until my turn as the Cossack. It should be noted here, however, that since Mummy treated my childhood colds with brandy (to Papa's chagrin), I was, in a way, weaned on spirit.

When said landowner was elected Prime Minister some years later, I helped Pinto escape to Australia.[20] My friend knocked about down under during the Disco Era before returning to Currachee, but by then the Prime Minister had imposed prohibition in a gutless attempt to gain currency with the excitable religious rabble. The clubs, bars and cabarets were shut down soon after. Many Goans left. It was the end of an age.

20. I suppose he could have fled to Canada or the United States of America—if I were compelled to leave I would escape to San Remo like the White Russians—but the Australian Consul General at the time, a certain His Excellency Darling, was known to us, so I leaned on him to help a man out.

ON RITES AND RESPONSIBILITY (OR TAKE FIVE)

THE GOAN ASSOCIATION IS housed in an imposing double-storeyed stone edifice featuring arched windows and cornices and pilasters flanking the entrance. There is a library and wine shop downstairs, typically manned by a ruddy tubby chap whose mouth is permanently fixed in a golden grin, and a vast hall upstairs where concerts and plays and marriages are staged with great foon fan—not to mention the annual Valentine's & Independence Day balls. It's always cool inside because the walls are thick and the ceiling is high and the doors open out to a shaded alcove featuring a fountain. As you enter, you pass sequential portraits of past presidents whose solemn expressions suggest a tale that is best not to broach with the members of the storied institution.

I find Felix in his tatty tuxedo and dark glasses towards the far end of the hall, leaning for effect, nursing one of those deadly bottles of feni. 'I looked at him,' he is saying, 'he looked at me, then I said, "Why don't you sit on the trumpet, mister!"' There is a roar of laughter from the audience, a cast of pirates arranged in a circle: the barkeep, magnificently named Titus Gomes, and two others, a walnut of a fellow with bushy whiskers, and a ponytailed character in a Hawaiian shirt who elbows Pinto upon my advent.

As if parting a stage curtain, Felix proclaims, 'Ah, the Cossack cometh! Happy birthday, you rascal!' Turning to the trio, he adds,

'He might be a Musalman, but he's all right!' They hoot and toot and raise empty glasses. 'Get the birthday boy a chair, and some hooch.' Although I rarely partake in libation anymore on account of sugar and gout, I cannot refuse my old friend. I down a Patiala peg[21] and wince. It feels warm going down; it feels like the old days.

'I was going to hold a party for you, man,' Felix begins, 'but you don't have any friends anymore and mine are dead or in Australia—it's the same thing. You know, I've been everywhere in that penal colony of a country—Perth, Sydney, Melbourne, Adelaide, I've even been to that big rock in the Outback—and I tell you, I'm happier in this godforsaken place any day of the week. *How ya goin?* they ask. *What tribe ya from?* 'Goan, man,' I say, 'Pakistani,' and they think I'm saying Papua New Guinea. G'day, mate, good on ya. Sure, I played gigs there, good gigs, or good enough, but here I've got a name, a place—'

'Context—'

'You have a way with words, Cossack.'

'That's what I do.'

'I walk into any hotel in this city and somebody comes running, *Good afternoon, sir, good evening, sir,* because they know I'm an old-timer. I've survived, banjo. The other day, I was at the Intercon, and who do I see? Do you remember that bacha, Yusuf? He'd ask me to call him Joe, and I'd say, "Joe, help me carry the equipment back to the Foxy." Now he's a big seth—he's got buildings on the beachfront. *Anything you need,* he said, *you call me.* But what do I need? I need a drink, my trumpet—I need people to know that I am the best bloody trumpet player in the country.'

'They need to know you knocked out a prime minister—'

'Exactly, man, exactly!'

'Aun-houn,' Titus Gomes chimes in, in pidgin.

---

21. The story goes that the Maharaja of the Princely State of Patiala invented the measurement to beat the team of visiting Irishmen on the cricket field. They, of course, fell for it.

'Enough jib-jab!' Pinto proclaims, biting his trumpet. 'Time to jam!' As the others conjure a double bass, an accordion, and a dhol because the snare drum is torn, Pinto says, 'I know what you want to hear, Cossack.' Tapping his foot, he adds, 'Happy birthday, old friend.'

What follows is an awesome rendition of 'Take Five,' more Puente than Brubeck, more marching band perhaps than jazz: Titus beats the edge of the dhol tentatively with a bamboo stick, reproducing the sensation of the introductory movement of the number, that peculiarly syncopated 5/4 beat—duddud-dudda-da-da-da, duddud-dudda-da-dada—whilst the walnut strums the double bass as if this is the moment he has been preparing for since the Dawn of Time. When the trumpet enters the medley, I shut my eyes. You have to shut your eyes.

'Take Five' is like you are flying, arms extended, inhaling the beach at Seaview on a cool December evening, duddud-duddud-da-da-da, duddud-duddud-da-da-da. You see floodlights lighting up loping camels, and miniature families huddled around miniature stalls preparing corn on charcoal. If you are lucky, you see a woman dancing in the surf, her wispy aquamarine dupatta fluttering in the breeze. If you are luckier still, you see the silver-grey fin of a dolphin cutting the silver-grey waves, duddud-daada-da-da-da, duddud-daada-da-da-da.

THE FELIX PINTO QUARTET play into the night. They play Armstrong and Getz, selections from the ragtime canon, and even a couple of Bollywood numbers.[22] They play until they are tired and sottish and can play no more. When they are done, the walnut

22. Recall the lyrics of 'Shadmani': 'Aaj to nasha aisa charha, pucho na yaron / Mein to aasman pe hoon, mujhay neechay utaro,' or *Don't ask me how drunk I am tonight, friend / Can you help me get down from the clouds?* The number was de rigueur at weddings once. Now it's all just dances I don't dance and dish-dish boom-boom.

dozes in a corner, squeaking through his nose, then Pinto, clutching his drooling trumpet, puts an arm around me and burbles, 'I need a favour, Cossack.'

There was a time when I could extend favours, when I had resources, succour. I was a different man then, a known man, a scion of a respected family. Whilst I have nothing, am nothing, the Caliph of Cool still believes I can help. 'Of course, old friend,' I slur. I do not want to disappoint, or disappoint immediately.

'Is my grandson, Bosco. My daughter's in a pickle and her husband's a doper, so you need to put him up for some time. You know things. Teach him something—character building and all that jazz.'

When I say I do not believe I have had the pleasure of meeting said Bosco, a dark, gangly lad of twelve or thirteen emerges from the shadows, wearing a parenthetical moustache and a chequered shirt too big for his frame. For all I know, he might have been standing there all night. 'Say hello to Uncle Cossack,' instructs Pinto.

'Hello, Uncle Cossack.'

Lo and behold, a ward is thrust upon me. It is the damnedest development.

ON RECONSTRUCTING MEMORY AND MAN

VERILY, MEMORY IS A tricky wench.[23] It catalogues images, episodes, reifies yesterday today, but recent research cited in *Reader's Digest* suggests yesterday might change tomorrow, or the day after, in the mind. It's all murky, molecular, but makes you what you are. I can attest to the fact that when I rake through the soil of my memory, there are certain episodes impressed in it like pebbles: I remember a fearsome cat with a severed tail stalking me in the garden, remember waddling inside the Lodge, teary, and my grandfather setting me on his bony lap, cooing in Gujarati, 'Tamay kaim cho?' viz., *You okay?* Although he never completed school (he dropped out in the seventh form) he could negotiate the Queen's English because he had to: like his contemporaries—Messrs Merchant, Mistry, old Ebrahimji Sulemanji—he had business with the Britishers. When I would shove my foot in his soft shoes, for instance, he would chide, 'No naughty pun!' I was six when he passed. I bawled when I beheld his shrouded corpse, bawled louder when I was told that he was going to Heaven. *There are rivers of milk there!* 'But he didn't drink milk,' I sobbed. 'He took tea only!'

My father spoke English to me (so I have little Gujarati), and generally cultivated an English air: he sported trilby hats and used the

23. The opening sentence of fellow Khoja Badr-ud-Din Tyabji's *Memoirs of an Egoist* comes to mind.

word 'pardon' as a threat. One of my earliest memories features a smart young man in seersucker,[24] pulling into the driveway in a cool blue Impala, the staff standing at attention. Whenever somebody invokes him—*Your father used to say*, or, *If only your father were alive*—some other incarnation materializes, though the canonical Papa, rendered in oil by a family friend, resides in the parlour downstairs:[25] Jinnah cap perched on head, charcoal sherwani extending to the knees, he stares back, stands tall, fist on hip, commanding, indifferent. We all aspired to be that figure. Perhaps that's why we all fell short.

When one thinks about it, my eldest brother Hidayatullah looked most like him, down to the Roman nose, though he was a breed apart—loud and bolshie, even as a boy. Next in line, the fair and lean Bakaullah looked more like Mummy, and though temperamentally sober, he would become severe with age. Neither took interest in our flagship business, the Olympus. Hidayatullah did spend time in other hotels, carousing with the scions of established families, whilst Bakaullah, Comrade Bakaullah, fraternized with the local Communists, or Soorkhas, who populated Zelin's and Café George on Preedy Street. He organized discussions on rooftops and street corners (attended by the likes of S. Sibt-e-Hassan) and rallies in support of farmers and the labour movement, but his career as an activist came to an abrupt end when he was nabbed by the authorities outside the Volk's House, the Soviet 'cultural centre,' for 'subversive and suspicious activities.' After spending four months in Central

---

24. Unbeknownst to most, I know for a fact that 'seersucker' is derived from the Urdu *khir* & *shukar*, or 'pudding' & 'sugar.' Pudding! Sugar! Hoo! Ha!

25. Said friend was the late great Pakistani Jewish painter Samuel Fyzee Rahamin, protégé of one John Singer Sargent. The latter is often neglected by Western art critics, whilst the former has been all but forgotten here, though in recent years I managed to sneak into a secret room at the Mohatta Palace to see many a canvas.

Jail—Hidayatullah, a major in the army by then, lobbied the Inspector General (IG) of police for an early release—Comrade Bakaullah left for points West, or rather, the Near or Middle West, to become a dyed-in-the-wool capitalist. In his new incarnation, he hounded me for running the family into the ground. That is slander, libel, bovine faecal matter.

It is a fact that, unlike the Major or Comrade Bakaullah, I was not a sportsman or academically accomplished.[26] I was a sensitive child, a curious soul; I lolled in the garden, talked to myself. When the neighbourhood children congregated to play tennikoit or gulli danda in the vacant plot adjacent to Apollo House, I made figurines in the flowerbed recalling the local sphinxes featured at fairs and mud-men recalling the Priest King of Mohenjo-Daro. Although the zoo was around the corner—you could hear the lions roaring at night—I had a fetish for ants, beetles, dragonflies, creatures that comported themselves with quiet resolve. And whilst the others awaited the tun-tun-wallah, I awaited the cycling librarian's delivery of *National Geographic*. Mummy called me 'Anokhay Mian,' viz., *Master Unusual*.

Papa attempted to draw me out, taking me on excursions, mano a mano:[27] there were jaunts to Empress Market and Gandhi Garden and a memorable trip to the shabby shrine of Mungho Pir—patron

---

26. Hidayatullah was tennis champion at the Gymkhana, then at St. Lawrence. He was also a swimmer, runner—he ran the fifty metres—and later, took up skeet shooting. And Bakaullah topped in Senior Cambridge, then again at NED—the famous Nadirshaw Eduljee Dinshaw University of Engineering & Technology.

27. Typically, however, excursions were en famille. I remember when the entire clan was stuffed into the Impala to Ranikot, the largest fort in the world. We camped in the open under a powdery spread of stars, attended to by our staff. I also recall spying Badbakht Begum's ras malai buttocks as she relieved herself in the bushes.

saint of the Sheedis, the Afro-Pakistani community.[28] Gawking at the crocodiles lazing in a murky pool, I remember Papa telling me that the frightful reptiles were 'just big lizards,' said to have been the lice shaken loose from the saint's head—'A giant, he was?' I asked. ('Primus inter pares,' he remarked cryptically.) When Papa narrated a story of how the mighty Sheedi general fought the British, losing ten thousand men to the machine gun, a leathery old man within earshot invited me to bang on a sheepskin drum—dhug-dhug, dhuga-dhug—a rare honour. I can also remember quarterly pilgrimages to the Toy Trading Agency where I once picked up a locomotive labelled 'Made in Occupied Japan,' but as I grew older, Papa bid me to put away childish things. Circa nineteen hundred & fifty-four, he took it upon himself to make a man out of me.

During oppressive Currachee summers,[29] when families we knew made their way to hill stations up north—Murree, Ziarat, or the emerald abode of that Fairy Queen—Papa put me to work in the kitchens of the Olympus. I peeled potatoes until my fingers bled, chopped onions until I bawled—it was trial by fire—but burn by burn and by and by, I learnt to negotiate the involute ecosystem. It helped that the chef, a jolly Goan named Pereira, took a shine to me. He had been recruited from Agha's Tavern, the finest steakhouse in Currachee, on the condition that he had absolute dominion over the kitchen, and there was truth to it: I remember him telling Papa once, 'You do your work, man, I do mine.' Nobody dared confront Papa, save Pereira. I also recall him telling Papa, 'Boy's a natural'—I could,

---

28. Sheedis maintain *sheedi* is a variation of the Arabic *sahabi*, or 'companion.' Some claim descent from the Prophet's (PBUH) associate, Bilal (RA), whilst others, the Qambranis, claim descent from Ali's (AS) coterie.

29. The summer lasts from April to July. August & September is the Monsoon. Then there's what can be characterized as the Indian Summer.

after all, prepare beef bourguignon and coq au vin—but I am not certain my father was impressed; he was hard to please.

Consequently, save the two years I spent at the American University in Cairo during the Suez Crisis—I read Political Science—I devoted myself to becoming Papa's Aaron (AS) or Ali (AS). After all, if I could not become Papa, I could become his man—politics or science had nothing to do with it. At the tender age of twenty-two, then, I was virtually running the Olympus. I had a card printed on ivory paper that read: 'Executive Manager.' I wore spotted kerchiefs, felt important. Papa could be proud.

I remember it all as if it were yesterday. But yesterday is no more.

ON THE HAZARD OF SPIRITS
(AND HIGH TEA)

THERE IS A PROVERB in Gujarati that goes *Jagya tya thi savar*, which amounts to 'It's morning whenever you wake' in the Queen's English. I am uncertain of the import but the day after my platinum jubilee, I wake beside my bed, marinating in my smoking jacket. There is a pounding in my head and a pounding at the door, dhas-dhas-dhas-dhas, but I am a sack of potatoes. Of course, at my age every gesture demands Herculean stamina: it takes me three, four swings to peel myself off a divan, knees cracking like biscuits, and I have dispensed with socks because I have not been able to touch my ankles since Tiananmen Square. Somehow I manage to hoist myself up, mouthing that old shanty, 'Hurrah, and up she rises,'[30] and traverse the expanse of the room as if braving a sandstorm. A patina of crust glues an eye shut, but I perceive a disembodied visage at the door. 'Who is this?' it squeals.

'This is who?' I reply through my fingers, chuffed that even in a state of raw, gut-churning lassitude, my capacity for inductive logic remains functional. Stepping aside, Nargis the Opossum reveals a bony, fawn-faced boy regarding his joggers. *I don't know him,* I begin to say, *don't know much at this particular juncture of history*—but instead find myself mouthing the curious appellation: Bosco.

---

30. After a solid night of drink, Felix is wont to hum the traditional version of 'What to do with the drunken sailor?'

'Bosco?' Nargis repeats.

'Bosco,' Bosco confirms.

'I found him wandering around downstairs. I was so frightened. You know, I'm alone in the morning after Babu and the children leave—'

'Bully for you!'

'Really, Abdullah Bhai!'

'Come on, lad.'

'What's wrong with you?' she asks with arguably earnest exasperation.

Quavering, 'Heave him by the leg in a running bowline,' I shut the door on her and slip back into a fugue. There are days, indeed seasons, when one is felled by fate again and again, and on such occasions one wonders how and why one keeps getting up. It might be a matter of habit rather than faith but who knows? I know this much: when I come to, I find my trousers around my knees, a syringe lying next to my pulpy, pallid thigh & Bosco sitting on his haunches beside me, chin balanced on palms, whispering the Memorare or some other esoteric supplication.[31] 'I'm fine,' I mutter. 'This happens all the time.'

Extending a stringy hand, the lad attempts to yank me up but it's the cordial whiff of the alloo bharay parathay[32] and pickled mangoes that compels me to my feet. The March of History attests to the

---

31. It might have been the Guardian Angel or Miraculous Medal Prayer, prayers we all learnt as children, courtesy of our Catholic schooling. One does enjoy the foon fan of Catholicism, even if the papacy has been mostly occupied by disagreeable characters, save Popes Francis & John. One wishes our very own Cardinal Joseph Cordeiro, the dark horse candidate for Pope once upon a time, would have been elected. Imagine, just imagine.

32. In case Bosco is unfamiliar with the dish—who knew if his mother made alloo bharay parathay—I volunteer an explanation: 'Think of these as pancakes filled with mashed potatoes, sautéed in cumin and chilli powder.' 'I know what they are,' he mumbles.

fact that there is nothing like hunger to transform a Thinking Man into a Man of Action. And there is nothing that sates the soul like Barbarossa's luncheon spread. Master Bosco and I sit under the fan in the veranda and lunch like kings.

I would like to ascertain the nature of his familial travails, apprehend the boy's familiarity with the scourge of diabetes, enquire about his habits, hobbies, crushes, but he keeps stuffing his mouth as if he has led a life of privation, reared, as it were, on a diet of grass and shrubs. I ought to lecture him on the Protocols of the Sunset Lodge—First Things First: Stay Clear of Nargis the Opossum—but fain watch him eat; his entire being informs the act. I offer him paratha after greasy paratha and he keeps tucking in. The only request he makes is for a napkin—I wear a striped plastic apron, for napkins don't fit the bill, so to speak—and a bottle of pop, Pakola. 'Ah,' I proclaim, 'a man after my own heart!'

But what the dickens do you do with a ward? Not quite the Boswellian type, is the boy Watson to my Shaukat, Aflatoon to my Socrates? The trajectory of the query leads me to the library where amongst the gazettes and pamphlets stacked on the floor and yellowing articles cut out from magazines dating back half a century,[33] I happen across a gilt-spined decalogy regarding the Intellectual History of the Ancient World. 'Your grandfather told me to build your character,' I say, 'and they say there's no better place to begin than Greece.'

---

33. I possess issues of Burney Sahab's excellent *Outlook*. There is no doubt that articles such as 'An Exposé on the American Role in the Dismemberment of Pakistan' have as much resonance today as they did then. I also have clippings of my friend Badruddin Ahmed's brilliant 'Gardening Notes' from the *Mirror*. One ought to note in passing here that Mohammad Aslam Mian's *Flower Gardening in the Plains of Pakistan* is also an invaluable resource, though the prose is somewhat flat. W. Firminger, Woodrow & Johnston have also made meaningful contributions to the field since the Brits have the need to categorize everybody & everything.

Stuffed like a taxidermist's bear, a Yankee Grizzly, I retire to my chamber for a siesta ad interim, dreaming of that pair of obsidian eyes, but before being swept far from the shores of consciousness, I am roused by the slate-faced, iron-haired housemaid known universally as Bua, informing me that I have been summoned downstairs for high tea. It is a decidedly odd development: the family dines together once a month but seldom fraternizes otherwise. Moreover, strictly speaking, teatime is over.

Anticipating a dressing down, I don my lucky tomato-red silk shirt (one ought to look proper if one does not always behave properly), comb my kinky hair to the side for good measure (though it will spring back shortly), buff my crisp nails (even if they require clipping not buffing), and glance at the mirror to assess whether a shave is required (though I have never been capable of whiskers). On the way out I tell Bosco to hold the fort—there is no reason to subject him to the Opossum again—and pick up a couple of finger-shaped balloons because the Childoos always expect a gift; an egg crate would do. Oh, if only realizing joy were so easy!

Lumbering down the staircase, lightheaded from the balloon blowing, suddenly, uncannily, I have the sensation of being observed again—I think I sense that phantom firefly from my dreams. As I pause to collect my breath, my wits, I survey the gate, the length of boundary wall, but my cataract eye renders me practically blind in weak light.[34] Then I hear the cartoon voices of those crazy little Childoos: *Choo-choo (choo-choo), chuk-chuk (chuk-chuk).* Verily, they have the power to banish ghosts!

---

34. 'They just snip it, man,' Felix once said about cataract surgery. 'It's like clipping your nails.' But then, I rarely clip my nails. It's a grand waste of time. Ditto for dental health: Doc Rumi, my dentist, was always flabbergasted, but squeezing caterpillars of toothpaste over a toothbrush day in, day out is taxing, especially if you don't have teeth. And barber visits? They say man is evolving towards hairlessness. I look forward to it.

When I enter the parlour flinging balloons in the air, they run to me in mismatched slippers chanting *Cha! Cha! Jan!* as if welcoming a politician. 'You must let Chacha Jan sit!' Nargis cries. 'You're in his way!'

'Not in my way,' I pant, 'they're never in my way.'

Palming my cantaloupe knees, I say, 'I want one kiss on this cheek, and one on the other.' Guddu capably complies but Toto, a famously inept kisser, licks my face as if licking ice cream. A wilful, spirited character, he is also known for conspiring against his elder-by-twelve-minutes brother—there is no doubt in my mind that he will purloin Guddu's balloon by bedtime.

As soon as the two march off, Babu embraces me, an awkward gesture partly because we are not the embracing sort, and partly because I am in medias res. 'When they were up, they were up,' I hum, 'and when they were down, they were down—'[35]

'Sir?'

'Cheers, partner.'

'Happy birthday!'

Drawing my attention towards a wreath with the proportions of a tractor tyre, the sort that embellishes the grave of a bureaucrat or brigadier, Babu says, 'Isn't it special?' as if he fashioned it himself.

'Yes, but I'm still alive—'

'God is merciful!'

Babu contends he sent word the day before via Barbarossa to join the family for supper, a claim that cannot be supported because the old man oft cannot recall the number of toes on his feet, but I play along: I say I was out with a friend but do not mention the friend or venue because Nargis is the sort who consults the Holy Book to make the most mundane decisions—I swear she flipped the pages

35. 'And,' you might recall, 'when they were only halfway up, they were neither up nor down.'

to determine whether she ought to serve Polka ice cream during the Holy Month—and sees Signs of Judgment Day everywhere. If she only knew I was as drunk as a wheelbarrow the night before.

When the cake arrives—the spongy, saccharine sort, the sort that can kill a diabetic—I think *Good God* but say, 'Good job!'

'Nargis organized it,' declaims Babu.

'Always so thoughtful.'

Whilst Nargis and I do not have an equation, she is probably a good girl, or good enough: she takes care of her family & unlike me, is integral to the household, even if she does not appreciate the Lodge: I have heard her bemoan the seepage, broken tiles, weedy backyard on various occasions. There is no doubt that she would immigrate to the suburban wasteland of the Defence housing schemes if she could afford it. She has my blessings!

As the seven candles are ritually lit,[36] I call out to the bacha party, knife in hand like Abraham (PBUH) at Moriah. They gambol in like drunks, howling *Hay-pee Baad-deh Too-yoo!* They take mousy bites, chew with mouths agape. During the commotion, I fold the deathly collops from my plate into a napkin & shove them into the recesses of my trouser pockets. You do not want to die with cake on your face.

BABU AND I SIT facing each other afterward, contemplating the walls. I don't know my youngest brother particularly well—after all, I departed for college soon after he was born—and what do you discuss with an IT manager at a Shariah-compliant leasing firm? 'Say,' I begin, 'why don't you play table tennis anymore? If I recall correctly, partner, you excelled at it. You won that trophy—'

'It was for third place, in class seven—'

---

36. I prefer those other candles, trick candles, the variety that don't extinguish in a breath. After all, why do we have to hammer the fact that existence is evanescent?

'That's qualitatively better than being seventh place in class three—'

'I wanted to talk to you about something, Abdullah Bhai—'

'There is no doubt in my mind that there is a conspiracy to deride the noble sport of table tennis by characterizing it as ping-pong—'

'You know this house, it's like a clock.'

As Babu wipes his flat forehead with a gesture calling attention to the hair plugs sown across the gleaming surface of his scalp, I shift my weight from one cheek to another, wondering how I fit: am I a hand, spring, tourbillion? 'What are you getting at, partner?'

'Let me start again,' Babu says, changing tack. 'When Papa, bless his soul, was alive, things were different. And now things are different. Wouldn't you agree, Abdullah Bhai?'

'You have ably stated the obvious.'

'I mean to say our circumstances have changed, and there's so much upkeep required in this house, and we can't expect—'

Before the conversation can scrape further, I'm saved by the bell. But the thak-a-thak-a-thak-a of a Derby cane against the floor undoubtedly heralds another brother, the eldest, Hidayatullah, *Major Sahab to you*. Although success might have eluded him in recent years—he flipped real estate during the construction boom in the early eighties and has been living beyond his means ever since—he sits on several boards, presides over the Rotary Club, cultivates local consuls general & mandarins in the capital. He is not known to frequent these parts. *I'm stuck up*, he maintains, *it's the spondylosis*. 'How old are you, shehzaday?' he asks.

Peeling myself from the sofa and yanking the waist of my sagging trousers, I reply, 'Seventy, sir.'

'Seventy, my foot!'

'Does he look seventy?' Babu interjects.

Nargis shakes her head like a new bride.

Whilst I have oft been told I do not look my age—it is, perhaps, one of the few benedictions of corpulence—I sense conspiracy in this easy effusion. 'I am flattered—'

'I remember,' the Major continues, 'he would be messing about in the house and lawn in the afternoon, nanga-patanga—'

'I wore nappies—'

'I remember you trapped worms and beetles and made those little muddy men.'

'In the sweat of thy face shalt thou eatst bread,' I mutter, 'till thou return unto the ground.'

'You've finally started reciting the Koran, shehzaday?'

'Will you have cake, Hidayatullah Bhai,' Nargis interjects, 'and biscuits?' Nobody has offered me any biscuits & I do relish a biscuit, a splendid genus, incorporating everything from the modest saltine to the vanilla wafer.[37] 'Please sit,' she adds, 'please sit.'

As the confections are passed around the room, the Major enquires, 'What are you doing these days?'

'Me? Oh. Well, sir, I'm working on several urgent projects, essays, articles, monographs—one on historiographical sensibilities, another on culinary anthropology and, of course, the mythopoetic legacy of—'

'I have always said that raw talent is like sewage: it needs to be treated.'

'Sir?'

'When will we see the fruits of your labour?'

'It's a matter of time.' I notice my red silk shirt is wet in twin crescents under my chest. 'I'm ironing out some didactic tics—'

'I'll be dead soon, shehzaday.'

'Avoid the cake,' I mumble under my breath.

---

37. I have recently discovered these scrumptious dark chocolate wafer rolls at Agha's. I can inhale an entire tin of the confections as a snack, especially after some hash. But I must exert self-control.

Whilst we sit about like a family, discussing this, that, the other, foreign policy, physiotherapy, the flower show, I find myself speculating about the objective of the Major's visit. The clan only gathers at marriages and funerals, a night or two during Muharram, and on the second day of Eid. The Major's third wife, a Kashmiri who wears too much rouge, has been to the house a few times, usually for the Childoos' joint birthday. Nobody assembles for mine.

'We have to think about the future,' the Major is saying, digging into his chair.

'What about the future?' I blurt.

'The past is the past but the future belongs to them,' he says with a vague nod towards his audience, the conspirators. 'We have to think about square yardage and equity. We have to think about the Lodge.'

And suddenly it all makes sense. Suddenly, I pass gas; when vexed, I pass gas. It sounds like a bleat and smells like French Onion Soup. I glance at the painting on the wall facing me—a forested vista cut by a winding bottle green stream; regard the adjacent Dutch tapestry depicting cherubs feting each other, which has been in our possession for at least seventy years; and study the porcelain plates beside my arm, featuring round-faced Chinese dames of an arguably homosexual bent inhaling a plucked flower. I notice two heirlooms—the Bohemian cut-glass stallion & the ivory horn—are missing. Presumably, they have been sold. I will not allow myself to be sold!

Rising in a huff, I announce, 'There was a Certain Man in Russia Long Ago! He was Big and Strong and his Eyes were Flaming Gold!'

The audience is rendered speechless. I am out the door, however, when I hear Nargis whisper, 'Is that cake in his pocket?'

ON HOW HISTORIOGRAPHICAL SENSIBILITIES INFORM THE POLITICS OF PRESERVATION

IT IS SAID THAT on the continent of Europe and in certain swaths of the Americas, the Trajectory of History is considered linear. Homer, old Pliny the Elder & that curmudgeon Marx might have posited other paradigms, but since the storied Enlightenment and subsequent Colonial Conquests—the former strangely informing the latter—the Caucasian tribes have broadly believed that history is a Chronicle of Progress.

The Chinese, on the other hand, have always maintained that History is Cyclical. After occupying the centre of the world for an epoch, they experienced an epoch of profound turmoil, barbarism, bloodshed, war;[38] after inventing bells, noodles and printing, plastromancy, metallurgy and fireworks,[39] they were swept aside by

38. There was even a period known as the 'Warring States Period.' It went on for two hundred and fifty years! Imagine: that's as if the American Civil War continued to this day!

39. Whilst researching acupuncture when my back gave way several years ago, I compiled a list at the Club library of the following Chinese inventions: the animal zodiac, pinhole camera, cannonball, landmine, coffin, golf, football, high-alcohol beer (the regular variety was invented in Iraq), lavatory paper, the toothbrush.

insidious opiate winds, a brutal occupation; and after Great Leaps Forward and falling flat on their rumps, they generated muscular economic growth that is eclipsing what the Caucasians call the West (but the Chinese consider the East). The motto of the Chinese could be: *We Might Be Eating Grass Now. But Wait a Millennium. Things Will Change.*

Then there is the Musalman. It is said that we subscribe to a third historical paradigm, that of the Golden Age. We hearken to different times, different eras, whether the Caliphate of the Pious (termed CP4 hereafter) or the Splendour That Was Andalusia. Of course, the period of the Caliphate was not particularly rosy: the second caliph cuffed the elected successor to the community circa 632 CE,[40] then instituted severe punishment for inebriation; his successor was knocked off by vexed protestors demanding the head of his good-for-nothing governor; and the Mighty Ali (AS) was mired in civil wars before being felled by the first bona fide fundamentalists of Islam.[41] In our collective memory, however, CP4 is an oasis in the Sahara of history.[42]

One would think that the Musalman predilection of looking back would compel them to preserve the past, but that is nary the case. Like children with dynamite, the Bedouins running the Hijaz have

40. And Saad ibn Ubayda (RA) never recovered. Madelung's brilliant *Succession to Muhammad* provides a comprehensive account of the events subsequent to the Prophet's (PBUH) death. It will make a Shia out of you.

41. It is no secret that the Khariji Imperative has returned with a vengeance today. Many Kharijis, by the way, settled in Beloochistan. Go figure.

42. Of course, our notions of history are more complicated than the above three paragraphs would suggest: the Great Ibn Khaldun articulated the most sophisticated historiographical analysis known to civilization; Marx was fundamentally a cyclicalist; and we have not even touched the Buddhist or for that matter, the Papuan conception of history. According to the Hindoos, incidentally, we inhabit the Age of Kali.

been tearing down monuments willy-nilly. In 1924, the graveyard that housed the Prophet's (PBUH) first wife was razed, and two years later, the mausoleums of the Prophet's (PBUH) daughter & grandson as well. When we did not protest, the Bedouins blasted the Seven Famous Mosques.[43] In their place, they constructed shopping complexes, retail banking outlets, those Currency Dispensing Machines. And imagine: they constructed public toilets on the Prophet's (PBUH) wife's house!

Verily, Islam became better the further it moved away from the desert. It is a matter of fact that a drop of water from a secret fountainhead only nourishes land, peoples, civilizations when it picks up momentum. The Torrent of Islam thusly originated in the Hijaz before widening into a river in Syria, Persia, Anatolia, North Africa, then opening into a sea that touched the rest of the world. Unbeknownst to most, Islam first reached the Subcontinent not on horseback but via the coast.

Whilst there has not been any wholesale destruction of the Bedouin variety in the Subcontinent, historical preservation has been wanting.[44] My brother Tony told me that his childhood policeman friend, Hur a.k.a. Hawkeye, presently Deputy Inspector General (DIG), narrated the following story: 'Yahoodi Masjid, or Magen Shalome as it was known, came under my watch when I served in Garden. When I heard that the land mafia was eyeing the property,

---

43. Said mosques belonged to Salman Farsi (RA), Abu B. (RA), Omar the Caliph (RA), the mighty Ali (AS) & his wife.

44. We preserve Sufi tombs, but the hundreds of stupas dotting the land are rotting like carcasses under the sun. It is said that the cremated remains of the Gautama are hidden in eighty-four boxes of silver from Patna to Kandahar. The Biharis have preserved some, whilst the Pathans of late are intent on destruction. Between the poles, one of the Last Swaths of the Muslim World to have been colonized, the Scindees of Scinde, practise supreme neglect.

I went to investigate. The caretaker, this old lady named Rachel, said most of her kind had left after the wars with Israel. All her documents were in order—title deed, expense reports[45]—but when I tried to secure the site, my superior resisted. If I were a better man, I'd have stood up for it.' The synagogue was razed in the summer of '88. That's not even yesterday.

Secular constructions, broadly speaking, do not command much interest or attention. Take Mohenjo-Daro, or for that matter, the Olympus. Constructed by my grandfather by 1919, a relic of the First World War construction boom, the establishment was indeed unique, arguably the only aesthetic outpost of the Hapsburg Empire in the Subcontinent.[46] I do not believe any Hapsburg availed of our hospitality but if any Raja or Rana sojourned in the city, he would be stationed in one of our Deluxe Suites. Several sipped Scotch in proper Baccarat crystal, played the Baby Grand to an empty lobby, long after the world changed.[47]

Our fortunes began changing with the dictatorial edict shifting the capital to the Poonjab—occupancy rates fell when foreigners left

---

45. Hawkeye mentioned a card that read, 'Circumcisions: 4 annas; Bar Mitzvahs: 8 annas.'

46. At the time, more than half of the town's real estate was owned by the Great Edulji Dinshaw who famously financed schools, dispensaries & the storied engineering college that continues to function & bears his name.

47. If the Brits had vision, the Subcontinent would have been arranged sensibly, like Europe. After all, the Subcontinent was a collection of 572 states. Partition is a preposterous misnomer—what was there to part? The best arrangement would have been a federation of five, six unions: the Republic of the Indus, United States of South Asia and so on. The Bengalis would have been delighted to have Bengal all to themselves. (Ditto for the Poonjabis & the Poonjab.) But the British imposed their bizarre vision for disparate peoples, disparate lands for an area larger than Europe. Europe might be some subcontinent; we are the Continent.

for greener pastures—and there was also the silly war in '65, an inept attempt to redress the legacy of colonial gerrymandering. Who visits in a Time of War? Exogenous shocks aside, the hoteling landscape also changed: the Shadow Lounge lost out to the Intercon's Nasreen Room, Palace's Le Gourmet. Moreover, as the boundaries of the city expanded exponentially, we found ourselves relegated to the periphery.

Then there is the Sunset Lodge (named thusly because the vista of dusk from the veranda was said to be spectacular). Conceived by the renowned Moses Somake,[48] a local Jew who also designed Uncle Jinnah's residence, Flagstaff House, the Lodge was fashioned in what they call the Indo-Gothic mode. The central structure, hewed from yellow limestone quarried in Gizri, is flanked by semicircular turrets featuring narrow windows. A stairway ribbons down one side and another down the back, leading to the garage and annex that once housed the domestics' quarters. There are three bedrooms downstairs plus a parlour furnished with oak wainscot where Papa would host bridge nights on a plush green table (now lodged in the kitchen), and three and a half bedrooms upstairs, not including the garret. Bosco inhabits Tony's tiny old room which still houses his collection of multicoloured bongs and remains plastered with posters of Hawaiian Elvis Presley and sixties pinups, including Jean Seberg wearing not much more than a hat. My parents' erstwhile abode serves as my bedroom & library, drawing & dining rooms.

I would like to believe that the Lodge will remain when I am gone, rearing successive generations of the clan, but I might be mistaken. Whilst I inhabit the Master Bedroom, I am reminded that I am not Lord of the Manor.

48. One has heard of the renowned architects of the time: J.A. Shiveshankar, Jamsedji P. Mistry, Durgas Advani, M. Nazareth, Gulshan Jalal & Khemji.

VOLUME II

ON ROADSIDE METAPHYSICS
(OR THE CURIOUS CASE OF THE PHANTOM FIREFLY)

ONE AFTERNOON DURING THE Holy Month, I experience that indistinct but unmistakable sensation of being followed. It occurs in the broad vicinity of Empress Market, environs I know like the inside of my pocked, pallid thigh; once upon a time, I would accompany Papa to the landmark to purchase meat & vegetables for the kitchens at the Olympus, clutching an extended finger, cloth bag slung over my shoulder. The structure's sturdy walls and imposing tower reminded me of a storybook castle. Indeed, some of my fondest childhood memories reside in the stalls and alleys of this sprawling compound—a musty, indeed magical realm,[49] inhabited by that spirited, mercurial species, the butcher: Original Heir of Man. If you do not know what you want, he jeers at you like a harlequin, but if you do, and Papa did, he is an obliging djinn: a sleight of hand would yield a cut of clod or silverside. At the time, of course, I could not distinguish tongue from tripe, but I have since developed the sense and sensibility that allows me to appreciate the modalities, indeed, the majesty of meat.

---

49. Not so long ago, a Hindoo tailor told me that Empress Market was built on a site where the Brits hung political prisoners after an uprising. The story goes that after the hanging of a Hindoo rebel, flowers would appear on the site every morning. The authorities posted guards and then, in a tizzy, rounded up the members of the family and banished them from the city. I have searched for the marigold bouquet. One day, I might find it.

But I am not in the market for protein or produce; Barbarossa procures the meat for the household—I suspect he serves up blinded cockerels on occasion—and my roots, tended lately by one Bosco, are famous across Garden. I have been lecturing the lad on Topics in the Horticultural Sciences since he has been in my stewardship (what has it been? a fortnight? two?) addressing matters that include the Requisite Water for the Healthy Development of Vegetation in Sandy Loam and Coastal Subtropical Conditions.[50] Brow furrowed, legs crossed, he takes notes. There are, however, secrets about various processes—the Modulation of pH Levels in Soil with the Use of Milk, for instance—that I cannot, or rather, will not disclose. You have to learn some things by doing, by living. And Bosco is doing.

No, I am on my way to pick up reference books required to tackle the only enterprise of any consequence in my life, The Mythopoetic Legacy of Abdullah Shah Ghazi (RA) (and, if Lady Luck smiles, several dog-eared copies of a local digest that features Lesbian trysts[51]). The fact of the matter is that I need to get out of the Lodge, and my head. Although not temperamentally paranoid—anxious, yes, but not paranoid—I sense a sulphuric conspiracy. There have been intimations even prior to the Major's visit.

THE OTHER WEEK, FOR instance, I woke to an unfamiliar mechanical clamour, deriving from the general vicinity of the vegetable garden. To

50. I suspect that changes in the hydrological cycle are causing Global Warning via evapotranspiration. Put differently, put simply, more water is evaporating into the atmosphere than before. If you're an avid gardener, somebody who has been at it for decades, if there is a crust of dirt lining your fingernails, you will know. Nobody cares here. Maulvis, for example, pray for Judgment Day. They want the world reduced to dust.

51. Bless the Lesbians and their trysts. Bless publications that appeal to both head & hand.

my shock and weak-kneed horror, a large diesel generator, veritably as alien as a UFO, materialized by the boundary wall, belching smoke. My calculations suggested that the device occupied 17 per cent of my patch, ravaging the zucchinis and cherry tomatoes that garnish my cold pasta salads. When I protested to Babu that evening, I was told in a tenor reserved for recalcitrant children that the 'loadshedding situation' had compelled him to acquire a second-hand, Korean-manufactured 6 kVA generator.

'I'm not concerned about the capability of the dashed contraption! I'm concerned about its placement, partner, and the smoke—look at that smoke!'

'We had no choice.' *We who?* I would have liked to ask. 'You see,' he gestured, 'the line from the street enters here from the grid.' The fact had the force and function of a full stop.

But it's not just a matter of generators: if I were to construct a treehouse for the Childoos in the old banyan in the backyard (a project I have been mulling for years, even if I do not possess the stamina or know-how), there would be strident demurrals, drama. And a treehouse is a major infrastructural undertaking; I even have to inform the authorities if I solicit the services of a plumber when the commode gets backed up. A plumber, for God's sake! One cannot even relieve oneself without negotiating the dashed administration!

I feel somewhat unstable, somewhat unhinged. I am in good company: everyone turns lunatic in the Holy Month, or worse—small, testy, sanctimonious. In fact, the only time one feels the presence of God during this disconsolate period is when one happens to be on the streets at the break of fast: the city seems uninhabited then, and in the resonant silence, there are Intimations of Providence. But the streets remain raucous until then, teeming with the faithful, hurried, harried, haggling over the price of fritters.

Consequently, I find myself walking in circles. But I am not a famous walker: my gait is laboured due to the girth of my thighs and recurring gout in my knee, not to mention the cotton sack slung over my shoulder, weighed down by a thermos of water, a box of cardamom biscuits, a spare pair of knickers, and a volume of Müller's *Sacred Books of the East*. And my size, complexion, the drama of my parasol[52] presumably attract gawkers, street children, the attention of pye-dogs—try as I might, I cannot avoid notice. But I have attracted something odd, ineffable, today, like the shadowy fireflies that flit across the field of vision in the sun. Perhaps it's the heat; perhaps, Ateed or Raqeeb[53]—it is, after all, the Holy Month.

By the time I arrive at the narrow environs of Afghan Alley, populated by merchants lounging on rolls of fabric, swatting flies, I am parched and panting. Just as I raise the rim of my thermos to my maw, a hoarse admonition rings out: 'Kya karti hay?' or *What are you doing?*

Turning, I find a lupine lad sporting a fanned beard. 'Kya lagta hay kya kar rahi hoon?' I reply, or *What does it look like I'm doing?*

'Tum musalman ho?' he persists, or *You a Musalman?*

I am asked to elucidate my relationship with God in the bright light of day—a parlous query at the best of times. What to say? What to do? When I was young, of course, I would have run. The boys

---

52. The relic provides only a pretense of shade. Isn't it perplexing that Umbrella Technology remains so horribly primitive well into the Twenty-First Century? We should have developed umbrellas with fans by now, like John Steed's whangee-handled marvel.

53. Those in the know know that Ateed & Raqeeb are those clerical angels perched on our shoulders, recording our deeds from puberty to the grave in respective ledgers in shorthand. Those in the know won't, however, tell you that it is the accounting for good deeds that ultimately does us in. Who would disagree that Good ought to come from within rather than without?

chased me in the playground at Jufelhurst[54]—the Brothers Ud-Din I recall, neighbours, nemeses—chanting, *Fatty Boy, Fatty Boy, turn around; Fatty Boy, Fatty Boy, touch the ground.* Although I was chubby if not quite corpulent, and the jibes were not particularly clever—sticks, stones and that whole thing—there were occasions when I was tripped or biffed as well. Returning home, I would shove my head in Mummy's ample bosom, red-eyed, and lie, complaining of headaches. Since she suspected migraines, she took me to a hakim, an autistic chap who lived on a farm amongst goats and a broken Jeep and prescribed proprietary medieval remedies packaged in satchels tied with string. The foul concoction wrought of reddish powdered leaves turned glutinous and slimy when mixed with milk. I suffered it daily even though it made me retch, suffered it for Mummy's sake.

And later, much later, I attracted violence for different reasons: when I would brush against some young hothead at the Shadow Lounge, I would be mistaken for the Goliath to his David. As a result, I learnt to avert my gaze, slouch, shrink into myself.

But not anymore; I am too old, too large. Breaking wind, I holler. 'This is Currachee! This my city! I could be Catholic, Protestant, Pentecostal, Hindoo, Amil, Parsee. I could be Shia, Sunni, Ismaili, Bohra, Barelvi, Sufi, Chishty, Naqshbandy, Suhrawardy, Wajoodi, Malamati, Dehria, anything, everything. If you want to ask such questions then go back to Kabul!'

As the commotion attracts attention, I find myself surrounded by five or six chaps, intent on mischief if not a riot. 'O you who believe,' the boy persists, flies swarming around his head, 'fasting is prescribed for you as it was for those before you, that you may become pious!'

---

54. I must note that Jufelarians are some of the finest graduates in the country. But no more: one hears that the Building Control Authority wants to tear the edifice down. Ms Sybil D'Abreo, who built the school in '31, would undoubtedly be turning over in her grave.

'The Prophet (PBUH) said, "What is better than charity and fasting and prayer? Keeping peace and good relations between people!"'

And for the next five, ten, fifteen minutes, a dashed eternity, we are locked in an excitable roadside doctrinal debate that features piecemeal quotation of scripture, anecdotal evidence, tenuous analogies, madcap allusions, CP4. After a chorus of *alhumdulillahs*, the learned perspectives of grandfathers, uncles, the neighbourhood maulvi (a veritable Renaissance Man) are invoked. I want to say, 'Bhaar main jaye tumhara chacha!'—viz., *To hell with your uncle!*—but instead attempt to communicate that there are manifold realities, and they have no claim on mine.

'My piety,' I proclaim, 'is between God and me. How dare you intervene!' They can do what they want to do—shave their moustaches whilst letting their pubic beards run amok—only if I can do what I want to do: drink water in the middle of the street in the middle of the Holy Month. I am a diabetic for God's sake! My God allows it if theirs does not. 'If you're sensible, then your God is sensible,' I proclaim, 'but if you're a dolt, your God's a dolt!'[55]

My antagonist swats my flask to the ground. The horde smells blood. *Fatty Boy, Fatty Boy, turn around; Fatty Boy, Fatty Boy, touch the ground.* I am ready. I have been ready since my birthday. It will be a good death, a noble death. But before I am knocked down, kicked in the ribs, beaten to watermelon pulp, and interred at the end of the urine-stained alley, I perceive movement from the corner of my eye.

Turning, I behold a looker in the fray, an equine-faced, flinty-eyed dame in a low-cut canary kameez and tangerine pyjama. 'Oye!' she cries like a traffic warden. Leaving me to my own devices, the horde

---

55. For the record, the exact words I employed were: *Agar tum bawlay ho to tumhara khuda bhi bawla ho ga.*

turns on her, jeering & jostling, shoving & shouting, 'Scamp!' 'Hussy!' 'We will break your legs!'

Although it's an opportune moment to flee, I am not a bad man, a dishonourable man; I stand before my Godsent saviour like a boulder and declare, 'You pray five times a day, keep your fasts, but this is the way you treat another human being? A lady? Shame on you! Shame on you all! If this is your creed, I am a Kaffir!'

There is a pause, a moment pregnant with peril—the smell of sweat is thick in the air like spoiled meat—then one of the lads picks up my flask and hands it to me. I guzzle a quart before my audience in one glorious swig—verily, water tastes like wine when one's thirsty—then beckon to the dame with a wave of the hand. Hopping over a crate like a lady, she grabs my hand like a man, and we dash like Bonnie and Clyde, leaving the faithful to contemplate exercises in eschatology, epistemology & logos.

'I am very grateful to you,' I say, hailing a taxi.

'You should be,' she replies matter-of-factly.

I ask her name. I hear *Jugnu*. I ask where I should take her. 'I am with you,' she announces. I look into her fantastic, indeed obsidian eyes. I am certain I know her from somewhere else.

ON POETICUS, FURORE
(OR COME, IF ONLY TO LEAVE AGAIN)

ANY CIVILIZED HUMAN BEING can tell you that in the Taxonomy of Verse, the ghazal is not only unique because of the associated protocols of rhyme, refrain and metre,[56] but because as a form it

---

56. It has come to my attention that there is a community of poets outside Our Swath of the World that has adopted the ghazal, concentrated especially in the otherwise insular United States of America: Merwin, Rich, Wideman. Of course, the Yanks, consummate innovators, have altered the concerns of the form—I came across the following verses penned by Heather McHugh, for example, at the second-hand book bazaar at Regal Chowk recently, 'Ghazal of the Better-Unbegun':

> Too volatile, am I? too voluble? too much a word-person?
> I blame the soup: I'm a primordially stirred person.
>
> Two pronouns and a vehicle was Icarus with wings.
> The apparatus of his selves made an absurd person.
>
> The sound I make is sympathy's: sad dogs are tied afar.
> But howling I become an ever more unheard person.
>
> I need a hundred more of you to make a likelihood.
> The mirror's not convincing—that at-best inferred person.
>
> As time's revealing gets revolting, I start looking out.
> Look in and what you see is one unholy blurred person.
>
> The only cure for birth one doesn't love to contemplate.
> Better to be an unsung song, an unoccurred person.
>
> McHugh, you'll be the death of me—each self and second studied!
> Addressing you like this, I'm halfway to the third person.

functions only to address love, particularly the unrequited variety. Imagine if the limerick were exclusively devoted to pain, say, arthritis, or the villanelle pertained only to matters of geological time; and the triolet—what about the triolet?[57]

Recall that the lover in the ghazal is typically a fool, a masochist; the Inimitable Ghalib, for instance, wrote, 'I will be dust before you realize I am here.' Why couldn't he have just dispatched a note? 'Madam, you stir me. Yours, G.' Note or not, the lover is doomed from the beginning, and the beloved is typically elusive, illusive, cruel until the end; and sometimes God. Consequently, every word is a metaphor. Indeed, the homologous conceit suggests the Multidimensional Dominion of Love: the ghazal asserts that divine and profane love are fundamentally, organically the same stuff. That is elegant, profound, tip-top.

But I'm no philologist, poet, no authority on Urdu[58]—I cannot pen ghazals, much less rearrange the topography of contemporary poetry. After the incident at Afghan Alley, however, I find myself composing spontaneous doggerel in my head, affected, as it were, by afflatus, and God has nothing to do with it—I cannot recall the last time a dame smiled, just smiled at me, and this dame has saved my worthless life.

AS WE SIT SIDE by side on the ride home like children thrust together by serendipity, I find myself stealing glances at Jugnu's slender nape,

---

57. There is no doubt that the flat topography of contemporary poetry requires a fundamental reconfiguration. Who wants to read another poem marrying mundane diurnal rituals that characterize modern life with profundity? Only the other day, I came across a peculiar poem entitled, 'I Am Intimate with My Brush,' purporting to pertain to love, life, the human predicament.

58. I'm technically Gujarati-speaking though my Gujarati's poor. My mother's tongue was Urdu though she was technically Pathan. We are all fundamentally cultural salads.

swimmer's posture, and the zircon stud embellishing her aquiline nose, reminding myself not to stare. She has no such compunction: when I stutteringly, circumspectly, enquire whether it was she who spied on me the other day, my birthday, she looks me in the eye, and declaims, 'Tum nangay thay,' viz., poetically speaking, *I observed you in full plumage*. The response induces a couplet—'Dallying outside, she spies a small indiscretion / Admittedly, I'm no Priapus, a peacock perhaps'[59]—and colour in the cheeks.

Changing the subject, I ask, 'What were you doing in Afghan Alley?' She offers but a smile in response. One can only discern this much: the dame wafts talcum powder and tobacco and is Cool as a Cucumber. As we swerve through traffic, for instance, my leg keeps knocking against hers, behaviour generally unbecoming of a gentleman, but when I apologize, she places a long reassuring hand on my gouty knee. 'Koi nahin,' she avers—*No worries*.

At the Lodge, however, I deport myself in an uncivil manner again: when we arrive, I realize I cannot invite her in. How can I? There is always somebody if not somebody else installed in the parlour—Babu and Nargis, Barbarossa or the Childoos—somebody always coming or going, especially in the Holy Month—Nargis' neighbourhood gang, housebound malcontents who find solace in the sermons of a revivalist preacher, that famous swine Chambu, manager of my garment-dyeing business, or our squawking relatives, Badbakht and Gulbadan Begum,[60] who drop by unannounced for supper at the drop of a hat—and at that moment I espy Bua lurking in the shadows, undoubtedly conspiring with her good-for-nothing husband and good-for-nothing son.

---

59. Recall the following ancient verse: 'Obscenis, peream, Priape, si non / Uti me pudet improbisque verbis / Sed cum tu posito deus pudore / Ostendas mihi coleos patentes / Cum cunno mihi mentula est vocanda.'

60. We had nicknamed them Gulbadan, or Rose Body, and Badbakht, or Bad Luck, and it stuck.

Imagine if I am seen going up with a dame! Imagine if the authorities got wind of it! It would be a dashed debacle! There is a social law that few acknowledge: Relationships Are a Function of Logistics. Consequently, I fix a time to meet at the zoo the following day on the benches outside the Reptile House—what the Yanks would call a date—before dispatching her into the night with a small fortune for carriage. It breaks my heart, but what to do?

Lying awake in my quarters, staring at a gecko on the prowl, I plan a picnic in my head as if planning a banquet—silk napkins, silver cutlery, the candelabra. There will be pakoras and hunter-beef-and-butter sandwiches, bottles of pop, Pakola; strawberries, chocolate syrup, and ice cream! Although I might not be able to arrange entertainment on short notice—snake charmer, Mariachi Singers—I will charm her with jokes, droll anecdotes, poetry:

Would have offered samosas, tea,
My jackfruit maybe—
But how to get in? And out?
Rendezvous day after, we agree, at dusk.
Sky purple before dawn,
And bloated like a belly;
Distant gunfire, or firecrackers,
Restlessness pervades, and dew.

I should have woken with the cock and crows at first light, but instead wake on the morrow at midday like a delinquent, panicked and palpitating: the probability that I can organize a picnic banquet is next to nil—a soufflé rising in a sandstorm.[61] Girding my loins,

---

61. I have it on good authority that our young friend HH managed a Pavlova in a makeshift tin-box oven in Murree. Man Bites Dog? Ha! How about Man Makes Meringue on the Mountain!

however, I reckon I can, at the least, fry some samosas. But those in the know know that the manufacturing of a samosa requires stamina and nimble fingers, and mine are like cigars—more Toro Grande than Petit Robusto. Consequently, flattening the doughy balls into paper-thin discs is trying, fashioning the miniature cones, testing. No matter! I am a man possessed!

As the skinned potatoes for the filling come to a boil, I am reminded that my only pair of linen slacks is stained with frosting, and since Barbarossa must be cocking about, and Bua conspiring with her husband, I retrieve a cauldron from the kitchen myself and squat on my haunches in the loo for the first time since the Tit-for-Tat Nuclear Tests in '98, scrubbing like Lady Macbeth. There are fireworks. I pass out in the tub.

When Bosco stirs me—'Hypotension again, Uncle Cossack?'—I pop up like toast from a toaster, hot and bothered: the samosas are not sorted and the trousers are wet along the lining. 'Dash Murphy,' I thunder, 'and dash his law!'

'Who's Murphy?' Bosco asks.

'He discovered the fourth law of thermodynamics,' I reply. 'Read up on it. I'll quiz you when I'm back.'

Ad interim, I conduct my own Experiments in Thermodynamics: after sliding limp fritters into boiling corn oil, I place my trousers in the oven at 10°C—an inspired gambit. But just then, Murphy strikes again: I hear a howl from downstairs and descend, thighs chafing, to find Toto has banged his nose on the swinging doors. Guddu weeps in fraternal sympathy. Since neither Nargis nor Bua is in sight—they would have undoubtedly resorted to that absurd strategy of beating the villainous table—I settle them on the settee and narrate the fable about the Lion & the Mouse. The moral of the story is not really relevant: the trick is to divert attention immediately. If only I had children of my own to spoil! But I am only capable of spoiling samosas: the first batch is burnt, and badly.

Collapsing on the floor like Toto, I mull my precarious place in the universe, certain I have been Born Under a Bad Sign, before Barbarossa emerges, transistor tucked under his arm (playing that old number, 'Khayal rakhna'), wet rag slung over his shoulder (the one he uses to polish the beaks of cocks with palm oil) to save the day. 'Leave me to,' he says in English.

Kissing my Godsent saviour on the head—he smells of naswar and cockerel and sunflower oil—I rush to brush my dentures, administer a sponge bath, don my lucky red shirt and splatter eau de toilette across my jowls, only to recall that my trousers remain in the oven. Mercifully, they are not singed.

I feel pleased with myself, but Murphy, that lout, is relentless: on my way out, I find Chambu in a dark safari suit stretched on the deck chair on the lawn, waving as if we are childhood friends reunited at a beachside resort. 'Boss!' he calls.

It is a matter of fact that you can appraise the Measure of a Man from his teeth and toes: Chambu's teeth recall yellowing Scrabble tiles, his sponge slippers expose talons, and once he seizes you by the scruff, he will eat your brain like a buzzard.[62] 'We are both gaseous individuals,' he might begin, 'and you know how dangerous gas can be.' You might ask, *What to do?* 'Boil two grains of jaggery and a slice of ginger in water and take a tablespoon before and after lunch and dinner. It will make you a new man, a better man.' *What an elegant elixir!* you think. *It might just revolutionize gastronomy, revolutionize me!*

As soon as Chambu opens the battered portmanteau that always yields a set of ancient files, a tape recorder, a can of olive oil and a

---

62. It was not always like this: his progenitor, a good man, a dedicated man, dropped dead of congestive heart disease in the employ of the accounts department at the Olympus. Before his demise, he exhorted us to take care of his son. Who knew the boy would turn out to be a swine?

packet of dry fruits—'for the Sex Drive,'[63] he claims—I holler, 'Not interested in your nuts today!'

'You know I would never even think to bother you unless there is an emergency, unless Hell is upon us, and to be honest, to be very honest, Boss, Hell is upon us—'

'Hell is below—'

'The inspectors are threatening to cut off power,' he continues, brandishing a file, 'because we do not comply with the new wattage quota for industrial units—'

'But it is not an industrial unit—'

'If you do not come with me this very instant, you will regret the decision for months if not years, because if they shut the power, we lose our contract, and if we lose the contract, the workers will not be paid, and if the workers are not paid, they will show up at your place and there will be a riot.'

'I cannot come right now!'

'Do not tell me I did not warn you,' Chambu shrugs, turning on his heel. Oh, such blithe skulduggery! 'You can deal with them yourself if you like.'

'How much do you need?'

'Just a lakh, Boss,' he chirps.

'I am writing a cheque for twenty thousand.'

'You know, that might just work if the cheque does not bounce, but I cannot promise—'

Somehow I manage to make it to Gandhi Garden at the instant the muezzin stridently announces prayer, and slumping on the bench, picnic basket in tow, I imagine the fraternity of animals—the elephants, baboons, wallabies—breaking fast together. The

63. It's a misconception that nuts have a salutary effect on the sex drive, but Mummy maintained that almonds benefit the eyes, walnuts the brain, and peanuts the earlobes, each shape corresponding to a particular part of our physiology. Sometimes I suspect I am walnut deficient.

probability of a reunion with Jugnu is arguably as ludicrous. I hum an old tune, cross and uncross my legs, careful not to crease my trousers. But Jugnu doesn't show. I have only mosquitoes for company.

> Quiet bench, picnic basket,
> I am left bereft in the twilight.
> Come, I say out loud, to nobody in particular,
> Come, if only to leave again.[64]

---

64. I doubt that I would have impressed Jugnu with my doggerel—to be honest, it's not even entirely mine. The following verses penned by my young friend A. Allawalla, writer, raconteur, might be more apt:

> I should have been born a son-of-a-bitch,
> Not needing to love;
> Instead, here I am, a derelict,
> Upon the shores of sin,
> Unable to even wave at ships floating away like tulips...
> So where to go,
> With your thorn-shred feet and broken bits of heart?
> Where indeed?
> And indeed how,
> Should I fall in love one last time?

ON CONSEQUENCES OF THE SOCRATIC METHOD (OR SHADOWBOXING)

THE TAPER FLICKERING IN the parlour downstairs upon my return from the zoo announces loadshedding, and the smell of gasoline in the air suggests that the generator has packed up. I bang my knee on the way upstairs, bruise my rump searching for a candle stub or two in secret drawers in the pantry. Bracing for a dark night of the soul, I settle amid the clutter of my desk—bureaucratic-blue files and calendar diaries dispatched annually by banks, and notepads filled with decades of scholarship in ballpoint ink held down by an onyx ashtray, a round tin of Danish Butter Biscuits and other provisional paperweights—intending to make meaningful progress on the only project that promises certain succour, The Mythopoetic Legacy of Abdullah Shah Ghazi (RA), but it is still and sticky and I am supremely distracted. I feel like a dotard for lingering at the Reptile House, washing down fritter after fritter with thermos-brewed tea. Oh, the heart's a hungry huckster! I even missed the Childoos' bedtime.

I am known to wander downstairs just before bedtime with idle queries—*Anybody interested in these issues of National Geographic?* or *Anybody notice the geyser rattles like a box of ping-pong balls at dawn?*—prompting the Childoos to hop and cry 'Cha! Cha! Jan!' at the same time. They tug me to their room as Nargis steams in the background, sit me down on the edge of their bed, and insist on a story. My repertoire only includes the classics: the timeless adventures of the world-famous mariner Sindibad al-Bahri,[65] Podna Podni, the tale of an unjust, uncharitable Raja who is upended by a sparrow,[66] and a permutation of *The Wizard of Oz*,[67] in which I substitute the Scarecrow, Tin Man and Lion with the Childoos and me. Typically, I play the Lion, but after the fiasco at the zoo I am more like the Scarecrow—hollow & alone.

But I am not alone! *Bosco!* I think. 'Bosco?' I call. Perhaps he has abandoned me as well—everybody eventually abandons me. The lad is not in his room or the library, pantry, wardrobe. I find him on the roof, perched on an overturned basin, reading in candlelight like young Abraham Lincoln. Alarmed by me, my shadow, a sudden storm cloud, he nearly topples over. 'What,' he asks, recovering, 'is a moral man?'

Struck by the odd, unexpected query, I squat for the second time in twenty-four hours. 'A moral man,' I reply, warm tar clinging to my slippers, 'is a man who does good things.'

'But what is "good"?'

What on earth has gotten into this boy, I wonder? Although we have come across each other in the last few days, we have only

---

65. I have it on good authority, incidentally, that said sailor was a local, a denizen of Scinde. There is no doubt that our heroes have been forgotten, neglected, or appropriated.

66. Those familiar with the story—and most of us are—are aware that the fable is thrice punctuated by the following rhythmic refrain: 'Sarkando ki gari bani / Do maidak jotay jain. / Raja mari podni / Hum larnay marnay jain.' Ha!

67. When they are older, I will explain to them that the story is really an atheist allegory—the Wizard, after all, turns out to be a fake, a fraud—although I understand that there is a vocal constituency of economists who maintain that *WoZ* concerns the politics associated with the abandonment of the Silver Standard: the Gold Road gets you nowhere. But economists, like mechanics, are not to be trusted.

exchanged greetings and nods, as if we have been revolving in proximate but parallel orbits. There is no doubt that Master Bosco has spun out of control since. 'Good,' I sagely continue, 'is what is beneficial to yourself and to others.'

'Does it have to do with justice?'

It occurs to me that this peculiar, problematic line of enquiry is a youthful malady, an intellectual infection, a virus borne by gadflies. 'Sure,' I begin, 'but justice is not a samosa. It's an idea. It has a certain genealogy and context: in the jungles of the Papua, for example, justice dictates devouring an antagonist. Justice might be characterized as collective consensus—those dashed Saudis, they hack limbs, and I can tell you, lad, it doesn't always work. In the United States of America, the mecca of civilization itself, blacks are wrongly incarcerated, routinely sentenced to death. You tell me: is that justice?'

The candle flickers; Bosco fidgets. I notice his shoes, beige-brown joggers, are punctured at the toes. 'But,' he blurts, 'what about the angler?'[68]

'Ah, the dialectical angler! And what about the tinker, tailor, the famous candlestick-maker?' The whole creaky hermeneutic apparatus—not unlike the jurisprudential tool of qiyas, I might note—is intrinsically flawed. One could spend the entire night in the company of dimwits, exchanging parables. I'm a large, untidy man with a proclivity for public debate as of late. What of it? Recall the Goblet of Hemlock, the Rule of Thirty Tyrants? Timocracy? 'In this time, in this country,' I continue, 'I believe the role of a ruler is to provide order.'

'What kind of order?'

'We could talk about social and political order but why not discuss environmental or economic order? Everybody evacuates into the sea

---

68. I might mention in passing that history books ignore the fact that, after Plato's death, Aristotle took up marine biology on the island of Lesbos. After years of yapping, he eventually got down to more meaningful matters.

from Rio to Bombay. That's why Bombay duck tastes so good—you taste yourself in it. I could make a moral case against inflation, and her grotesque sibling, hyperinflation. Inflation kills but nobody talks about it. It's a conspiracy. We all talk about democracy, about freedom, but you can't eat freedom.'

I pause to allow Bosco a retort but he does not interrupt because the matter, the discipline, is obviously outside his purview, not to mention the purview of those chatty Athenians. It had also been outside mine until I developed gout: I picked up economics mostly from discussion programmes on this new CNBC channel in the waiting room of my GP's clinic.[69] 'I want to read the treatise of that philosopher,' I continue sententiously, 'who champions economic enfranchisement over political enfranchisement.'

Although I am pleased with my exegesis, Master Bosco shrugs. The boy has undoubtedly overdosed on the cerebral acrobatics of the Greeks—we all have—but perhaps he is prey to something else. There is no doubt that he too is suffering a dark night of the soul. I must distract him. 'Don't you have a girlfriend?' I ask.

'I go to an all-boys school.'

'Hobbies?'

'I forgot my yo-yo at home.'

'What's really vexing you?'

When the lad looks up, I behold that rabbit face, the powdery parentheses on either side of his mouth suggesting a moustache, a pair of bulging black eyes conveying contempt, disdain: *What would you know,* he seems to say, *you sad, fat old man?* I want to tell him that I wasn't always like this, that I was somebody else once, young,

69. I ought to mention that I stopped frequenting my GP a few years back—it's too late in the day to jumpstart my batteries. I should also mention that I am not entirely unschooled in the Discipline of Economics: I have read Rosenthal's translation of *Muqaddimah* by Ibn Khaldun, the Father of Sociology, Anthropology & Economics.

energetic, full of promise; I was known, a scion of a great family. I ran the Olympus, one of the most prominent institutions in one of the most animate cities in the world. Instead, I begin, 'Divorced from experience, ideas are meaningless. I suggest staying away from the philosophy section in the library for the time being. Read literature instead. I will put together a reading list for you. Fiction is the lie that tells the truth.'

Scrutinizing his holey joggers, Bosco says, 'If I can't put things right, if I can't do what I should do or must do, I'm no longer a good man. Do you know what I'm trying to say?'

Nodding, it occurs to me I have it all wrong: the matter is not theoretical. It could have something to do with his parents, presumably the father. The two might have quarrelled. I can imagine a rancorous exchange, a slap, a scene—the boy walking out, slamming the door behind him. Or was he thrown out? In either event, I know a father's ire. I want to embrace the lad, put his head against my heaving bosom, but instead, say, 'We will have to visit your home.' As his custodian, it is my responsibility to investigate.

'Not a good idea, Uncle Cossack.'

'Good ideas don't always work. That's what the Greeks never understood. That's why it took two millennia for them to understand the digestive system.'[70]

Before repairing to the Lodge, Bosco blows out the taper, then looks up searchingly at the sky. Hobbling on pins and needles, I point out the buttery impression of a crescent in a cloud. It is exquisite.

---

70. Instead of sitting on their sore, sallow rumps pontificating, the Great Greeks should have put scalpel to cadaver to learn the functioning of the circulatory system. It would have changed the trajectory of scientific enquiry. It wasn't until the advent of Islam that anybody did any hands-on work. Bad air! Four humours! Ha! And imagine: doctors the world over today actually take the Hippocratic Oath. Hippocrappus!

ON MATERFAMILIAS
(OR THE MAN UPSTAIRS)

AS OUR RICKSHAW RATTLES past the sprawling police station and the old tram station on Commissariat Road that has since become the Coast Guard headquarters, past Prince and Capri cinemas[71] and the Seventh Day Adventist Hospital where Tony was born, towards the residential end of Saddar, I find myself speculating about the boy's relationship with his father: Bosco is a serious, sensitive, decorous sort—another Master Unusual—and his father, like mine, might be impatient, imperious, one who does not suffer fools gladly. There is the distinct possibility, then, that he might not countenance me either. The boy does not let on either way; riding in front with the driver since there was no space in the back, he has not uttered a word since we departed.

There had been a scene at the Lodge earlier: Bosco refused to take me, and refused to say why. He might not have known himself. When pushed, however, he declaimed, 'It's not that I am not thankful for your hospitality, I am, but I don't want to be here and cannot be there.' The lad only relented when I bribed him with a first edition of *The Long Goodbye* (a veritable classic in the annals of literature), one of Papa's beautiful old felt trilbies (at least a size too big for the

---

71. Since there were 119 cinemas in the city once upon a time, almost 50 in Saddar alone, bus stops were often named after venues: Jubilee, Lighthouse, Paradise, Rex, Ritz, Khayyam in Nursery Market, Crown on Mauripur Road.

circumference of Bosco's head), and the promise to make him a good man (even if my experience is spotty). It seemed to have worked.

We disembark outside a narrow, grey, four-storeyed edifice wedged between a surgical supplies store and an abandoned lot, a stone's throw from the familiar pink Gothic spires of St. Patrick's Cathedral, undoubtedly one of the finest constructions in the city.[72] I have attended baptisms and marriages at the institution in the old days, and Midnight Mass with Uncle Ben, City Collector and Cointreau-maker.[73] The event took place around the back, beneath a marquee, because the structure could not accommodate all the teeming faithful. I mouthed all the words to the hymns that rang into the night—we are, after all, products of a Good Christian Education.[74]

We enter via a sliding steel gate that leads to a dim corridor wafting disinfectant, Bosco cryptically mumbling something that sounds like *nonchalance*. The stairwell is dauntingly steep. I am certain that I will die in a stairwell one day: the headline will read, large man falls down on the way up. Hoisting my trousers, I haul myself up the flight fitfully like a circus elephant only to realize at the stairhead that Bosco is not behind me. It occurs to me then that he must have

---

72. Other favourite landmarks include the Port Trust, Frere Hall and D.J. Science College. There is a veritable trove of architectural delights scattered across the old city, but the land mafia is working double-time to level our heritage. Make it anew! Mary Road changed only yesterday. I understand Bholu Pahalwan's family is behind the riotous development.

73. The recipe was a secret but one night, several drinks into that night, he told me. I have, however, since forgotten. It's funny: the important things in life, one forgets.

74. Of course Tony, who completed his primary schooling from Jufelhurst and Senior Cambridge from St. Pat's, was once hauled up by the nuns along with his chum Hur, a.k.a. Hawkeye, for sneaking into the loos of St. Joseph's Convent next door. Tugged by the ear to the principal for a proper caning, he said, 'We wanted to witness God's beauty.'

mumbled *no chance* as I had forged ahead. I have no choice but to continue on my own—second flat, he had said, on the second floor. When I knock on a set of splintered double doors twice, and once again for good measure, a lady's voice peals, 'Yes?'

Addressing the keyhole in a wheezy pitch, I begin, 'Good afternoon. I'm sorry to disturb you but was hoping for an audience. I am Abdullah, known once to all and sundry as the Cossack—'

'You're mistaken, mister. You want the man upstairs.'

I stand in the dark a few moments, contemplating, calculating: some count from the mezzanine up, some from the second storey—and some never make it to their destination. Cursing the lad, fate and the gradient, I climb another flight, sweating, seeing stars, streaking comets, and knock on the door of the flat immediately above the one below. A hatch promptly slides open, and a probing, disembodied eye materializes. 'How many?' it enquires.

'One?'

The eye squints. 'Two thousand.'

Out of idle intellectual curiosity, I hand over a wad of currency in exchange for a heavy brown bag rattling with bottles. *Now what, friend?* I ask myself, *Now where?* I consider abandoning the expedition—*Oh dash it, dash it all!*—but tell myself I have to give it one last chance.

'You again?' the lady exclaims.

'I am a friend of the Caliph of Cool—'

'Please leave before I report you—'

'I am the custodian of one Bosco.'

When the door opens, I find myself face to face with a smart, dark, freckled lass in a nurse's uniform who stands in the frame like a sentry. 'One cannot be too careful these days,' she says. 'Come in.'

The flat is neat and spare, and the clean aroma of cinnamon permeates the still air. The walls are painted a hue of aquamarine that recalls an aquarium. A portrait of the Lord, wreathed with a garland of drying roses, hangs in the centre. There is a shelf housing several stacks of magazines, a battered Scrabble set and a forlorn black-and-white polka-dot backpack on one side of the room, and several cane chairs arranged around an oval table on the other. Parking myself at the head, I ask, 'Do you mind if I sit down?'

'Suit yourself—'

'Could I trouble you for a glass of water, and a pillow perhaps?' The ride has stirred anarchy amongst my piles.

Combing her greying bob with the flat of her hand, she considers the request. 'I have to leave soon,' she replies. 'My shift begins in exactly seventeen minutes. What can I do for you?'

'Aren't you going to ask about Bosco?'

'No.'

'You don't care?'

'Have you come here to ask whether or not I care for him?'

'Not really,' I reply, but this seems odd, very odd, unless, of course, the lass before me is not Bosco's mother. She might be a sister, aunt, a cousin twice removed? 'I wanted to stop by to ascertain the situation.'

'What situation?'

'With the father?'

'The less you know, Mister Cossack, the better,' she says. 'It's best you leave.'

I stand up and nod respectfully, as if I have lost a game of snakes and ladders: there is nowhere to go but down. As I shuffle towards the door, however, the thought of the stairs emboldens me. 'Miss,' I begin, turning on my heel, 'excuse my impudence but I'm an old man—I would like to believe I am entitled to a certain decorum. I did not travel across town, climb those treacherous stairs, for a glass of water. I won't leave unless I have been adequately briefed about the circumstances surrounding Bosco's departure.'

The girl manages a smile, revealing a perfect set of pearly teeth. 'I'm sorry, Mister Cossack. I'm a little overwrought these days … Let me fetch you that water.'

'And a pillow please.'

After bearing a glass of lukewarm water and producing a small tasselled cushion, she pulls up a chair, and sighs. 'I don't know where to begin.'

'Please try.'

'Bosco's father lost his job at the Council two years ago and has, let's say, developed some very bad habits. He hasn't been much of a father or husband, or a man. I need somebody to stand up to these people. I've lived here all my life. What should I do? Where should I go?'

'Who—wait, what?'

'The land mafia, Mister Cossack, the land mafia.'

Jesus, Joseph and Mary! The cloak and dagger suddenly makes sense: Bosco has, in effect, been dispatched to me for protective custody. As we all know, the land mafia is not some ragtag ruffian outfit—no, it is a fearsome, formidable institution anywhere in the world, one that possesses the power to create and destroy entire cantons, communities, if there is a meaningful Rate of Return in it.[75] If they co-opt the police and local government machinery, what is a lone nurse with pearly teeth to do? And a heavyset phenomenologist? Draining the glass of lukewarm water, I feebly suggest, 'You might consider getting the courts involved.'

'I don't have the resources to hire a lawyer.'

---

75. Mac, a friend of Tony's from St. Patrick's who left for the United States of America with him, said he would cower in his portion of a 'brownstone' in the hamlet of Harlem, afraid the local land mafia, who routinely set buildings on fire to collect insurance, would set his place ablaze. Since then, he has become a real estate baron, the proprietor of several multimillion dollar properties, but the point is that pyromancy is one of the dark arts at the disposal of the land mafia. In the white-hot heart of the flames, they can perceive single-family homes with remodelled kitchens and parquet flooring: Eden.

'I have some contacts in the legal community,' I blurt. My advocate, however, the legendary, mercurial Kapadia, has a mixed record: in the lawsuits that Comrade Bakaullah has brought against me, I have won one, lost one, and one is outstanding.

'What can a lawyer do? Stand guard outside? They have intimidated me and my family. Believe you me, I'm tough—I can abide threats and insults, I can even take a knock, but Bosco...'

I want to clasp my head, heart, but will not allow myself to despair before the lass. 'Rest assured, Miss,' I declare stoutly, 'I will look into this.'

The nurse smiles again—it might be obvious to her that I am talking through my hat.

'Thank you for your hospitality.'

Before shutting the door on me, she hands over Bosco's backpack and whispers, 'How is he?'

'Don't worry.'

'I know he's in good hands.'

'Could you, by any chance, also give me the yo-yo?'

Standing in the dark as if teetering on a cliff on a moonless night, I take in the sour air of the corridor before making my way down, cradling a brown paper bag and backpack, yo-yo stuffed in pocket like a stale macaroon. Bosco emerges from the shadows, adjusting the brim of the trilby like a gangster. 'You and I, my friend,' I say, handing him the backpack, 'have the same problem.'

'What?'

'Two words: Cosa Nostra.'

'What?'

'You need to read Puzo.'

'Who?'

'Don't worry,' I reply. 'I've got a plan.'

I have no plan.

ON THE POSSIBILITIES OF LOVE & LITERATURE (OR A MOSTLY SENTIMENTAL EDUCATION)

AS APPOINTED FATHER FIGURE, mentor, what you will—there must be a Teutonic term incorporating all three like freundlicheziehvater—one makes adjustments: one sleeps earlier, rises earlier, and after breakfasting, repairs to the balcony. Bosco works on exercises in astrophysics or alchemy, subjects outside the purview of my knowledge—he has been given homework over the summer—whilst I write; then we undertake Readings in Literature together, a scattershot course derived from my dusty volumes: (1) Cooper, James, *The Leatherstocking Tales*; (2) Defoe, Daniel, *Capt. Singleton*; (3) Hughes, Thomas, *Tom Brown's School Days*; (4) Chandler, Raymond, *The Long Goodbye*; (5) Puzo, Mario, *The Godfather*, etcetera.[76] Yo-yos be damned—what better way to become a good man? Several sessions into our regime—we must have been reading *Hero of Our Time* or some dreary tract that ought to make any sensible reader cringe—I suggest we recite from the Romantic Canon, *The New Golden Treasury*. I clear my throat, adjust my robe, and address the street, arm's distance from the railing: 'In Xanadu did Kubla Khan / A stately pleasure dome decree!'

---

76. I always wanted a Godfather & later, what I would characterize as a Dogfather—somebody to introduce me to the underbelly of the city. But after my turn as the Cossack, I managed on my own.

Though initially dubious, Master Bosco cannot help himself after my rousing rendition: stepping up to the railing in the zippy joggers I purchased—Velcro straps, suction cups on the soles—he squeezes his fingers into fists like a nervy, determined pugilist, enunciating, 'A savage place! as holy and enchanted / As e'er beneath a waning moon was haunted / By woman wailing for her demon-lover!' There is catharsis in it.

The recital, the display of raw lung capacity, is an attempt to make the lad sensitive to the joys of poetry, though not unlike the Courtship Practises of Certain Tropical Primates, it is also informed by the possibility that the vociferous verses will attract the attention of *my* demon love. Whilst the probability that she is sauntering outside, flashing those obsidian eyes, is insignificant, it's worth a cry.

Our strolls are partly informed by such misplaced expectations as well. Donning a bush-shirt, shalwar & deerstalker one evening, I tell my confrere, 'You need to make use of those joggers.' Avoiding puddles, red spews of tobacco, Bosco follows as if flouncing down the aisles at Bata. We walk to the Gymkhana where once upon a time, amid great foon fan, the Agha Khan was weighed in gold, and then the other way to the Imambargah where we congregate to commemorate the martyrdom of the Prophet's (PBUH) grandson.

Ordinarily, however, Bosco & I gravitate to the zoo. I tell him of the time when the gentry promenaded in Gandhi Garden: Mr Fida of Lover's Lane, the Alvis of Chestnut St, Mr Lanewallah, Director of Zoology. And there would be marriages in the winter,[77] those famous red grapes in spring which Tony and I picked off the vines like toffees. What times! How I miss Tony, my brother, my boon companion!

Gandhi Garden, like Currachee, has changed in the intervening half century. The main entrance, once due east, has been shifted

77. In '58 or '59, if I recall correctly, H. Alvi wedded S. Karambhai there, despite the inclement weather.

south, within the compass of a shabby unpaved parking lot populated by loitering goats. Although the fee remains nominal—five rupees for minors, ten for adults—the park has been claimed by the sort of families who lob popcorn at the lone American Turkey. The amusement park, featuring noisy mechanical rides, is a vulgar development. The Shalimar Lawn, however, remains lush and well-tended. Our regular round takes us past the Reptile House, over the slat footbridge (Tony called it the Bridge on the River Kwai) spanning the basin of hoary crocodiles soaking in bright green water, around the cage of the delightful wallabies, the aquarium shaped like a bosom, and the plaque that reads: THESE LAWNS ARE NAMED AFTER THE LATE T.L.F. BEAUMONT, PRESIDENT, CURRACHEE MUNICIPALITY & CHAIRMAN COMMITTEE NOV. 1905 TO MAR. 1910. The regime is welcome for both of us. Bosco and I eat well, sleep well, and wake invigorated.

ONE MORNING THE CHILDOOS appear after overhearing us reciting *Twelfth Night* on the balcony. Naturally, we put on a show. When I emerge from my quarters in Mummy's purple, hand-embroidered kaftan folded with pins, Guddu and Toto chortle and clap. There is no doubt that great theatre engages young and old, academic and rabble alike. Just before Act 2, however, just as Bosco cries, 'Thy tongue, thy face, thy limbs, actions and spirit / Do give thee five-fold blazon—' Nargis happens upon us.

'This is what happens up here?' she yawps uncharitably. 'Unholy spectacles? Men dressed up as women!'

'But,' Bosco interjects quite unexpectedly, 'Uncle Cossack is a woman dressed up like a man.'

'And you?'

Bowing, broom in hand, he states, 'The Duke of Illyria at your service.'

'Not right!' she cries.

'Auguries of Judgment Day,' I mutter.

'All wrong!' she elucidates, storming off with my nephews.

'Perhaps she doesn't care for the comedies.'

'We could do *Coriolanus* next time,' Bosco quips. 'With puppets, of course.'

Ha!

Another time, one of our famous familial squawkers, Badbakht Begum, shows up, threatening to interrupt our regime since there is nobody downstairs. Once upon a time, Badbakht was one of the fairest, most coveted maidens in the land; it is said she resembled Mummy, a telling though misconceived comparison because nobody could be as comely as Mummy. The irony was that Badbakht was so fetching & accomplished—she is MA-pass—that she never found a suitable mate, and then it was too late. Although we grew up together, she never took an interest in me except during my turn as the Cossack: our only rendezvous went awry, however, when I found myself under the sheets with another cousin, Gulbadan, during a power outage.

'Madam,' I cry through the crack in the door. 'We are in quarantine! We have the Bug!'

'Oh dear,' Badbakht exclaims. 'Which one?'

'Naegleria,' I blurt—a malady I heard being discussed in passing on the transistor.

'The brain-eating amoeba?'

Slapping my head, I turn to Bosco. 'Listeria,' he whispers.

'Listeria,' I repeat, 'it's listeria.'

'What's that?'

I repeat what Bosco whispers to me: 'Bacteria ... found in unpasteurized milk ... smoked seafood ... hot dogs ... a cousin of botulism.'

'It's contagious?'

'No but it's foul, funky, fetid—'

'Okay, okay, okay. Get better, Abdullah. I'll wait downstairs.'

Bosco raises his hand. I slap it. The lad is turning out to be a fine companion—attentive, sporting, endowed with a certain humour.

I WOULD LIKE TO take him on a field trip to the shrine of Abdullah Shah Ghazi (RA) but I reckon he will take more interest in a jaunt to Sandspit for the nesting season of the green turtles. The expedition requires an automobile, as a rickshaw ride to the beach would devastate my rectal harmony for weeks. There are three parked in the garages in the back—Papa's legendary '58 Impala, a burgundy BMW 1600, and Felix's old Foxy, which I purchased during the lean times as a favour to him—but since not one functions, I am compelled to borrow Babu's Starlet. Feigning a headache one evening, I wander downstairs for a pair of paracetamols and purloin the keys when my brother wanders off to retrieve the bottle. It's a cinch.

But I have not driven since the invention of the Digital Video Disk, and downtown is a jungle. Lorries lumber up and down Bandar Road like elephants, motorcyclists like a sounder of boars. Slowly, steadily, high beams blazing, hands clutching the top of the steering, I negotiate the artery to the port. Although the traffic thins towards the end of Mauripur Road, save the occasional swinging gas lantern, gloom pervades. Past the deserted checkpost leading to the narrow bridge over the salt flats, one can only discern one's coordinates in time and space by the crunch of the gravel and the sighing sea. Parking by the mangroves, we disembark like Ninja Warriors on a mission but there is nothing to do except sit on the warm sand & wait.

It is a gorgeous evening, the sort that reminds you why one resides in Currachee: the stars are like spilled sugar across the sky, and the breeze is cool and salty like lassi. 'There was a time we picnicked here through the year,' I whisper. 'We would take a boat in low tide. We would sing songs,[78] play cards, charades, badminton, hurl ourselves into the waves. Then we had sandwiches, rolls, Pakola.'

There would be others, doughy children, lasses in polka-dot one-piece bathing suits, and once we even ran into our genial, tubby then-PM. When Papa introduced me to him, he noted, 'If you weren't so fair, you could be my son.' Papa also introduced me to green turtles. There is something marvellous in the rituals of the ancient creatures. *Where do they come from? Where do they go?* I still do not quite know. Nobody knows. It's one of the Bona Fide Mysteries of the Universe.[79]

Suddenly, Bosco falls on all fours. I cannot see anything at first, but gradually discern a shadow inching towards us. The form settles not more than a metre away. I can make out a head, a variegated carapace, massive flippers. It is larger than me and presumably older. It has travelled thousands of kilometres, propelled by currents, by will, and knows what it has to do. If only I had been bestowed with such uncanny instincts!

Still as statues, we watch the creature digging in the dirt, flippers working like spades. Once the nest is fashioned, a trench of sorts, the clutch is laid, a secret spectacle that lasts about an hour, after which she covers the hollow and drags herself into the sea. Brushing our clothes, hands, we make our way back as well. We will not witness the hatchlings waddle towards the waves—feeble, frightened and motherless. Most will die immediately, devoured by pye-dogs and gulls. The world is oft cruel, bizarre, a series of tragedies.

The drive home is fraught. Few realize that the roads of our city are most treacherous when clear. During the stretch between the

---

78. I recall crooning numbers from Madam's *Dopatta*, and Ahmed Rushdi's classic, 'Bunder Road se Keamari.' The jaunty latter tune often plays in my head when I'm travelling in a rickshaw—my theme music on the move.

79. I suppose nobody really knows how the universe functions—I don't even know how magnets or xylophones work, much less air conditioners or airplanes. But much like Socrates, I know what I don't know.

village and the roundabout, the inevitable happens: avoiding a wobbly bicyclist, I swerve into an open gutter. The momentum carries the automobile over but we suffer a spectacular flat. 'Changing a tyre,' I announce, 'is one of the prerequisites for manhood.' Acting on my instructions, Bosco proceeds soldierly, raising the car with a rickety jack, unscrewing the lug nuts counterclockwise, dragging the spare from the dicky and installing it on the hub, drenched in sweat. The remainder of the expedition is uneventful save the ominous wheezing deriving from the chassis. But there is pandemonium in the morning.

Upon discovering the flat, Babu barges into my quarters at half past seven. 'This is the height of irresponsibility!' he shouts. 'You're my elder brother—I should look up to you, but—but you behave like a child!'

Listening to the harangue, hands clasped over my chest, I observe that the hair follicles forming the border of my brother's hairline are stunted like seeds arrayed in a frosty trough. I would like to ask him how he afforded transplant surgery, an extravagance of the young, the vain, the wasteful, given his precarious finances. Instead, I declaim, 'I'll pay for the damages.'

'Of course, you'll pay,' he shoots back uncharitably. 'And I'll only accept cash. No cheques!'

'Of course, partner, of course—'

All the excitement must have roused Bosco: I notice him half-awake in the background. I signal to him with my chin to leave but he stands squinting idiotically, pyjama riding up the leg. 'This is all because of this—this runt!' Babu screeches. 'Who is he and why is he here?'

'This is unambiguously my fault,' I reply. 'You leave the lad out. He's not your business.'

'Then I will make him my business!'

'No, partner, you will not.'

'This is my house—'

'No, it's not!'

Although things have been said that ought not to have been said, there is no sense in standing around like attendants at an asylum. Turning my back on my brother, I slide my arm around Bosco's shoulder and usher him away. 'That was a bad dream,' I tell him. 'Poof!'

MY DREAMS COME TRUE one muggy evening, perhaps a fortnight later: as the fiery sun is setting over the leafy horizon of the zoo, I notice a familiar figure on a bench, beedi wedged between fingers. Slipping Bosco a twenty, I say, 'Why don't you go feed the lemurs?' As soon as he disappears around the corner to purchase bags of choice popcorn, I head over and ask, 'Is this seat taken?'

Jugnu glances at me with quick black eyes, then looks away. Wearing the same canary-yellow kameez she was wearing the second time fate introduced us, she is looking even more striking than I remember. 'I waited for you that night,' I say, settling beside her.

'Why?'

'I wanted to thank you properly.'

'You're welcome, Abdullah Sahab.'

She might be preoccupied, or worse, uninterested. I don't care; I will not let her go this time. The hell with Babu, Nargis, the Dictates of Propriety! Sidling closer, I say, 'I would like to invite you over for dinner.'

'Why should I accept your invitation?'

'Because ... because I cook very well: I can make biryani with apricots that will make you teary with feeling ... chicken heart karahi that will fulfil you in a spiritual way ... authentic fisherman's prawn masala and disco aloo—'

'Acha, acha,' she says with a grin. 'Main chakar maroon gi,' she adds, or *I will stop by*.

'When?'

'Soon—'

'I'm taking you home with me now!'

When Jugnu attempts to leave, escape again, I begin singing that world-famous ghazal at the top of my lungs that begins, 'Aaj jaany ki zid na karo'—viz., *Don't insist on leaving tonight / If you leave, I will die / I will be lost / Oh, please don't go.*[80]

Passers-by stop in their tracks. Monkeys start turning cartwheels. 'Okay, okay, stop it!' Jugnu laughs. 'No hearts, no disco. You make me the best chicken karahi I have had in my life.'

'Done, hai!'

I have written a treatise on it.

---

80. Recall the rest of the ghazal, first sung by my late neighbour, the bespectacled crooner Mohammed Wali Khan: 'We are trapped in time's prison / But during the moment we are free / If we lose the moment, we will regret it for the remainder of our lives / Don't leave tonight...'

ON THE CULINARY ANTHROPOLOGY OF THE REGION

ANY CULINARY SURVEY OF the region would have to accommodate the historical vicissitudes that have informed this vast and veritably varied land. During the Oligocene Period, for instance, the Baluchitherium (a large, long-legged mammal with the bearing of a hippo) tramped through Beloochistan.[81] If there were any tribesmen then—by some accounts, Adam (RA) was tossed from the heavenly orbit during that time—one can wager a meaningful sum that they would have fashioned sajji from the ample flesh of the beast. Oh, just imagine the epic meaty succulence of such a speciality!

Whilst the western swath of the country might not always have been arid, undular, recalling Mars, we know that the gushing Indus cut through the other half, leaving a verdant delta and a riverine civilization in its mighty wake. But since archaeologists have not been able to decipher the pictograms on the tablets excavated from Mohenjo-Daro, the largest, most sophisticated city of said civilization, one is not privy to any primary source material on cookery during the Indus Valley Civilization. One can, however, divine the culinary ecosystem from the irrigation networks unearthed—the cultivation of rice and

81. There were others in other periods: Sulaimanisaurus, Marisaurus and, of course, the Pakisaurus.

barley, for instance, can be presumed—and the proximity of the cities to rivers would suggest that the people of the valley complemented agricultural endeavour with fishery.[82] One might speculate they were pescatarians. After all, fishermen have been trawling the waterways of the Interior for trout, palla, carp and bekti since time immemorial, and the sea has yielded croaker, barracuda and the sweetest crabs one has ever tasted (presently plucked for 'lollipops' on barges and beaches in and around Currachee).

One can also surmise that marine trade with Africa ensued along the Makran coast, though the exchange of silk, spice, nuts, ideas, bacteria was famously facilitated by the winding intercontinental terrestrial route known as the Silk Road. Globalization is not some recent phenomenon—it dates back three thousand years: laden quadrupeds from Central Asia, Han China and as far as Ancient Egypt traversed the craggy Karakoram, facilitated in time by the avenues built by Ashoka the Great Bihari. (The Romans got involved only later.) Built by Chinese engineers, local labour and the army beginning in 1959, the Karakoram Highway remains a vital trade conduit today between China and Pakistan. I know. In the spirit of commerce, I have traded a bottle of paracetamol for a bottle of Chinese vodka with the border guards manning the Khunjrab Pass. Verily, trade expands horizons.

Cuisine, then, is contingent on factors that include climate, culture, trade, technology, movements of peoples, and indigenous flora, fauna and foodstuffs. Rice and barley might be indigenous to the land as are pepper, cardamom and ginger, but coriander and cumin arrived via the Mediterranean shipping routes and the Arab World, nutmeg and cloves from China. And who would have known that the Portuguese

---

82. Further research must be pursued in an effort to understand the diet of the Indus Valley Civilization, employing the magic of biochemistry, or Scatological Anthropology.

brought chillies, tomatoes and capsicum? Or that the British brought potatoes? Tea?

One must also recall that Pakistan was the Mecca of Buddhism a couple of millennia ago. Taxila hosts extraordinary ruins and a museum that testifies to the fact, but there is evidence elsewhere, everywhere: stupas dot the land, and towards Kalam, Buddhist graffiti is scrawled on the sides of mountains—the work it would seem, of giants. It was, however, presumably the handiwork of ancient Pathans. I would wager that the famously fierce nation was once fiercely vegetarian. Although Buddhist cuisine is a misnomer—one cannot pepper supper with vinaya—the Eastern faiths developed elaborate dietary systems meant to achieve carnal & cosmic balance.

Controversy might dog the issue of the Holiness of the Cow—When? Why? What the dickens?—but it's certain that a hierarchy of foodstuffs was established based on Ayurvedic principles. Milk and coconuts were deemed pure, or sattvic, whereas meat, fish, eggs, onions and other tasty items were considered harmful, or tamasic. The classification recalls the peculiarly, if not entirely arbitrary, Judaic dietary prejudices which contrast with Islam's strict but relatively straightforward system of halal & haram.[83]

By the time the Bedouin faith took root in the Subcontinent, it had been tempered by the sensibilities of the Turks, Persians and Magnificent Moors. Textbooks have only recently acknowledged that table etiquette, from forks to courses to general matters of hygiene, were imported by the Europeans in the Dark Ages from the Musalman Civilizations.[84] Left to their own devices, the Gauls,

---

83. Shellfish, however, is considered neither good nor bad but discouraged, or *mukruh*, much like booze.

84. The innovations of Ziryab the Blackbird of Cordoba, gourmand, musician and boulevardier, are documented in Mark Graham's excellent *How Islam Created the Modern World* (1427 AH / 2006 AC)

Franks & other dirty denizens of the Cold World would be stuffing roasted offal into their maws with foul fingers.

One of the most comprehensive primary source materials for regional cuisine might date back to the fifteenth-century court of the Sultan of Mandu.[85] I have not been able to secure a copy of the *Ni'matnama* but have managed to procure an expert translation of the *Nuskha-e-Shahjahani* (or *Recipes from Shah Jahan's Court*) from a bright & comely PhD scholar in Musalman Intellectual History.[86] One learns that the Mughals were preoccupied by rice, a Persian fetish: there are a hundred and thirty permutations of pulao in the *Nuskha*—one hundred and thirty!—each differentiated not simply by ingredients or technique but by presentation.[87]

---

85. Mangarasa's sixteenth-century cookery book in verse, *Soopa Shastra*, must be mentioned. The coda sounds impressive, featuring snacks, drinks, desserts and banana curries, but I don't read Sanskrit.

86. Known to me by her mother, SB, a famous beauty of her time—she is an understated, uncanny tour de force.

87. I can furnish the following for illustrative purposes:

The Cooking of Orange Pulao

Meat:	1½ āsār	Lemon:	3pāō
Rice:	1 āsār	Egg:	1
Ghee:	3 āsār	Onions:	½ āsār
Saffron:	1 māsha	Ginger:	2 dām
Cinnabar:	1 māsha	Almonds:	2½ dām
Cinnamon:	4 māsha	Raisins:	2½ dām
Cloves:	4 māsha	Pistachios:	2½ dām
Cardamom:	4 māsha	Grain Meal:	1 dām
Sugar:	3 pāō	Salt:	2 dām
Pepper:	1 tānk	Caraway Seeds:	1 damṛī

Take ⅓ of the meat and mix in the ground spices with a stone. Take the roasted chickpea meal and the white of the egg and a little ghee, onions

One has aspired, on occasion, to replicate the Mughlai processes—one would like to sample just a lick of the regal delicacies—but even as a reasonably able cook, the High Art of Mughlai Cuisine is outside the purview of one's capabilities. But then, more experienced cooks are rarely up to the task: I have sampled poor Mughlai fare around the fort in Delhi—my fingers were caked with turmeric most foul after a plate of purported murgh Jehangiri—although some joints in the old city of Lahore approximate the experience. In any event, the Mughals were eventually done in by the British Colonial Enterprise.

Of course, the Subcontinent was a collection of states then, not a cogent political entity. The centripetal forces that swept European nations into states in the eighteenth century were also sweeping through the Subcontinent from Bahawalpur to Hyderabad to the Maratha hinterland, but the insidious Exogenous Shock of Colonialism jarred political development. Colonialism yielded only mildly appetizing culinary experiments that include the phenomenon

---

and ginger [and] mix with the juice of 1 lemon and knead together. Make flat cakes out of this, then put the fruit/ground-meat into the belly of the cakes and close them up to look like oranges. After having hardened them in hot water and baking them in ghee, throw them into ¼ āsār of sugar syrup. Throw over it the colour of the saffron and vermillion levelled, such that it has the colour blue of coriander ... When the syrup dries up, take the remaining meat and make *yakhni*. Strain the *shorba* through a muslin cloth. Garnish the meat and *shorba* with cloves fried in ghee, then mix in ½ āsār of sugar syrup. Pour the caraway seeds into a pot, layer the meat in and add the spices and 2 wooden ladles full of the sweet *shorba*, and put it all on the fire until the *shorba* is absorbed into the meat. After that, bring the rice to half boil, soften in the *shorba*, then add it over the layer of *yakhni* [and] give it a flame for about 6 min (¼ *gharī*) and then let it cook in its own steam. Pour some ghee from above. When presenting the pulāō in the dish, place the 'oranges' on top.

of Mulligatawny Soup—daal served in a bowl. If only the French had won at Pondicherry, we might have been dining on curried escargots. Another staple of Anglo-Indian cuisine, Country Captain Chicken, is an academically interesting local permutation of a British maritime recipe. But it's nothing to write home about.

Although there is great variety in our cuisine, the national dish of Pakistan has arguably become chicken karahi. You will find it anywhere you venture—North, South, Left, Right. I have had it in Kaghan, Naran, Gujranwalla, Tando Mohammed Khan. The ubiquity of karahi is a function of many factors, from the Economics of Red Meat to the construction of the Grand Trunk Road by the brilliant Bihari, Sher Shah Suri. In Currachee, some of the finest karahi joints, from Bombay Restaurant in Cantt Station to Mecca and Medina along the Super Highway, are run by Pathans catering to their trucking brethren.[88]

I am a karahi cognoscente. I can contrive at least twelve different variations, some soupy, some dry, some with khara masala, some with bhuna masala; one involves onions, another eggs, and I could serve karahi avec beurre blanc sauce for French company. You have to work with what you have and if you do not have much, or much time, you can attempt the following:[89]

A nice plump chicken, cut into pieces
Four medium-sized red tomatoes
A handful of black peppercorn, cumin and coriander seeds
A heaping teaspoon of salt

88. The best this connoisseur has sampled is from the Interior—from Hala.

89. I am not certain of trademark laws, but I ought to mention in no uncertain terms that I would like to formally trademark the recipe as the Cossack's Quick Karahi.

Boil the chicken pieces in a pot of water on high heat for ten minutes, throw in the tomatoes, sliced in quarters, and after grinding the peppercorn, coriander and cumin seeds with a pestle, sprinkle them over the concoction. Salt to taste, of course, and cook for another twenty.

That's it. It's done.

ON THE CONVENTIONS OF MODERN COURTSHIP (OR HAD WE BUT WORLD ENOUGH)

UNDER COVER OF DARKNESS courtesy of summer loadshedding, Jugnu and I repair to the Lodge for a candlelit soiree—Babu and I cannot agree on the modalities of restoring the generator.[90] The gloom would have been exasperating at any other moment in history but I am grateful to the power shortages—the electricity typically goes for two hours—because Jugnu cannot perceive my corrugated brow or the archipelago of sweat across my chest; I have not had a dame over since the Signing of the Maastricht Treaty. Abandoning Jugnu in the veranda—'One minute,' I beseech, 'just one minute'—I change into my flimsy filigreed mauve batik before groping my way to the kitchen where I locate a taper and a bottle of Roohafzah, and mix a tablespoon into a glass of water. But the saccharine sherbet will not suffice; no, the success of the evening hinges on Master Bosco securing from the butcher a nice plump cut of chicken for my quick karahi, as Barbarossa is AWOL (participating, I would suspect, in a cockfight).

---

90. I have organized my finances in such a way that I receive an annuity, or rather, a monthly stipend of forty-one thousand rupees, not a princely sum but one that suits my requirements: drugs, gardening items, foodstuffs and Barbarossa's pension (though I suspect his livelihood is the cockpit). The problem with the arrangement is that I cannot afford capital investments—commode, generator, whatever—unless I draw on the principal, and if I draw on the principal, the monthly monies-in-hand is diminished.

It's a winning recipe, strategy, but what to do, ad interim, what to say? Mercifully, Jugnu initiates small talk: 'Big place,' she remarks.

Situated on a four kanal plot, the Lodge is indeed vast by present standards, and from our vantage, rather transcendental at night: we can perceive the swaying silhouettes of the peepal & jungle jalebi trees, and the lone ashoka in the moonlight. But the bright light of day reveals that the grass is wild and yellowing, and the boundary wall is cracked at intervals. Jugnu may or may not realize that a house does not come apart suddenly, dramatically—it goes chip by chip, not brick by brick: you reckon you will attend to the masonry when you have a moment and sufficient currency, but then a fixture in the facilities snaps and the wiring in the pantry rots and the window becomes unhinged, but you make do. I have to make do with myself: I notice the gibbous flesh bulging in rolls through the shirt I have decided to wear for the occasion. 'Big,' I mumble, 'very big.'

'How long have you lived here?'

'I was born in this house,' I reply, 'spent my childhood in this garden,' I add, raising an arm as if balancing a tray on my palm, 'but tell me, how long have you been here?'

'I am not from here.'

'Oh?'

'You can say I am visiting.'

'Visiting,' I repeat. Whosoever sojourns in Garden anymore? 'Where from?'

Sipping Roohafzah as if sampling a glass of Riesling, Jugnu considers the query, me. 'Lyari,' she finally replies.

'Lyari,' I repeat.

Once upon a time, Tony and I would cycle through Lyari, one of the oldest cantons of the city, not more than nine, ten minutes as the crow flies, to play with a friend who would become one of the most prosperous hoteliers in the country, but of late it has become what broadcasters term a No-Go Area due to the sclerotic municipal dispensation and resultant warring mafias. Once upon a time, Lyari was renowned for producing footballers, cueists, Olympic boxers,[91] but of late one only hears of the fearsome don known as Langra Dacoit. I cannot help but wonder, *What's a dame like this doing in a place like that?* but before I can get in a word edgewise, Jugnu interjects, 'Do you have anything else to drink?'

'Tea, coffee, maybe?'

'Toddy, tharra?'

'Feni!' I blurt, 'I have feni'—the provision of sauce inadvertently purchased from Bosco's bootlegger neighbour. When Jugnu shrugs, I continue, 'I might have a few drops of Chinese vodka somewhere—it works with Roohafzah—and plenty of wine distilled from my brother's grapes!'[92]

'Vine chalay gi,' she says, or *Wine will work*.

The way she enunciates the word suggests to me that though she might not have ever experienced wine, she understands it is something to be had. Scampering inside—'One minute,' I say, 'give me just one minute'—I unlock the Bombay sheesham armoire in the powder room that houses my important papers and Tony's special distillation. The bottles are bottle green and labeled T.K.O. 1999 in cursive and feature the rubber stoppers that once fitted ice cream soda.

---

91. Tony, a boxing enthusiast, for instance, has mentioned the middleweight Hussain Shah.

92. I ought to mention that Tony is not the only vintner I personally know. There was a prominent educationist who concocted a tart jug brew, a thespian turned lawyer who made vodka from sugarcane, and a lovely lady in Parsee Colony who makes a sort of Beaujolais nouveau and a sweet plum wine in the winter. One has lost interest, one has fallen out with me, but once a year I do still negotiate my way through Soldier Bazaar to pick up a couple of bottles of the plum stuff. A bottle a year never hurt anybody.

Pouring two proper Baccarat goblets to the brim, I toast my company, bottle under arm like a regular sommelier. Although unfamiliar with the etiquette, Jugnu mirrors the gesture before draining the glass in a single gulp. The dame can drink, but before I can ask her what she thinks of it—I taste jamun, *Syzygium cumini* and notes of pipe tobacco—she asks for another.

'Now,' she instructs, lighting a crisp beedi, 'play music.'

Scampering inside again—'Two minutes,' I say, 'just two minutes'—I fetch the old clockwork gramophone and crank it up. As Clifford Brown's trumpet fills the air, I slide into the deck chair and find myself transported to some nearby stretch of the galaxy, a Ring of Saturn, before a voice reels me back: 'You keep leaving me.'

'Oh please forgive me, Jugnu Begum. I am not a good host. I am not suitably attentive, or entertaining—'

'But you are attentive, very attentive.'

'Thank you—'

'And entertaining.'

'Really?'

'You were entertaining even before we met, Abdullah Sahab.'

Blushing like a beet, *Beta vulgaris*, I clear my throat. 'Please,' I say, 'call me Abdullah.'

Jugnu straightens her back, raises her chin, gathers her hair, and as she ties her tresses in a bun behind her head, I observe her long neck, the dark, musky patches under her arms, and the impression of her custard apple bosoms. 'Abdullah,' she enunciates, causing palpitations in the vicinity of my heart.

But the moment, pregnant with possibility, is interrupted by a knock. Cursing fate, I attend to the door to find Bosco, King Bosco, beaming, announcing his advent with a raised packet of chicken. 'I will have to leave you once again, Jugnu—I have to prepare dinner—but I should be back before you finish the bottle. In the interim, Bosco, King Bosco, will entertain you. He is a charming and thoughtful lad who one day, no doubt, will conquer the world.'

Chuffed by the introduction, Bosco bows before taking my place on the deck chair. 'Pleased to meet you, Madam,' he says, extending his hand. The lad is a natural.

'You are gentlemane,' I hear Jugnu say in English.

When I throw the pink pieces of chicken into boiling water, it occurs to me that I am missing the ingredient that makes karahi karahi. Slinking down the stairs, I tiptoe to the vegetable patch for tomatoes, afraid of being discovered—as usual, I feel like a thief in my own house. The batik, I reckon, will surely give me away—after all, Apparel Doth Proclaim the Man. But I manage to escape without incident.

When the dish is done, the three of us sit like a family around the round plastic table with folded tissues for napkins. The sweet, pungent aroma of crushed coriander and cumin seeds wafts like good tidings in the night air. It's a picture-perfect night, a picture-perfect occasion, but before we can scrape the last of the soupy, spicy tomato mess, calamity announces itself with a Gestapo knock at the door. I look at Bosco, Bosco looks at me, then I heroically announce, 'I'll get it.'

I find Nargis the Opossum, candle in hand, lurking like an apparition—she must have noticed the batik! 'Abdullah Bhai,' she begins, 'can I have a word?'

'Of course, dear.'

'Do you mind if I come in?'

'No!' I squawk. 'It's so dark inside ... and you know my place is always in such a terrible mess ... I wouldn't want you to take a tumble.'

'I just wanted you to sit down because I have some sad news: Hidayatullah Bhai's brother-in-law died.'

Scratching my head, I attempt recalling the deceased, but since the Major is much married, thrice at least, he has a legion of brothers-in-law. It is quite possible that I bumped into the man sometime, somewhere, at the GP's, Agha's Supermarket, but I probably would not be able to identify him in a police line-up. 'What a tragedy,' I commiserate. 'He was a fine soul.'

'The soyem is tomorrow.'

'Right-O.'

'Hidayatullah Bhai phoned to say, "Tell Shehzada he must show up."'

As I wonder what my brother has up his sleeve now—the Major has always fancied himself a strategic thinker—somebody turns up 'In the Mood' and Nargis' eyes dart into the darkness behind me. 'You know,' she stalls, 'Babu would have come up to tell you himself but he's putting the children to sleep, so I thought I would tell you before you went to bed—'

'Very thoughtful of you—'

'You seem to be having a late night.'

'I have a late night every night, Nargis Begum—you know I work at night—'

'It sounds like you're not working too hard—'

'It's only, what, ten?' It suddenly occurs to me that the electricity returns at ten! Shutting the door halfway, I mutter, 'I'm educating Bosco at the moment, playing old jazz records—'

'I've always been curious about your jazz music—'

'I'll schedule a session on the fundamentals of form in the coming days, but I ought to be getting back because the needle is made of fibre—'

'The soyem is before sundown,' she cries from the stairwell. 'We can take you along with us if you like,' she says, adding something about Badbakht Begum joining us.

'Cheers.'

Bosco is teaching Jugnu the Cha-cha-cha when I return, his bony hand on her angular waist. 'Uncle Cossack,' he pants, shirt unbuttoned to the navel, 'you must know how to do this better than me. Want to try?'

There is nothing else I would like to do at that instant, no other place in the world I would want to be, but Nargis is on the prowl and the electricity will return any second. 'I have received some bad news,' I tell Jugnu. 'There has been a death in the family. It breaks my heart, but I must ask you to leave.'

'But Uncle Cossack,' Bosco interrupts, 'she hasn't even finished her wine.'

'Then she will just have to return tomorrow.'

Leading her down the steps and out the gate, I implore, 'Come tomorrow, please come tomorrow.'

'Give me taxi fare,' she demands, promising nothing.

Handing her sufficient fare to get from Garden to Timbuktu and back, I repeat, 'Will you come tomorrow?'

All of a sudden, streetlights illuminate the street. 'You will find out.'

Then I dash for cover.

ON THE DEATH OF CIVILITY
(OR BRASS TACKS)

THERE IS THE WHIFF of dung and incense in the air at the Major's. The mourners, slow and sombre like giant tortoises, negotiate plastic chairs under the cream marquee stretching over the lawn. Espying tea in the far corner, and a spread of samosas and limp hunter beef sandwiches, I post myself by the pickings as the maulvi takes the microphone, mulling other possible culinary options at funerals: bharta filled vol-au-vents, khagina quiches, kachoomar spring rolls with coriander dip. There is no doubt that funeral menus[93] require a fundamental review. And what about funeral rites?

In this time, in this country, one prays, reads bound chapters of the Holy Book, counts date pits, but I only pray at shrines, cannot understand Arabic, and if I were to pick up a pit, it would only be to toss it at somebody. It's not that one advocates for the retrograde conventions of the Bedouin variety; au contraire, one proposes the celebratory rites that characterize the Urs—the Reunification of Man with his Maker. Across the city, across the length and breadth of the country, the death anniversary of every saint at every shrine—Sehwan, Pakpattan, Abdullah Shah Ghazi (RA)—is commemorated

93. One understands that they do it right in two countries in the world: Ireland & Ghana. Denizens of the former famously hold wakes, drinking until they are sozzled, sottish, sick, whilst the latter revel as if celebrating a wedding. Oh, how I would like to die in Ireland, Ghana, the South Pacific! Oh, how is it to live before you die!

with song and dance until daybreak. I know: I have chanted and spun like a dervish, experienced fireworks of ecstasy after inhaling sweet, smoky mouthfuls of hashish. That's how it ought to be, and that's how I want to go: with a party. At funerals, I have oft considered accosting mourners with the following thought: Wouldn't it be marvellous if one knew when one was done? One could then plan ahead, order hors d'oeuvres, a band, dispatch invitations in bold cursive. It is not the inevitability of death but the uncertainty that kills.

Of course, in this time, in this country, not many would attend my going-away party. People are already avoiding me, casting pitying glances: *Never any good. Never got married. Look how he let himself go.* A neat greying man, the director of a vast public sector utility, smiles tightly, acknowledging me from afar. He knows I know that he was potty-trained at age six. I also descry that cigar-toting, bottom-groping politico with an overbite.[94] I knew his father, a dull but decent man who would be turning in his grave at the thought that his son made millions on aeronautical contracts. When I catch his eye, he pretends he doesn't know me. It doesn't matter—I might not wear a big watch but I have had half the platter of sandwiches. They will have nothing.

AS I STAND DABBING the corners of my mouth, a portly chap wearing an unruly crown of dyed jet-black hair joins me at the spread. 'Sad this,' he says, swallowing a samosa. 'God gives, God takes away. You knew him?' I shake my head non-committally as if to suggest: *Does anybody really know anybody?* 'Poor man, dropping dead. Thanks God he didn't suffer. I don't want to suffer. But I'm suffering.' Offering

94. There is a variety of man who believes he has scaled the summit of sophistication by dint of his command of cigar-related argot—the Wide Churchill, the Narrow Nostril—and naming a couple of single malts. There's a reason Scotch is blended: single malt tastes like paint thinner. My urine's sweeter.

me his card—FINE CARPET & RUGS IMPORT EXPORT—he adds, 'When democracy comes, business goes thup. What line you are in?'

'Monographs.'

'Oh,' he exclaims, without missing a beat, 'you must do bumper business.'

'Bumper,' I repeat.

The maulvi proclaims, 'Of those who reject faith, the patrons are the evil ones: from light they will lead them forth into the depths of darkness.'

Hell would be attending soyems forever, in the company of Babu and Nargis and Badbakht Begum, stuck with this chap at the sandwich table—he has just discovered the tamarind chutney. *Those two good-for-nothings,* somebody must be noting, *are only here for the spread.* 'Tell me something,' I say before deciding to abandon the carpet salesman. 'Wouldn't it be marvellous if one knew when one was done?'

'What you mean?'

'You think about it, friend. You think long, you think hard.'

Leaving him to ponder the Mysteries of Being, I tramp purposefully towards the house, stomach rumbling—I have had one sandwich too many and need to find the lavatory—but as I pass the vicinity of the zenana somebody squalls, 'Hai, mein khatam,' viz. *Oh, my life is over.* One can imagine the scene: draped dames, ruddy with grief, placating each other with sweaty caresses. I think I can discern Nargis' voice soliciting the number of a domestic—Nargis, God bless her, is always at it—but am drawn to another conversation towards the back of the marquee: 'Conscientious, hard-working,' a voice avers, 'so much potential, so much promise—'

'But he frittered it all way,' another asserts. 'If you ask me, he lost his marbles—'

I do not know the poor sod under discussion but empathize with him and his meagre marbles. 'He never quite found his footing.'

'Well, I don't know about you but I think he was fated to be a failure.'

'You're being unfair, darling. He tried. I know he tried but you can't discount luck in life…'

The sympathetic voice is familiar. 'Well,' it muses, 'Who knows? Maybe he's finally coming into his own.' Is it Badbakht?

Before I can investigate, the maulvi's homily ends amid a throaty chorus of amens and everybody makes for the spread. Trundling in the opposite direction to avoid the company of society, calumny, and to relieve myself, I slip into the Major's baroque mansion and settle on the commode in the ample facilities in the back. There is the scent of dried flowers in the air but it's no bed of roses for me: I watch myself grunting and groaning in the tinted mirrors surrounding me as I evacuate the sandwiches. Oh, the indignity of it all!

When I emerge, bruised and bloody, I am accosted by hands that might belong to my nervy Kashmiri sister-in-law or her son, my nephew—a toothy roué married to a former fashion model—but the wrestler's grip undoubtedly belongs to a retired army officer. I know: my brother has pinned me down on many an occasion over the years. 'I thought I would find you here,' says the Major.

'God gives, God takes away,' I blurt. 'Thanks God he didn't suffer.'

'We have to talk, shehzaday.'

Oh, I knew it in my gut, in my gonads: the funeral's a ploy! The Major probably poisoned his dashed brother-in-law with belladonna just to snooker me! 'Actually,' I bleat, 'I was just about to sample the sandwiches.'

'I'll call for a plate, a large plate,' he promises. 'Hut-huthut,' he marches forth, pounding his cane on the floor.

THE HEAVY BEIGE CURTAINS in the drawing room are drawn. They are always drawn. The Major's house has the ambience of a museum: marble floors and Doric columns, and paintings featuring bucolic alpine vistas and stylized profiles of stallions.[95] There is no doubt that the Major is a bona fide Renaissance Man. Following him into his wood-panelled study, I find Babu and Nargis sunk into a deep leather divan like children. Settling on a swivelling office chair with levers, the Major offers me a colourful buffalo-hide pouffe—a cunning strategy, a conspiracy.

'The tragic death of my brother-in-law has affected us all,' he begins. 'We remember him as an upright man. He cared for me and you and everyone around him. He was part of us and we were a part of him. That's the way it should be.' I know the street-side dentist better than the deceased but hold my tongue in deference to propriety. 'A death in the family serves to remind us of the important things in life,' he continues, 'Maut zindangi ki hifazat karti hay,' viz., *Death Safeguards Life*—an aphorism mouthed by talk-show hosts, pamphleteers. 'We've played a good innings,' the Major drones, 'and don't have many overs left. It's high time we think about the next generation.' Biting into a stubby pipe, he looks down at me. 'Well?'

Surveying the faces of the audience, I massage my forehead, my face, then report, 'My haemorrhoids are burning like faggots in a furnace.'

The conspirators wince for a moment as if a gust has swept sand into the room then Babu retrieves a heavy wooden chair from the corner and seats me with the deference of a courtier. 'You must be dehydrated, Abdullah Bhai,' he says.

'I will fetch a glass of cold water,' Nargis chirps. Such attention! Such hospitality!

'That would be lovely, dear,' I say, 'and those sandwiches?'

'They are on their way, shehzaday,' claims the Major, though he has not lifted a finger.

---

95. I don't mind the noble steeds—I actually prefer them to doves or to the feeble stabs at Modern Art by that society artist with the glasses and big nose—but these seem to be overdone.

'What exactly are you proposing?' I ask.

'We,' the Major announces, 'are proposing disposing of the Lodge.'

'One disposes of old magazines, mango rinds, not the family estate!'

'The house is falling apart!' the Major thunders. 'The roof is caving in. Who needs such a big place?'

'Nargis, Babu, the children!'

Babu, scrutinizing his palms, mutters, 'We don't really need so much space.'

'We should have done this long ago,' the Major continues, 'but you know that the court could not appoint a nazir to appraise the property because Bakaullah was away and Tony was in America and then there was the whole business of the lease renewal.'[96] The Major neglects to mention that nobody was interested in 'disposing' of the Lodge because property prices were depressed through the turn of the century.[97] 'Better late than never,' he is saying. 'Bakaullah is in a bad way, and I have to support my children, and what about Guddu and Tota?'

'Toto—'

'How can you deny them their right? We all need money, shehzaday. We all have needs.'

'I also have needs—'

'Liquor?'

---

96. In the nineties, leases for many properties in Garden lapsed and the renewal cost was something like Rs. 1,300 per square yard or almost Rs. 6 million in total.

97. These America- and Gulf-return types are in search of 'investment opportunities,' and there is no doubt that because of its square yardage and location, the Lodge has become a bona fide goldmine. Many have sold out over the years—Mr Silveira, the Mascarenhas, Ghulam Mohammed & Sons. Amrohi's brother, the formidable poet Jaun, was reportedly compelled to move to Buffer Zone. How can a canton be called Buffer Zone?

'What of it?'

'It's haram!'

'Show me one place it is haram in the Holy Book and I will leave the Lodge tomorrow—'[98]

'You're a loafer!'

'I'm an intellectual!'

'Go do your thinking elsewhere!'

Where? In one of those new, exorbitant flats overlooking the smelly lagoon? I cannot afford that. Then what? A semi-detached Gulshan-e-This or Gulistan-e-That? The Major will say that I would be able to live like a king from the sale of the Lodge, but my needs are not regal and why should I leave heaven for hell? No, I will die on my own terms, in my own home. Am I selfish? Perhaps. But survival is a selfish imperative—the reason for the success of the *Homo sapiens* species! Passing gas, a cracker more than a thunderclap, I exclaim, 'I will not!'

'Don't be the dog in the cupboard—'

'Manger, sir—'

'You will be happy to know we've found a buyer, a carpet tycoon. He wants to build a high-rise—he will pay up to 60 per cent up front. Bakaullah is flying down to sign the iqrarnama!'[99] A carpet tycoon! Comrade Bakaullah! Surely the End of Days is upon us! 'We just need your consent.'

---

98. There are basically three verses in the Holy Bible that explicitly pertain to the consumption of alcohol: Al-Baqarah 2:219, An-Nisa 4:43 and Al-Mai'dah 5:91. Each offers a varying view. It is, for the record, mentioned a fourth time in a list delineating God's bounties. 'And from the fruit of the date-palm and the vine, ye get out wholesome drink and food.' Imagine that!

99. I might not know much about the law, but I know this much due to cross-questioning Kapadia over the years: according to the Colonial Era Land Transfer Act circa 1860 or 1870, the iqrarnama, or *agreement to sell*, is basically only a promise by a potential seller. It is not legally binding.

Bovine faecal matter! I can wager my stipend on the fact that Tony has not yet assented. They know they cannot accomplish anything without the written consent of Tony and me. And I decide I will get to him first. They also know that I happen to possess the title deed. Papa handed it to me himself.

'It will be a boon for us all,' the Major is saying. 'What say you?'

'I need to soak my rump in the tub.'

Just then, Nargis arrives with a glass of water. 'Too little,' I mumble, standing up, 'too late.'

'You cannot run every time we discuss the subject!' the Major exclaims. 'You need to commit now! You will commit now! The express train doesn't wait for the passenger!'

'Let me think about it.'

'You need how long?'

'Six, maybe seven years?'

'Nothing doing!' he hollers. 'You have three weeks, and three weeks only! Any later and I'll sort you out! The courts will sort you out! You have no locus standi!'

'Locus standi, my foot,' I declare, marching out. 'Exit, Cossack.'

AN ORAL HISTORY OF THE COSSACK ERA

'YOU SEE, AFTER THREE years of praying, praying for inspiration or direction, praying for his mother's soul, he forsook propriety, society, family and our one and only God. He started the day in the afternoon with the equivalent of a three-martini breakfast. He evoked that mathematician Khayyam, proclaiming, "If there's no truth, no certainty, what does it matter if I in my ignorance am sober or drunk?" He staggered in Hawaiian shirts and an Elvis bouffant from bar to nightclub, from gambling dens to the brothels up and down Napier Road. Needless to say, he acquired a reputation overnight…

'One heard things. My clients were talkers. They said he was seen with a dancer of mixed parentage who was known to bare all on stage except her rainbow wigs, and also kept company with several society beauties known to be regulars at the Key Club. Once, they found his Chevrolet floating in the shallows beyond Bath Island—you won't remember but Bath Island was once an island—with him in it. They kept it out of the papers on account of his having been out with the wife of a serving provincial minister. Another time, he had to be rescued from jail for driving into a parked police car in the middle of the day. Then there was the straw that broke the camel's back. There was this band of hippies who had hitch-hiked from Bavaria and were running around town peddling hallucinogens. Our hero adopted them, lodging the hippies at the Olympus. When his father learnt of the arrangement, he had everybody thrown out, including his son…

'The story goes that one night at the bar at the Central Hotel, the young man happened upon a delegation of Soviet technocrats in town to advise the government on nationalizing industry—was it the steel mills? A bet was struck behind the bar and Abdullah found himself seated face to face with a Tartar and a Georgian and a dozen bottles of vodka. You know these peoples are famed for their capacity to drink. They laughed and postured and pounded shot after shot as if they were guzzling Roohafzah. Word spread. Idlers from neighbouring Metropole and Excelsior down the road showed up. More wagers were placed with the barkeep, some say close to half a lakh altogether. The Russians started to sweat and swoon. They cried foul but it was too late: at the end of the evening, our hero was the last man standing. He picked up a bottle of Cossack brand vodka and raised it to the cheering audience like a hero, then took a bite from the rim of his glass and spat it out. That night, he was crowned, no christened, the Cossack. The year was 1974…

'There are numerous tales and myths associated with the Cossack Era. Once, at the annual Fancy Dress Ball at the Burt Institute, it's said he donned tights and flitted up and down the hall all evening, telling the ladies he was Petipa's Don Quixote looking for his Dulcinea. He bedded two together. Another time, he and his cohort dressed as firemen, pumping beer into everybody's mouths through an elaborate contraption. Ironically, he set the lavatory on fire that night when he collapsed smoking a cigar…

'I can go on and on. I could tell you that one of the last visiting Lebanese dancers in the city was coveted by all, from landowners to the city's biggest businessmen. The Cossack dispatched a certain politician with her. He thumped up the stairs at the Excelsior, then thumped down half an hour later, proclaiming, "The bloody woman is a man!" He never forgave the Cossack…

'Some still call him the Cossack. I suspect he still sometimes likes to think of himself as the Cossack. But times change, you know, people change. He might have grown up or given up. He might have realized that he couldn't run all the way. He once said, "Whoever turns a bandit on God's highway will turn tavernward once he sees the light." I am not certain what he meant, but there you have it.

'You know, he comes from a good family, an old family, but sometimes you grow up too early or too late—sometimes you don't grow up at all. Sometimes you misplace your moral centre—it happens to the best of us. It's not unlike misplacing your spectacles, and can I tell you I often misplace those...

'He sobered not long after his father died, retreating into his head, reading literature, history, philosophy, philology, metaphysics, the horticultural sciences, what have you. He never really completed his education. He is a self-educated, self-styled academic, and hats off to him. I understand he has spent many years trying to begin some sort of project pertaining to "aspects of intellectual history" but I don't know much about it, so don't ask me.

'He came to see me when there were family disputes concerning Transfer Certificates—the Probate Courts. His brothers blamed him for everything, from their father's health to the health of the businesses. One of them lodged a case against him. I defended the boy because I didn't believe the apportioning of blame was just. I thought him fundamentally a decent fellow.

'You know, he had lived his entire life for others. One day he decided to live for himself. Is that wrong?'

Transcribed from a Telephonic Account Related to BB by Kapadia of Kapadia & Kapadia (Barrister at Law)

ON THE ART OF ENTERTAINING IN THE DARK (OR KISS ME DEADLY)

JUGNU COMES WHEN THE power goes, wearing reds and yellows and sucking a beedi. We drink, dine and dance under faint impressions of whirling constellations. There have been a few near brushes with the authorities below, the usual threat of Chambu, and sometimes a cloud of dogged mosquitoes descends, but by and large these lantern-lit evenings have been amongst the best of my life, like that number—*My lonely days are over, and life is like a song!* Such a period of amity in the history of nations is termed a Golden Age.[100] Of course, anxieties do conspire and circle the camp, but the idea, anticipation, the nightly promise of Jugnu has the effect of banishing disquiet to the periphery of my consciousness.

Jugnu is cool, quick, charming, mysterious. She will chat about everything from the inchoate shapes in the clouds—'That one looks like a buffalo from behind'—to the gusts of political change—'The war in the North is spilling to the South'—but rarely about herself. A veil separates her life outside the Lodge and

---

100. Gibbon states, 'If a man were called to fix the period ... during which the condition of the human race was most happy and prosperous, he would, without hesitation, name that which elapsed from the death of Domitian to the accession of Commodus.' Gibbon, of course, was wrong. What about Africa, South America? Akbar the Great's Rule? And Oudh?

one does not want to be seen peering in; but on occasion, when we are wet with sweat and flush with wine and the breeze stirs ever so slightly, the veil lifts. One has gleaned that she can read Urdu though she has not matriculated, that she has worked as a seamstress and beautician in prior lives, prior incarnations. She cannot cook or handle a fork, belches religiously after dinner (and says *Alhumdulillah*, God bless her), and After Eight chocolate mints make her giddy.

Of course, I am also aware of Jugnu's connection to Lyari, one of many cantons left by lily-livered politicos to the dogs.[101] I want to ask her about Langra Dacoit, the infamous don known for running guns, extortion rackets and other unwholesome endeavours. According to Chambu, resident expert on all matters including the machinations of the mafia, the fearsome don was recently nabbed by the authorities. Jugnu, however, remains tight-lipped.

In the effort to discern more, I offer to read Jugnu's palm, a ruse that has worked for swains the world over from time immemorial: placing her hands on my knees like a bold bride displaying fresh henna, she looks up expectantly. 'Phir?' *Then?* I explain that the left hand catalogues one's inheritance and predispositions, the right offers a snapshot of fate, viz., *kismet ki photo*: 'You must have noticed that the length and trajectory of these lines change over time. Fate, you see, is not set in stone. It's in your hand.' I might not believe such bromides, but it doesn't matter—nothing matters when her hand is cradled in mine. 'This is your brain line, long, elegant, and this one is your love line. I am happy to report that it is robust.'

101. Courtesy of Chambu, I know for a fact that there is not a single functioning emergency ward in the canton, or a blood bank, that residents have to clean the broken sewage lines themselves. One wonders where all the development funds go. Actually, one knows.

What else did her palm tell this amateur chiromancer?[102] Unlike my palms—clean, fleshy, and cut by three distinct divergent routes—Jugnu's are cross-hatched like raw silk, the telltale sign of an Old Soul. And she possesses glyphs I have never seen before—a confounding swirl across the Mound of Venus, a triangle in Upper Mars, etcetera. When I cannot discern the import of a particular pattern, I speculate: 'It seems that you were happy until you were, oh, about twelve years of age? Things changed thereafter and remained in flux for years. Now you're looking for something, somebody perhaps?'

Some nights she allows conjecture; some nights she retrieves her palm, changes the subject: 'Who is this Sara Awan?' I tell her that Sarah Vaughan was a legendary jazz singer who led a tumultuous life & died early. When she asks, 'What is she singing about?' I translate the following verse: 'Have you ever heard two turtle doves / Bill and coo when they love? / That's the kind of magic music we make with our lips / When we kiss...'[103]

WE ARE SPRAWLED IN the veranda late one night, sipping the dregs of a fine bottle of Tony's wine after Bosco has retired. Jugnu is sweating because she has been teaching the lad proprietary dance moves: Change-the-Lightbulb, Change-the-Lightbulb, Butcher's-Cut, Butcher's-Cut. The crevice of her breasts beckons, the zircon stud wedged in her neb glows—she evokes Nefertiti in repose. 'What are you looking at?' she asks.

Blood coursing from head to sole, I reply, 'You.'

---

102. I had picked up Mir Bashir's *Art of Hand Analysis* at Thomas & Thomas. Revered and respected throughout the world, Bashir was a rare breed amongst chiromancers—an empiricist: his library housed tens of thousands of prints.

103. It's something like this: *Tum ne kabhi / qabootar ki gayki suni he? / Jab tumhay mein chumta hoon / to aisi awaz aati hai / aisa jadu hota he.*

'Why?'

'Because,' I say, leaning closer, 'you are the most magnificent creature I have ever set eyes on.' Then I take a Leap of Faith: I shut my eyes and kiss her. She tastes like lipstick, tobacco, hope on the morrow.

Mercifully she does not swat me away. 'You are an interesting man,' she says, 'a kind man, but you need to be careful. You do not know me.'

'I like what I know, and I want to know more.'

'I have many issues.'

'Let me help.'

'If God cannot help me, how can you?'

'I have resources at my disposal,' I lie. 'I can get things done,' I lie again. 'But tonight I can help you forget.'

Tugging her to the dance floor, I place her hands on my chest and mine around her waist. We dance cheek to cheek despite the logistics of my belly for the remainder of the evening to the trill of the night birds & cricket orchestra. We kiss again. We do not go further. Why does it matter? We have time.

THE LAST TIME I experienced intimate relations was in the winter of '88. It was a hopeful moment in history—the gust of democratic change was sweeping across the land—but my relationship with Khaver, an aging television actress who had had supporting roles in several popular serials, was at best precarious. When I would visit her flat at Rimpa Skyline, bearing fragrant bracelets fashioned of jasmine and a bottle of Italian red wine, she would yell at me—*You're always late! What do you take me for? You don't know what it's like!*—before making spirited animal love. Sex, good sex, is fundamentally animalistic: it involves licking and sniffing and secret secretions.[104]

---

104. I would cook for her afterward whilst she sprawled like a Renoir, all rolls, folds & pendulous breasts, recalling the time she was courted

The closest Jugnu and I are to carnal congress is the evening she arrives dramatically drenched—a passing automobile has splashed soupy water all over her low-cut, Roohafzah-coloured shalwar. 'I am going to take a bath,' she announces. After expounding tubside on the idiosyncrasies of the plumbing system—the blue tap spouts hot water, turned counterclockwise—I repair to the balcony to entertain randy fantasies. Imagine a sodden beauty quietly soaping by candlelight in your tub! Imagine, oh, just imagine!

When she calls for a towel, I stand outside the door, clearing my throat, heart beating like a dhol, and when she bids me shut my eyes and enter—'Take nine steps'—I shut my eyes tight like a child anticipating a surprise: a peck, a caress, congress. But she is swaddled in a beach towel in an instant. I can only take in the wet, fragrant tresses cascading over her broad shoulders, the curly hair adorning her long legs. 'You're gentlemane,' she enunciates. What to do? Tug the towel? The moment passes like a thought.

ALTHOUGH IT'S MAGICAL HAVING Jugnu over night after night, the rituals that define relationships between two beings—lovers, friends or family—can slip inexplicably and intractably at any juncture into the Pit of Monotony. Conscious of the peril, I suggest excursions: Seaview, Sandspit, the spectacular beach of Kund Malir, the lighthouse on Manora Island. When I suggest spending an

---

by Bollywood, or the time she met the Dutch Queen Beatrix. A framed monochrome photo of the rendezvous (mediated, I learnt, by one R.S. Chattari, Chief of Protocol) graced the entrance hall. In comparison to the foreigner, a frumpy character sporting pointed dark glasses & a printed dress, Khaver looked like royalty. Other times, Khaver sobbed on the settee. In an effort to discern the cause of her melancholy, I would ask, 'Why are you crying, dear?' 'I don't know,' she would bawl, 'do you?' When she lobbed an onyx vase at me, leaving me with a hairline fracture, I left her. She took her life in '96.

evening at the shrine of Abdullah Shah Ghazi (RA) for qawwali and hashish, she replies, 'Things have changed there,' as if she's a regular. 'What about Colombo?' I ask. 'Tony is always talking about it. It's almost around the corner!'

Leaning back, wistfully scanning the horizon, Jugnu entertains the fantasies in her head with a half-smile but inevitably invokes certain 'responsibilities.' It seems to me as if she is trying to convince herself. Is she married? With child? Dying? Attending to the dying? Of course, if there are matters she keeps close to her chest, there are matters I do not readily divulge either: my piles, the uncertain fate of the Sunset Lodge, my failure to make meaningful progress on any project.

Then there is another matter, a queer matter lodged in my consciousness like a splinter: Jugnu's life line is like a snapped twig. When she asks, 'How long will I live?' I reply, 'You have nothing to worry about.'

But I am worried.

VOLUME III

ON SIGNS AND SYMBOLS
(OR BROKEN IN)

THERE ARE DAYS WHEN you know that God is in Heaven and All's Right with the World, and days when you sense Intimations of Judgment Day. Lolling on the balcony one steamy morning, content with myself, my morning constitutional, it occurs to me that I slept through the festivities of the Lesser Eid. There is no doubt that forgetfulness preys on polymaths, wastrels, septuagenarians, and there is no doubt I roundly qualify. It is a fact that such lunar conjunctures do not really matter to me anymore and we aren't much of a family anymore. But once upon a time, we would eagerly scan the dusky sky for the almond moon before heading to the bazaar for clothes, slippers, musty perfume (and Tony would insist on plastic watches, and dark glasses that he would wear to bed at night). We would attend the long sermon at the mosque in the morning, the short prayer after, then there would be embraces and the exchange of good wishes and food with family & friends all over the city. The only ritual I presently adhere to, however, is bestowing gifts or hard currency on the Childoos.

When I exclaim, 'By Jove'—the lapse is inexcusable—Bosco, nose in a novel, nearly tumbles over.

'What, Uncle Cossack, what?'

'I missed Eid!'

'I missed All Souls Night if it makes you feel better.'

'Why didn't you tell me, boy?'

'You know I'm undercover until this thing blows over.' After setting aside the Greeks, it seems the boy has taken to hardboiled noir. It's as if he is trying on different roles—I know; I have done it myself. 'Besides, God will understand.'

'God? I'm not concerned about God! I'm concerned about the Childoos!'

When I inform him about the urgent errand, he drawls, 'Just keep your nose clean and everything will be jake.'

I do not have time to parse the phrase. I grab my parasol and leave fut-a-fut for the toyshop in my pyjamas, trailed by Oliver and Felicity—I know all the pye-dogs in the neighbourhood by name[105]—and a handsome urchin with a caramelized mop of hair, chirping, 'Hello-Good-Morning-How-Are-You?' I don't reply. I have toys on the mind.

IN THE OLD DAYS we were content with wind-up monkeys or Ludo sets (with the exception of Tony who preferred dinkies) but in these modern times, Postmodern experts say,[106] children are taken with spectacle (with the exception of the Childoos who still enjoy egg crates): Automobiles Guided by Radio Waves, Trains That Transform into Robots, Rifles Emitting Sound & Fury.

---

105. Off the top of my head, there are also: the elder statesmen, Archibald & Buster; the pups, Lassie & Louis; and the territorial gangs that patrol the streets at night, primed for a row: John Wayne, Hecuba, Pax Romana on one side, Long Dong Silver, Gandu, Kuttay ka Bacha and Yorick on the other.

106. I picked up a slim volume on Postmodernity by a certain Borgmann at the weekly book market at Regal Square a couple of decades ago, but couldn't make head or tail of the phenomenon. I must say that I find the term singularly unimaginative and reductive. I have not yet met a Postmodern person. We are inherently tribal.

As a result, I spend an eternity at the toyshop pushing buttons, pulling levers, demanding demonstrations and calculating prices. Spectacle comes at great cost: the price of a child's construction set is equal to the monthly salary of a domestic, not to mention, a meaningful percentage of my monthly stipend. 'You get what you pay for, Seth,' the shopkeeper asserts, handling a box of multicoloured plastic pipes as if it were a case of vintage port on offer at an auction house. 'Kya kahnay,' he says, shaking his head, or *What can you say?*

The local businessman is a singularly savvy species, configured like Lamarck's giraffes to thrive in tough terrain, but I am neither fish nor fowl—a scion of a mercantile family famously improvident with monies. When the shopkeeper invokes retail prices, bulk rates, transportation charges, extortion costs by Langra's men, I sense that my cash will be tied up in toys for the near future. 'As God is my witness,' I interrupt, 'I am an old customer. I expect a discount commensurate with my unerring loyalty. I will make a deposit now and will pay the rest in a week's time.' And tucking the box under my arm, I march out like a conquistador.

BUT WHEN CONFRONTED BY Badbakht Begum outside the Lodge, I skitter past like a geisha. 'Is that for me?' she asks.

'Madam,' I reply, 'all the gifts in the world would not satisfy you.'

'Sometimes the simplest things do: a gesture, a smile, the regard of our near and dear.'

Turning on my heel, I consider my kaftan-clad, crayon-eyeshadow-wearing coeval and cousin-in-law twice removed: there is no doubt that her carriage remains regal, her skin, bright and rosy, her tresses, rich and red like a flame. And as she runs her fingers through her hair, I cannot help but wonder if she is flirting with me. 'Madam?'

'I understand you're burning the candle at both ends these days.'

What does she know? *How* does she know? Feminine intuition, unlike the patchy science of palm reading, is uncanny. 'Life is short,' I blurt. 'We must celebrate ourselves.'

'We could celebrate together sometime.'

'No doubt, no doubt,' I reply, scurrying inside.

Nargis the Opossum is ensconced on a love seat in the parlour, interviewing a middle-aged chap with a mop of wavy oiled hair, and a pot-bellied dame. 'This is Shafqat,' Nargis says, as if expecting me, 'and his wife, Parveen. They are interested in employment. Would you like to talk to them?'

Flattered by the unexpected offer to participate in household management, I lower myself into the settee, fold my arms like a monarch, and pose a couple of standard questions—Shafqat hails from Rahim Yar Khan and has family in the city, an uncle who does 'mechanic work'—before broaching the fundamentals: 'Tell me,' I begin, 'what is the tastiest part of the chicken?'

'The kidneys?'

'No. The skin.[107] And the tastiest part of the fish?'

'The head?'

'The tail.'

'Thank you, Abdullah Bhai,' Nargis interrupts.

'Please proceed,' I declaim, as if I have to attend to pressing matters of state. I do: I have to attend to my heirs.

Doodles and drawings embellish the door to the lair of the Childoos—an impressionistic rendition of a forest, a still life featuring a variegated watermelon, or if you like, Planet Earth & a black canvas, crayon-on-paper, Modern Artwork. Toto presides over the mayhem inside—stuffed animals, dinkies, marbles, crayons strewn across the

107. There is, however, a Culinary School of Thought that maintains that the oysters are the tastiest. The French call them sot-l'y-laisse which I understand translates to 'the fool leaves it there.'

floor—humming a version of 'Gentille Alouette'[108] that sounds like 'Jaisay Aaloo Hota.'

When I announce, 'I have something for you,' the Childoos hop up and down like Pagans Before the Feast. They rip the wrapping paper into confetti and get to work. Clearing an area to accommodate my rump, I sit amongst them like Gulliver amongst the Lilliputians as they construct an elaborate edifice wrought of plastic pipes. I have watched them build and destroy empires over the years, raptly, indulgently—it's a delight to be privy to simple pleasures, desires, straightforward objectives. My life might have been meaningful had I produced progeny.

When the Childoos grow tired of performing great architectural feats, they straddle my belly. Guddu grabs my chin. 'I knows the answer of the difficult math sum.'

'What?'

'Twenty-two.'

'That's brilliant, child, but what's the sum?'

'I forgots.'

Oh, the marvellous logic of the Childoos! I could stay amongst them for the remainder of the day, the remainder of my life, but I sneak out before tea for I do not want to make small talk with the insensible. It has been a good day. Why spoil it?

BUT WHEN I REACH my quarters, I find Bosco pacing up and down, teary and dishevelled and clutching an envelope. 'They barged in after you left,' he begins. '*Who are you?* they asked. *You look like a thief!* They asked me where you were but I told them I didn't know. *You give him*

---

108. One has observed that children's nursery rhyme preferences change regularly. It's uncanny. The last time I was over, the Childoos would not stop singing that ode to marine life: 'Machli jal ki rani hai / Jeevan uska paani hai / Haath lagao gey, dar jaye gi / Bahar nikaalo gey, mar jaye gi.'

this! they told me. *You make sure that he gets this, otherwise we' ll hang you upside down. Tell him that this is from his brother.*'

Poor lad: vulnerable at home, vulnerable at the Lodge. 'Come,' I beckon with open arms, but Bosco stands his ground, fists balled. 'I should've done something but couldn't. I'm completely useless!'

Embracing him, I say, 'This has nothing to do with you. This is my problem, my fault. Do you understand?' Bosco nods non-committally. 'You need to forget about it. Go freshen up. Jugnu will be here soon. We'll have a grand time tonight. I'm making my world-famous Chicken à la Kiev.'

When I unfold the note, however, I hear a portentous drum roll, the clash of cymbals. It reads,

> The past lies like a nightmare upon the present.
>
> Some loads are light, some heavy. Some people prefer the light to the heavy; they pick the light and shove the heavy onto others.
>
> And the LORD said unto Cain, Where is Abel thy brother? And he said, I know not: Am I my brother's keeper? And he said, What hast thou done? The voice of thy brother's blood crieth unto me from the ground.
>
> Vacate the premises immediately or FACE MY WRATH.

I do not understand the import of the missive but I understand this much: Bakaullah is in town. Judgment Day is nigh.

ON THE DYNAMICS THAT INFORM THE DISSOLUTION OF FAMILIES

YOU MIGHT ASK WHY we fell apart, but why do things fall apart? There are studies, proverbs and songs that illuminate the enquiry—numbers from the respective oeuvres of Chet Baker, Etta James, Frankie Valli and the Four Seasons come to mind—but I believe there is a more basic, indeed molecular, explanation. I might be known more for my vegetables than my scientific acumen, but I am aware that falling apart is more natural than coming together. As I understand it, said phenomenon is known as Entropy. Scientifically speaking, I also understand an entity, any entity, requires a locus. Show me a flower without a stigma & I will show you wilted petals scattered like a tragedy. Show me a galaxy without a heaving, breathing star & I will show you still life.

The Fall of the House of K. is not a particularly novel, mysterious, insoluble, perfidious or lurid tale. It is as commonplace as fallen leaves, as mulch. I am not certain where to begin, because to fit a narrative straitjacket on a series of conjunctures is not really my cup of tea, but if compelled I reckon I would mention the dry wintery evenings of a fateful year when the sea wafted the balm of seaweed and sedge, and Papa took to bed for the first time with 'a touch of pneumonia.' The rot that would finish him arguably took root then, but at the time, he persisted, swathed in a quilt, conducting his affairs prone, like an aging monarch. Members of his staff would scurry in and out and to and fro at odd hours, shuttling letters and documents that required signatures, and concoctions from Bliss & Co. Despite hoarse entreaties from our venerable hook-nosed Parsee GP—'You need rest, mister!'—Papa persevered. But his mantra, an echo, perhaps, of a Saying of the Prophet (PBUH) was: 'Kaam bhi ibadat hota hay,' or *Work, also, is a kind of worship.*

It is said that that is why Mummy lavished such attention on us. It is also said that since her family shunned her after her fleeting marriage to the Khan of This or That Khanate, she had nothing & nobody else. We knew otherwise. We knew that if we faced a problem, be it a bee sting or professional conundrum, she would roll up her sleeves. She was tireless and resourceful, even if she did not always succeed. She said she had failed when I decided to leave university and return to run the business, but once I was back she made certain that I realized my ambition to become Aaron (AS) to my father. Unbeknownst to most, Mummy solved many a matter at the Olympus, from staff retention to occupancy rates to the menu. There is that aphorism about Great Men, but those in the know know that Behind Every Man, There Is a Mother. There is no doubt that Mummy was the glue that kept us together, but we were not there when she needed us: nobody noticed that Mummy was suffering, that she had cancer, until it was too late.[109]

But I will not dwell on her demise—I cannot allow myself to become upended again. Instead, I will remember her gliding into the kitchen in the mornings in her robe de chambre to fix us extravagant breakfasts. 'Kya karti hai, Begum Sahab?' Barbarossa would grumble, or *Why does she do it (when I am here)?* 'Meray bachain hain,' she would reply, or *They are my children (and if I don't do it, who will?)* Tony and I would sit at the dining table side by side, feasting on scrambled eggs,

---

109. Many maintain cancer was rare then, but I suspect medical science did not have the requisite tools for detection.

sliced, sautéed potatoes, fried tomatoes and tall glasses of seasonal juice.[110]

Tony was a charming, bright-eyed lad—he would shake your hand when he met you, look you in the eye when he spoke, and converse about the Life of the Sun—but a famously finicky eater, known to be anti-egg, boiled, poached, scrambled or sunny-side up, not to mention, anti-apple gourd, lady fingers, fish curry, brain masala and sweetmeats.[111] I often caught him slipping sunny-side-ups into the napkin in his lap before disposing of them on the sly behind the credenza. When Barbarossa happened upon a cache of stinking, discoloured napkins in the gap between the credenza and the wall, he threatened to notify the authorities, but we all have a tendency to let it go with Tony. And undeterred, Tony began disposing of the evidence in the garden after. 'Egg, plant,' he joked. Oh, that rogue!

There was no doubt that we, the Second Batch of the House of K., availed of certain demographic shifts in the household: Crown Prince Hidayatullah had long left the roost, dispatched to the army by Papa[112] because he took no interest in the business (and because our family legal counsel, Kapadia, had reported that he 'entertained idle follies ... a proclivity for Dimple whisky and the company of women of loose character from the Excelsior'). Of course, when Hidayatullah appeared at the Lodge years later in a stiff khaki uniform, stomping and saluting and sporting trim whiskers, Papa nodded in appreciation. We were all in awe: Tony touched the epaulettes as if they were talismans, and Babu gave up knickers and table tennis. At that juncture in

110. For the record, however, my favourite breakfast is paratha & clotted cream sprinkled with sugar. There's nothing in the world like it.

111. Arguably, he was ahead of the times: I understand that it is now fashionable to be what is termed Vegan.

112. When Hidayatullah had pleaded for the navy, Papa exclaimed, 'What, what? Rum, buggery and the lash?'

history, nobody could prophesize that, though Hidayatullah walked and talked like a soldier, he would not rise through the ranks due to instances of insubordination. Nobody realized then that the Major would resent Papa for dispatching him to the frontlines.

Comrade Bakaullah was a different story: he rejected our father's enterprise on principle when he turned Soorkha. It might have been an act of rebellion, though all thinking men in the fifties sympathized with the noble principles of Communism—You Get What You Are Given and Give What is Needed. Red beret tilted over the forehead, tin of foreign cigarettes in hand, Comrade Bakaullah railed against the Inherent Brutality of the Capitalist Machinery in his trademark stentorian manner. Once when Comrade Bakaullah baited him, Papa declaimed, 'I provide for my workers, your proletariat people. What do you do? Distribute flags, peddle slogans? You can't eat slogans, young man.'

'I advocate ideas,' Comrade Bakaullah frothed at the mouth, 'and you cannot fight an idea!'

'You need to think up better ideas or get out of the business. You don't have the chops for it!'[113]

Perhaps Comrade Bakaullah took Papa's advice to heart: after escaping prison with the help of one Major Hidayatullah (Papa had proclaimed, 'Let him stay there, he might learn something'), Bakaullah was to find the Capitalist Enterprise in far flung Hijaz. When oil gushed out of the ground, shepherds became sheikhs, and sheikhs required expertise. Tall, articulate and committed, Bakaullah was undoubtedly Godsent: he advised the emergent oligarchy on matters from commerce to propriety, and as a reward for expertly negotiating

---

113. When I told Bakaullah that Marxism predates Marx by hundreds if not thousands of years—the Zoroastrian prophet Mazdak was the first Communist, preaching virtues of common good and community circa 500 CE & Inayat Shah (RA) established a commune in Scinde before the Mughals wiped it out—he growled, 'The hell does it matter?'

complex contracts with 'plundering neo-colonial forces,' he was offered a partnership with a prince in a transportation & logistics business that would command a regional monopoly for decades. Bakaullah was undoubtedly guided by the proverbial Invisible Hand.

In time, Comrade Bakaullah would find God in the desert—not just any god, mind you, but the tribal God of a tribal people. It was not merely a matter of genetic predisposition or geography, the Bedouin Way. No, he was a wounded man: in the summer of a fateful year, when travelling for the inauguration of a water park, a Dodge Monaco collided with his station wagon. Bakaullah's wife, my sister-in-law and friend, died immediately, his five-year-old, hazel-eyed heir expired later that night, whilst his daughter (known to all and sundry as Princess Surriya) lay in a coma for almost two years. Bakaullah attended to her every day, pacing and praying, but one fine day she left us. Verily, there are matters that pollute and fester and deplete our beings until we are nothing but husks.

The accident transpired long after that wintery evening when I was summoned bedside by Papa. Bunnet fastened on head, he handed me a blue file bound by string that opened to the following itineraries:

—PAGE 1—

Annual Ball
Caledonian Society

Host: Caledonian Society
Guests: President General Ayub, Mr N.A. Leslie

—PAGE 2—

Evening Party
Queen's Road Residence

Host: Prince of Bahawalpur
Guests: UK High Commissioner & Lady Symon, Austrian Minister & Mrs Hartlmayr, Canadian High Commissioner & Mrs Moran, Mr H.S. Suharwardy, Mr & Mrs Dinshaw

—PAGE 3—

Cocktail Party
PECHS Residence

Host: Mr & Mrs Mobed
Guests: Mr & Mrs Braganza, Mr Max Koening, Dr Khumbatta, Mr Dubas, Ms Patel, Ms Jenny, Mr Max Koening

As I held the documents in my hand like vellum, Papa instructed, 'Shake the hand of the host when you enter, commend them on the occasion, sample the spread, then slip out. You need not linger. You are attending these events in a professional capacity, in my stead. Do you understand?'

'Sir, sir, sir, sir, sir, sir,' I saluted. I understood that I had, in effect, been designated Ambassador of the Clan, at age twenty. The nominal nomination would cause certain rifts if not rancour even if the others did not qualify—Hidayatullah was already a serving major, and Bakaullah a card-carrying Communist—but at the time I was oblivious to the ramifications & determined to play the role with requisite serious-mindedness. I selected shoes and socks and a shark-grey suit[114] the night before, practised polite conversation before the mirror: *The weather has turned nippy, has it not?* Or, *Those melons, no doubt, are Central Asian.* One had to be prepared. The New Year

114. For all Papa's bespoke tailoring, he frequented Nawaz & Co.

was upon us, so I conducted research about it in the society paper of record, Aunty Zaibunnissa's *Monthly Mirror*:

> It's difficult to believe that [the New Year] is already here, isn't it? [Last year] is dead and buried [but] dear old December always dies with so much fun and frivolity that there's no sadness at all ... This year, December's last moments were filled to the brim with merrymaking. Hotels were crowded with enjoyment-seekers and everywhere a festive spirit reigned supreme.

Red and yellow buntings draped the walls at the Annual Caledonian Society Ball, magnificent flower arrangements bedecked the tables. Dames in dresses, in saris, promenaded with men in black tie, smoking pipes, talking about the bloodless coup. Presenting my invitation card at the door, I limply shook hands, wondering, *Who on earth are the Caledonians?*[115] & *What to do?* Although initially relegated to the periphery of the festivities, I would, in time, find my feet. I might not have known it but Currachee came of age then. So did I.

Of course, when Papa took to his bed for the second time, the last time, everything had changed: the Caledonian Society had disbanded by '77, '78, banking & manufacturing had been nationalized, Mummy had passed, and I had come apart. After spending a couple of years graveside—*what's the point,* I reckoned, *when you lose sight of essential matters, materfamilias*—I spent years drinking vodka until vodka was banned.

In lucid moments, I attended to the ailing patriarch who, by then, had taken up residence in the Olympus. The edifice was in a state of

---

115. Conducting research after the fact, I learnt that they serve ample malt refreshments, neeps, tatties & stuffed offal known as haggis, and venerate that poet known for his affinity for haggis. How does it go? 'Some hae meat but canna eat / And some wad eat that want it...'

disrepair, dilapidation: the shingles would get dislodged frequently by a gust or cloudburst, and slide down the slope of the roof to shatter on the esplanade. Pigeons made their homes in the interstices, and mangy strays roamed the ground floor, finding refuge in kitchen cabinets and under the bed. Papa fed them every day out of his leathery hands. They purred and urinated in corners. The feline is a despicable creature. But perhaps he required company. Tony was away, Babu no fun, the Major rarely showed, and Comrade Bakaullah sent missives from the desert, suing me for negligence. Sometimes an old-timer, some other broken, bereft captain of industry, would turn up with a story of woe, but by then most of the old-timers were lost to time.

One night, Papa summoned me bedside. I studied my father in the wan light—Adam's apple bulging, tongue heavy, eyes crusted around the rim. 'I want you to remember one thing,' he whispered. 'You will be judged by what you finish, not what you begin.' I did not quite understand what he meant—I was a bottle into the evening. 'You have not grown up the way I expected,' he continued, 'but you have been a good son.' When he handed me the title deed—the Lodge, I learnt, was in Mummy's name—I stammered, stumbled out. What to do? What to say?

The next day I found Papa dead.

ON THE DARK NIGHT OF THE SOUL
(OR MAN WITH A PLAN)

IN THE ANNALS OF Man, there have been peoples who have braved the murderous gales of the Arctic & Antarctic, peoples who have defied the bald, blanching sun of the Gobi & Kalahari, those who have inhabited trees,[116] those who have populated the open seas,[117] but there have never been a People Who Have Lived in the Night. One concedes that the Viking States experience evenings that extend for months, and in lost history books you will find cave-dwelling peoples for whom day was night and night was day—the Phruges of Anatolia, for instance, carved subterranean cities into volcanic rock more than a millennium ago—but Cave Life is a different matter, a different Mode of Being altogether.

I have lived, oft thrived, at night. Indeed, there have been stretches when I have not felt the warmth of the sun on my face but have seen the light: I have probed forgotten crevices of intellectual history, scaled cosmological peaks. Carpe Diem? No, Carpe Noctis! At night,

---

116. The Korowai & Kombai who inhabit the lowlands of West Papua scramble up & down trees unencumbered, members tucked into scrotums. They're hounded by missionaries insisting they cover up, bow to their God.

117. The Sea Gypsies of the Pacific, for example, inhabit the sea and suffer badly from the bends.

you are indifferent to the diurnal pantomimes that characterize the wakeful multitudes, from the Shaving of the Cheek to the Cataloguing of the Post. You do not have to contend with simple-minded sloganeering, the petty chatter that governs the age: *You're looking healthy, mashallah. How do you keep busy? Take care of yourself.* I will take care of nothing! I will devour a bowl of clotted cream with salted caramel ice cream to spite them!

But the night following the day I received the note from my lost brother, I recall why mankind eschews nightfall: night can be desolate, night can be absolute. You can hide from others but not from yourself. *You are an irredeemably idiotic old man,* I admonish myself, *you will lose everything, lose everybody, if you do not summon Will to Power.* But I cannot even summon the will to turn on my side. There is a tightness in my chest, as if I am girdled by bubble wrap, a throbbing in my left shoulder blade—I am certain I require an ECG, open heart surgery—and I can sense the cosmos conspiring against me: lying in bed long after Bosco has retired, I discern perfidy in the trill of the fruit bats, in the metronomic clicks that break the silence, in Jugnu's absence. She never showed. Consequently, I had dinner, Chicken à la Kiev, cold.

REREADING BAKAULLAH'S NOTE, I recognize the Gods of Modernity amongst the eternal injunctions of the Gods of Yesteryear, cognizant that Comrade Bakaullah, like his God, will do what he is wont. He always has. After attacking me in a series of lawsuits, he stripped me of my shareholdings in the family's principal business concerns, leaving me with the rump of the faltering empire—a recycling unit in the Industrial & Trading Estate (spun off from our paints & plastics business), a garment-dyeing operation, and a video rental service known to customers as Sunny Video. Bakaullah claims that I have run each into the ground. That's bakwas, bavardage.

There is no doubt that there is great scope in the recycling industry[118]—we are, as a matter of record, one of the world's leading recyclers—but Operation Clean-up, the brutal army campaign in the summer of '92, coupled with power shortages, conspired against success. In the end, the profit from the sale of the real estate barely covered dismantling costs. The video rental business, on the other hand, was a victim of changing dynamics, viz., the demise of the video cassette, rampant piracy, censorship. And though it is not incorrect to assume that I do not possess the patience for dyeing garments, it is no secret that my manager Chambu, that formidable swine, is in cahoots with the land mafia, that I do not see a paisa, that the industry, indeed the entire economy was in disarray after the Tit-for-Tat Nuclear Tests of '98. At the time I did not understand why Hindoostan pursued the exercise, why we reciprocated, but when I thought about it later, it was as clear as a winter morning: siblings always behave badly.

Whilst I might have had many matters on my mind—the Childoos' gifts, carnal congress with Jugnu, the moral and intellectual development of Bosco, the legacy of Abdullah Shah Ghazi (RA)—I am not a dashed fool; I have not forgotten about the matter of the Lodge. I recall phoning our family legal counsel, Kapadia, remember he agreed to meet, and remember he postponed our tête-à-tête due to some legal emergency—an outstanding case at the High Court concerning the scions of This or That Khanate. What to do? I must pull a hare from a hat.

---

118. I must mention that the son of my friend S. Sajjad, the world-famous sculptor, invented a contraption that has the appearance of a garden-variety geyser but transforms PET bottles into petrol. It's marvellous! Imagine: something from nothing!

THE LIGHT IS SILVERY after six, the clouds turgid and grey. The old crow cackles, a koel calls to his mate.[119] Soon the Lodge will stir, indifferent to the auspices: Nargis will rouse the Childoos, lead them to the lavatory, then to the kitchen where Babu will survey the city section—FIRST BATCH OF FEMALE FIGHTER PILOTS INDUCTED, BOXING CHAMPION OPENS FACILITY FOR YOUTHS—before turning to the editorial page. I have stopped taking interest in the news because it causes high blood pressure and who cares what others—people, mind you, no better than you or me—believe about foreign policy?

As I rise to retire, bleary-eyed and beside myself, I spy a solitary figure loitering at the gate. Is it Chambu? Bua's husband? The Grim Reaper? No! It's Jugnu! Sporting dark trousers, a chequered bush-shirt, and a cap that lends her the appearance of a contractor, she beckons with a wave. In all the excitement, I nearly trip down the stairs and crack my head open like a raw egg on the landing. 'This is the last time you will see me,' she announces, sack slung over the shoulder.

'What do you mean?'

'And I need money.'

'You cannot just leave me like this, Jugnu.'

'My name is Juggan.'

Digging into my pocket, I produce a handful of notes. 'I will pay for your story.' It's a mercenary ploy. It works: she allows me to drag her up to my lair.

---

119. I am always surprised when I glimpse a koel. Their calls to each other are passionate, emphatic, loud, but they are generally quiet, contemplative creatures that remain camouflaged in the flora & foliage. The males are Moroccan blue, their mates specked black and white, and both have blood-orange eyes. Indeed, they inspire birdwatching. Oh, how I would have liked to be a birdwatcher! So much to do, so much not done. I blame the crows.

Clearing her throat, as if poised to recite a ghazal, she begins: 'You have heard of Langra Dacoit?' Who doesn't know the Don of Lyari? 'He is known as a gangster, a killer, but I can tell you, he took me in when I had nobody, when I had nothing. I have been his keep[120] for the last four years. The day before I first saw you, he was picked up in an operation. They held him at Garden Station under remand. I was not there at the time—we had a spat that afternoon—otherwise they might have arrested me as well. There is an FIR[121] against him, but they do not have a case because no witnesses will testify. Last night, I learnt they are looking for me. I know things about him—'

'What?'

'I have no time to waste time!' she says, viz., *Time pass karnay ka time nahin.*

As Jugnu snatches the currency and flees like Taffy the Welshman, I reckon I ought to say something—*Come again, come often!*—but feel, *What to say? What to do?* The dame I love has shared the bed of another, a gangster, and is a fugitive from justice! Sitting like a paperweight considering the clutter about me—the rugs, canvases, candelabra, Betamax recorders—it occurs to me that I have nothing, that I cannot afford to let Jugnu go.

The last time I ran, the bully triad was chasing me on the playground, hurling abuses, swinging fists. I run for my life again, but it's like swimming against the tide. I can feel phlegm bubbling in my chest, uric acid coursing in my knees. I can feel gravity pulling me down to oblivion. Panting, sweating, thighs chafing, I tell myself I must turn

120. For your information, she used the word 'rakhayl.' Everybody ought to have one. Recall that old disco number that goes *Toot-toot, beep-beep.*

121. Those outside Bangladesh, Hindoostan, Pakistan and Japan might not know that a First Information Report, or FIR, is prepared by the police concerning a 'cognizable offense.' An arrest, then, is preceded by an FIR.

the corner. Somehow I do. I spot Jugnu a furlong away, tarrying at the bus stop under the TouchMe Talcum Powder billboard.

Clutching my thighs, swallowing mouthfuls of air, I attempt to call out to her but only manage a whimper. I attempt again but a bus noisily speeds past. It's like howling in a hurricane, a nightmare. Crumpling to the ground, I whisper to the earth like a madman, a majnun: *Come back, come back, oh God, come back.* Then I hear a voice speak to me in the darkness: 'Tum to sajday main gir gaye,' or *You've fallen in prayer.* I open my eyes to Jugnu squatting on her haunches beside me. 'You made me miss my bus.'

'The express train does not wait for the passenger.'

Mercifully, the bent neighbourhood radi-wallah appears on the scene like the volunteer fire brigade, helping me onto his rickety cart (claiming, erroneously, 'This can carry a buffalo'). Resting my head on yesterday's news, I grab Jugnu's hand and gasp, 'Come with me.' Although I have a habit of making promises I cannot keep, this time I actually have a plan. 'You need to trust me. Will you trust me?'

Jugnu squints at the gritty skyline, the slapdash billboards advertising shampoo and serials and prepaid telephone cards, the satellite dishes jutting from rooftops like finials, and tangled telephone wires extending into infinity. 'I trust you.'

The problem is, I am not certain I can trust her.

ON HOW TO GET THINGS DONE
(OR LIFE LESSONS)

CARTED ON MY BACK like a carcass, I ask Jugnu if she has somewhere she can spend the afternoon. She says she has a friend in Golimar. I tell her to meet me at the tollbooth off Lover's Bridge at seven sharp. 'We leave town. Okay?' 'Okay,' she sighs in English. I feel a pang when she boards a passing Victoria and waves like the queen, but for the first time in a long time, I am not anxious. Like Buddha after the Awakening, I know what has to be done: I corner Shafqat, Nargis' domestic-in-training, upon returning to the Lodge. 'I need your uncle, the mechanic.' Stressing supreme discretion with a hundred-rupee-handshake, the last I have to my name, I clamber up to pen the following dispatch:

> Dear Bakaullah Bhai,
>
> Concerning the note received, which I have read in its entirety, and appreciate for its erudition and unsentimentality, you should be happy to know that appropriate and necessary preparations are being undertaken forthwith.
>
> I would only humbly submit a request for a reprieve of three days, and three days only. You would understand that there are matters both great and small that require attention.
>
> I welcome you to the city as your brother, and hope you have a fruitful sojourn.
>
> Your loving brother,
> Abdullah (The Cossack)

Bidding Barbarossa with the dinner bell, I hand him the envelope and say, 'You know Major Sahab's house?'

'Yessur, nossur, cocklediddledosur.'

'Take this there,' I say, 'but you give it to *Bakaullah*.'

As I prepare to head out myself to run errands ahead of the expedition—bank, shrine, shopping—Bosco emerges bare-chested & groggy like a flyweight after a fight. 'Put on a pair of trousers and come along.' After the debacle the other day, I will not leave him home alone.

'What about our lessons?'

'We're bunking today. We should all know when to bunk. It's an important lesson in life.'

There is not much of a queue at the bank, but the teller, a chubby lass wearing maroon lipstick and a matching hijab like a bathing cap, insists on double-checking the obligatory paperwork, pointing out discrepancies between my signatures on different pages: 'One looping,' she points out, 'one not so looping.' She might be doing her job—I have withdrawn a small fortune—but is wasting my time. 'Allah-hafiz,' she says at last with a smile.

Stuffing the monies in and around my breadbasket, I reply, 'Khuda-hafiz. The correct usage is Khuda-hafiz.'

'But Khuda could be any god,' she chirps.

I look at Bosco, and Bosco looks at me. *Let it go*, he tells me with his eyes, but I snap: 'And I could hail from any faith. I could worship Ram, Zarathustra, Taus Melak. As a Musalman, you should be doubly, no, triply intent on accommodating others.' Summoning the manager, a small, suited, booted fellow with a shaved head, I declare, 'Your teller has a limited worldview. Please rectify the problem before my next visit. The customer, as you must know, is always right!' Marching out, envelope cutting into the soft flesh in the genital vicinity, I mumble, 'Important life lesson number two: don't let the insensible govern your life.'

WE FLY ACROSS TOWN in one of those new air-conditioned Radio Cabs—I am flush with currency for a change—listening to a programme playing 'Casino Classics, Northern Soul' on some new radio channel. I tell the uniformed driver to wait outside the dramatically striped rectangular seaside structure, the shrine of one Abdullah Shah Ghazi (RA). 'What now?' Bosco asks as we disembark.

'Follow me.'

After purchasing a bagful of wet rose petals from a roadside florist, Bosco and I deposit our shoes at the foot of the carpeted stairwell, then make our way up to the mausoleum. It is a relatively effortless climb because the gradient is not acute and one is stirred in anticipation of the summit. Upon entering the turquoise tiled chamber, Bosco gawks at permutations of himself in the mirrored dome above. The only other pilgrims present are two rosy-cheeked girls playing pat-a-cake on the far side, and a bent fellow clad in a long black kurta sitting cross-legged by the foot of the tomb, massaging his temple as if kneading dough. But in the evening, there will be no place to move.

Parking himself by the aperture that opens to the courtyard below, the blue-grey sea in the distance, Bosco repeats, 'What are we doing here?'

'You have your saints,' I explain, 'Saint Francis and Xavier, Valentine, Theophilus the Younger, and we have ours. Five men, good men, honourable men, brothers, settled here a millennium ago to escape persecution. Abdullah Shah Ghazi (RA) was one of them.[122] We protected him and now he protects us.'

---

122. They were, in no particular order, Jumman Shah of Garden (RA), Noori Shah of Liaqatabad (RA), Alam Shah of Jaa'ma Cloth (RA), Misri Shah of Defence Phase 6 (RA) and, of course, Abdullah Shah Ghazi of Clifton (RA). Some might claim Ghayab Shah of Keamari ought to be included, but I believe otherwise.

As Bosco contemplates the claim, I scatter petals over the marble tomb, kiss the headstone, utter a prayer for a safe, successful sojourn, slip a crisp green note in the deposit box, then make my way down to find my hashish dealer. Mufti, a retired angler with a ready, betel-nut-stained grin, is sleeping with his arm across his face in the shade of the awning outside the limestone cave in the back. When I tickle his ribs, he grins. 'You have forgotten me,' he groans.

'I have been busy.'

'You are the busiest man I know.'

'Not busier than you.'

'I am never too busy to smoke with you.'

'Soon, friend, but I am on a mission at the moment and need a good pao.'

Shaking his head in mock disappointment, Mufti reaches inside the rolled shawl he uses for a pillow and pulls out a plastic-wrapped brick of hashish. 'Not this,' I say. 'I want the strain from the North'—from the near mythical locale called Dara Adam Khel.[123]

Dislodging a couple of rocks from the wall behind him, Mufti wordlessly pulls out another tawny parcel, breaks it with long fingers, and hands a clump to me. It's redolent of damp earth, spring in the mountains. 'What are you going to do with so much?'

'It's a gift for my brother in the Interior.'

'Who's the boy?'

'My right-hand man,' I proclaim.

As Mufti reclines, crossing his arm over his forehead, canines exposed like a wolf after a meal, he says, 'I hear you have been keeping

---

123. Although not as foul as the stuff known as the fakirs' pitch, a powdery number mixed with henna & saliva, it's not as fine as the truckers' stash. Tony is a connoisseur. When he was in town, broke & broken, he discovered many sources: a pimp at a brothel past the Chinese dental clinics on Napier Road, seaside musicians at Boat Basin, and one Khan Baba, vagrant vegetable-seller who could be found once a week on an empty plot in Gulshan.

interesting company these days.' I would have pushed, prodded, at any other moment in history, but I do not have the leisure for horseplay and Bosco is out of sorts—I suspect I have somehow upset his delicate Catholic sensibilities. He confirms my hunch in the taxi. 'Are you religious, Uncle Cossack?'

'The call to prayer was whispered in my ear when I was born, and I will be buried with traditional rites, whether I like it or not. So I was born a Musalman, will die a Musalman, but in the interim, I wonder.'

'What?'

'I wonder what is good, what is bad, does morality have anything to do with God? I wonder if we all misunderstood the message except the Mandaeans or, say, the Yazidis.'

'Who?'

'You don't know? At the dawn of time, God famously wrought a being out of the dust of the ground and told his angels to bow before His latest creation. One angel stood up, and cried, *Surely, you jest, sir! Surely, you jape!* I will not bow to anybody except you, my Lord. You can imagine that God was livid, red in the face. You can imagine he turned to the recalcitrant angel—you know what recalcitrant means?—and glowered in a way nobody has glowered before. After an epic silence, God said, "You know, you're right! You passed the test! You are hereby appointed my Vice-Regent on earth!"'

'That's not how it goes.'

'It depends on what you grow up believing, and God knows, I'm all grown up. There might be something outside of us but perhaps it's just Mother Nature. You know what I mean?' The boy stares out the window vacantly. 'Look,' I say, 'one day I will present you my magnum opus, The Mythopoetic Legacy of Abdullah Shah Ghazi. It will be a brilliant treatise that will explain everything—'

'Don't you know,' Bosco interjects, 'my father's also mixed up with drugs?'

'Oh,' I blurt. 'I only smoke for spiritual reasons—'

'When my father began using,' he continues, as if he hasn't heard me, 'he sold our flat to a bootlegger upstairs. Now he's forcing us to leave.'

Suddenly, it all makes sense. But what to do? What to say?

As we pull up to the Lodge, I ask, 'How would you like to go on holiday?'

'Where?'

'It's a surprise. Pack a couple of things.'

'I only have a couple of things.'

'Just don't tell anybody.'

'I'm not the talkative type, Uncle Cossack.'

WHEN WE ENTER, I find Shafqat loitering at the gate, accompanied by a round man sporting a beret and a Hitler moustache who does not appear to be an uncle or a mechanic. Surveying the premises like a detective, I lead him to the garage housing the Chevy Impala, the lissome burgundy BMW 1600, and the sunken black Foxy—I dare not borrow Babu's Starlet again. The air inside is redolent of diesel and leather, and afternoons spent playing hide-and-seek with Tony who often hid in the Impala's vast dicky—a dicky that can accommodate three suitcases, a bicycle and a goat. Who would have believed then that I would be playing hide-and-seek again at the ripe old age of seventy?

When the mechanic states that VW parts are the easiest to procure, I tell him I have always been partial to the Impala,[124] though

124. The front grille suggested a dinosaur's grin to me as a child. As a teenager, its contours suggested a spaceship from *Amazing Stories*—one might still be able to get copies at Khori Garden—a conception of the future grounded in an aesthetic of the past. One has oft mulled an 'Ode to Americana' that would begin, *Thou foster child of art & mechany* ... Tony put it differently: 'She's a real piece of work, ain't she?' The Impala is undoubtedly a voluptuous machine: if automobiles today invoke the waifish lasses on the covers of magazines at doctors' offices, the Impala evokes the Ava Gardner variety of dame—beautiful, buxom, full of grace.

the easiest automobile to repair would have been the family's fourth vehicle, Papa's sable Toyota Crown Super Saloon. Although nobody was allowed behind the wheel, we all knew that Tony would take it out on the sly—the odometer always betrayed that he had driven to Xanadu and back. But when it comes to Tony, of course, we had a tendency to 'let it go,' perhaps because he possesses that nebulous quality known as duende. Then one day after Papa passed, Barbarossa informed us that the Crown had been stolen. Some suspected that Tony sold it when strapped for currency, but nobody made much of it. After all, *Tony's Tony!*

'How long have they been there like this?' the mechanic asks.

'Ten, maybe fifteen years.'

'It will be expensive, boss,' he says, sucking his teeth, 'and there's not much time—'

'I understand if you're not interested,' I interrupt. 'I'll call somebody else, but I hear you're top notch.' The fellow pulls in his chin. 'If you can do the job by five, I'll compensate you handsomely, more than the going rate. You need to decide now.'

'Okay, okay,' he says.

'But nobody can know what's going on,' I add. 'Not your wife, mother, lover, and certainly not anybody you encounter here. This is a secret project. Understand?'

Returning to my quarters, I find Barbarossa standing like a totem by the exercise bicycle, bearing the same damn fool envelope entrusted to him a few hours back and a lean black cockerel under his arm. The old fox might have lost the way in the wasteland of Defence Housing Society—I myself routinely get lost on those narrow, nonsensically named streets: Badar, Badban, Baharia, Bakwaas. 'What happened?' I cry.

'I went, came back.'

'With the same envelope and a cock!'

'Same envelope,' he replies, exposing his gums, 'but different letter inside.'

Snatching it from his hand, I read: '(1) Your request is hereby granted, provided you deliver a month's rent. (2) You owe funds of Rs. 46,000. (3) Remuneration required in cash forthwith.'

Raging—'Dash it all!' I cry—I pace furiously up and down the veranda like Hajra Between the Hills, red in the face and unctuous with sweat, until Barbarossa grabs me by the arm and says, 'A sound of the broken pot will never ring true, my son.'

What pot? What sound? It doesn't matter. Kissing him on the forehead, I say, 'There's one more thing you need to do.' Jamming a wad of currency in his hand, I instruct, 'Give this to Bakaullah. He wants the rent? I'll give him the dashed rent. And leave the cock in the back for God's sake.'

Then I retrieve Papa's leather valise from the powder room. I pack two shirts, two pairs of trousers, the knickers drying like dried flounder on the clothesline, along with my toothbrush, a bottle of cologne, a week's supply of insulin and the block of hashish. I throw in a box of powdered minestrone soup I enjoy for its addictive synthetic tang, a set of cutlery, a corkscrew, a candle stub, and a packet of AA batteries for good measure. I might have thrown in the toaster if there had been space. I am not known to be an expert packer. I never go anywhere.

AS THE AFTERNOON LAPSES into evening, I have clipped my crispy nails, shaved the hairy growth on the pudgy periphery of my ear, and sponged my damp crevices—I am ready for anything, everything—but the car is not ready at five or six but seven, and at seven rounding Gandhi Garden is complicated. The intersection at the Sayfi Apartments is an impasse because they always station some damn fool copper there, a dogsbody from Gujranwalla who, in the midst of an epic jam, can be found probing the inside of his nose.[125]

---

125. I am fairly certain that the traffic police manufacture jams so that they can justify their loutish existence. I've seen them stopping traffic at

Stashing the valise in the back, I hand the mechanic an envelope and arrange myself behind the wheel. 'Not enough, boss,' he says, thumbing the notes. 'The fuel pump alone—'

'You know where I live, and you can ask anybody in Garden: the Cossack always keeps his promise'—an aphorism I coin on the spot.

Just then I perceive movement in the parlour, a ruffling of the ancient floral curtains. Who is it? Nargis? Bua? Babu would not take kindly to an expedition involving the family heirloom. 'I have to go,' I exclaim. 'I have to go now.'

Bosco jumps up front, sporting a pair of russet drainpipe pants, Bata joggers, and the trilby (that Jugnu somehow sized for him). Stroking the leather seat, he says, 'Cool wheels!'

'Life lesson number three,' I mutter. 'Travel in style when you can.'

Barrelling past the automotive spare parts distributors, the life-sized statues of the giraffe and Asian elephant, and the small green-domed shrine—traffic is strangely thin—I turn the corner at the frayed grey bungalow that marks the boundary of Garden. I stall kerbside before the tollbooth, surveying the avenue leading to Lover's Bridge. Jugnu is nowhere to be seen.

'Why's it so quiet?' Bosco asks.

The tollbooth seems abandoned and the sole paan-wallah is shutting shop. Something is indeed awry. I attempt to honk the 'Lullaby of Birdland,' our proprietary Morse Code, but since the horn has not been repaired, I just bang on the steering wheel like a bongo drum; I cannot play the role of the forlorn lover with dignity; I am not Ranjha, Ror Kumar, the canonical type.[126] I roll down the window for

---

roundabouts. You don't need Johnnies posted at roundabouts. That's why roundabouts were invented.

126. Recall that there are seven legendary sets of lovers in our mythopoetics: (1) Heer / Ranjha, (2) Momal / Rano, (3) Dhaj / Ror Kumar, (4) Lila / Chanesar, (5) Noori / Jam Tamachi, (6) Sassi / Punnu, and (7) Umar / Marvi.

a breath of air. The warm breeze carries the tincture of rubbish and smoke in. Perhaps there is a fire somewhere?

'What are we doing here?' Bosco asks.

In the rear-view mirror, I espy four ruffians marching in the middle of the street, swinging hockey sticks like scythes. They might be boys looking to join a game; they might be gangsters. We are, after all, a stone's throw from Lyari. 'Lambs to the slaughter,' I mutter.

As I prepare to escape, Jugnu, my Jugnu, emerges like a shadow, clad in a charcoal shalwar kurta buttoned to the neck, and a driver's cap that recalls a picaro. 'There's trouble in the neighbourhood,' she says, getting in the back. 'The war has begun.'

And we are off.

ON THE CONSEQUENCES OF FELICIDE

(OR HEGIRA TO THE INTERIOR)

WHEN THE CITY BECOMES unsettled, shops shutter, traffic thins—the Great Involute Urban Machinery comes to a halt. You stay indoors and listen to the transistor, to bulletins concerning 'miscreants riding pillion' and busses set ablaze in far-flung cantons. When you turn off the news because the news upsets, the news is bad, you hear only the whistle of kites and the protest of crows. Sometimes, you can perceive smoke on the horizon, sometimes nearer, but the next day or the day after that, it is as if nothing happened, as if a storm has quietly passed. The city is vast: it could rain in Federal B and remain sunny in Pipri; there could be picnickers frolicking on the beach when there's gunfire off the highway. You have to read the signs, take caution: if you happen to be on the streets, you do not stop at red lights; you drive through and drive fast.

ALTHOUGH THE MAIN ARTERIES seem clear—we pass the airport, the temple in Malir, the Lanewallah farmhouse[127]—the drive

127. The proprietor of the old Sayfi Apartments—the abode of my Jewish friends—still owns a farm in Malir. After making a left at the temple, you negotiate a filthy warren of alleys until you reach an unremarkable gate that opens into an Edenic compound housing fruit trees and flowers & a small swimming pool. We would swim in the summers there, and barbeque by a

could still prove to be treacherous: swaths of Scinde are tricky after dark; dacoits famously patrol the roads unencumbered. It's Out of the Frying Pan & Into the Fire. As we hurtle into the darkness, I ask, 'What war?'.

'The war of succession,' Jugnu replies.

Naturally, Langra's incarceration has consequences for the dispensation in the area, but that does not explain the scene at the tollbooth. 'Who,' I ask, 'were those boys with hockey sticks?'

'I heard Langra's men are looking for me.'

'Why?'

'They want to get to me before the police do.'

Good God! The dame's in a proper pickle. What if we were followed? What if we are stopped? I only possess a corkscrew for defence. I have also not slept in twenty-four hours, the meat in my lower back has turned brittle (as the Impala's Flexomatic six-way power seat[128] is jammed) and, after the Steel Mill, I encounter Stygian gloom. It's not just that there are no streetlamps or moonlight; no, it's my cataract eye. I should have had surgery years ago but I do not want to die of septicaemia in a hospital. I want to die at the Lodge. But not yet.

Jugnu says, 'Abdullah?'

'Yes?

'Thanks you,' she says in English. 'You are the hero.'

---

bonfire in the winters. You can, it seems, make heaven anywhere, even in the midst of Malir. I have wondered: What if after you die, God asks, 'So how was Heaven?'

128. Papa explained to me that the basic model cost the princely sum of $2,600 whilst the full monty set you back $3,000. The latter featured front and rear armrests, dual sliding visors, crank-operated front ventpanes, an electronic clock (which no longer functions), and the aforementioned Flexomatic six-way power seat.

Grinning like a schoolboy, I run over a passing mammal: there is a bump followed by a crack—the fracturing of a mongoose skull or the snapping of a feline spine. The Impala skids violently, veering left then right before spinning to a halt. Jugnu, who possesses the reflexes of a lioness, is unscathed, but Bosco grazes his head on the headrest. I am buffered by my gut but my soul feels mangled: I do not need a carcass on my conscience—I am not a dishonourable man.

By the time I pull kerbside and extricate myself from the seat, Jugnu is inspecting a heap a couple of metres away. There is the smell of burnt rubber in the air and the rot of marsh. We are on the outskirts of Haleji Lake, more than an hour into our jaunt, more than an hour from our destination. 'It is a cat,' Jugnu announces. 'It is alive.'

'Oh God,' I cry. 'Now what?'

I watch Jugnu wordlessly gather the carcass and disappear into the bramble—I am certain I hear puling over the whisper of the breeze in the reeds. When I ask what she did, she states, 'Animals live, animals die.'

'But we're not animals!'

Jugnu instructs Bosco to fetch my valise from the car. The lad dashes off as if his life depends on it. When he returns, Jugnu pulls out my flask, pours a cup of water into the top, then splashes it across my face. Shaking like a wet dog, I yawp, 'Why did you do that?'

'You need to cool down.'

The gambit succeeds. And suddenly, I know what to do: dig a grave. I claw doggedly, but I have clipped my nails and the crust is hard because the rains are late this year. Pouring water over the earth, I retrieve the cutlery from my valise; a fork and knife can come in handy when fashioning a grave.

After Jugnu lays the carcass inside, we sprinkle handfuls of dirt on top, read a prayer, the fatiha as I remember it,[129] and stick a crooked stick in the ground. There is catharsis in it. There is always solace in ritual.

'We're not going anywhere,' I announce. 'If I drive again, I will kill again. We camp here tonight.'

'Aren't we in the Interior?' Bosco asks. 'Aren't there dacoits in the Interior?'

'You know about the dacoits?' The boy, a bundle of nerves, nods vigorously. This is not the sort of holiday he would have imagined. 'I'll park inland,' I say. 'We'll sleep in the car.'

But it's one of those miserably muggy nights. Since the windows have to be left open, bloody-minded mosquitoes feast on our damp flesh. It doesn't matter; sprawled on the backseat, arm akimbo, I feel febrile, finished. The last image I remember before lapsing into unconsciousness is of Jugnu perched on the bonnet: she lights a beedi, glistens in the dark.

WHEN I WAKE, I am alone, save for a hefty, hirsute, lethargic mosquito—Bosco and Jugnu have either abandoned me or have been taken by dacoits—and feel like runny pudding: sweat soaks the accordion folds of my neck and the pockets under my bosom down to my grape-sized haemorrhoids. The sun, a golden whorl, blinds, and the leather beneath burns. Glancing around, I make out low bushes of thistle extending into the blinding horizon and the only intimation of civilization: a vacant chicken coop with a corrugated tin roof. I angle my arm to unlatch the door. A gust of dust blows in. Good God!

After a searing, sodden eternity—it might have been minutes, it might have been hours—Bosco appears, dishevelled, despondent.

---

129. I believe I also remember another short prayer, one of the quls, but I don't remember much more.

'We've got to go back!' he says. 'There isn't a tree for a kilometre. I had to poop in the open.' I would like to tell him that there is nothing like evacuating in the wide open but I am too drawn to respond. Then Jugnu materializes and declares, 'I'm not going back.'

'I can't move at all,' I mumble.

'What is the matter?' Jugnu asks.

'I'm dying.'

'We are all dying, Abdullah.' Placing a hand on my forehead, she says, 'You have fever.'

'You might have sunstroke!' Bosco exclaims. 'Or worse, heat tetany! You need salt, Uncle Cossack, salt!'

'There's soup in the bag.'

Using the automobile lighter to light a clutch of twigs in a forgotten bird's nest, Jugnu prepares the minestrone by boiling water in a discarded corn oil tin—it's as if she was born in the wild, suckled by wolves. When she feeds the soup to me, I feel relatively revived. 'We press on,' I slurp. 'After all, Tony and the city are equidistant.'

'Who's Tony?' Bosco asks.

'My brother. You'll like him. He's a charming rogue.'

'But what about the dacoits?' Bosco asks.

Jugnu says, 'I know their kind.'

After breakfast, after the supplies have been stowed, we are ready to move. But as I take the driver's seat, Jugnu declares, 'You won't drive.'

'Then who?'

'Me.'

'Have you driven before?'

'No,' she replies matter-of-factly.

ON TRAVELS IN SCINDE IN TIME AND SPACE

THERE ARE TWO ROUTES into the Interior from the city. One travels through the central districts via a functional four-lane highway patrolled by vigilant police cars. Brush and scrub and the odd keekar tree speckle the relentlessly flat, tawny terrain, broken only by petrol pumps and ramshackle eateries that offer a decent plate of daal. The rocky folds of the Kirthir range rise in the distance, but after the bridge spanning the Indus, the environs turn verdant: muddy aqueducts circumscribing plots of wheat, flappy banana trees, and mango orchards in and around the erstwhile provincial capital of Hyderabad. One passes fluttering black flags on either side of the road—the seal of the House of Ali (AS)—and on each flagstaff, open silver hands reach for the sky. In Scinde, everyone reveres the House of Ali (AS).

The other road traverses shabby cantons of Currachee populated by recent immigrants from the north and west.[130] One passes bus depots, wandering cows, rubbish in heaps, graffiti on the walls. There was nothing in the vicinity twenty years earlier save the Steel Mill, a structure that recalls the failure of the Socialist Enterprise. Beyond the periphery of the city, you can sense the presence of a lake from the

130. They live in Pipri, Razaqbad, Qazafi Town. I know because Barbarossa fights cocks in these localities several times a year.

flocks in the sky. Unbeknown to most, the sea extended inland early in the topographical history of the region. There is ample evidence for it: if you veer off the road, you find seashells encrusted in rock. One might also come across other relics off-road, at Bhambore[131]—'The Gateway of Islam'—or the sprawling necropolis of Makli, or the ancient town of Amarkot, the only Hindoo kingdom of Pakistan, the birthplace, you will recall, of Akbar the King.

One understands that there is now a third route off the Super Highway that shoots straight to Sehwan along the range, the seat of the greatest of saints, Lal Shahbaz Qalandar. Every evening after the call to prayer (except during the first ten days of Muharram), drums sound in the compound—Dan-da, dun dun! Dan-da, dun dun! Dan-da, dun dun! Danda, dun dun!—heralding frenetic movement: men and women from high and nigh in shiny hats and embroidered kurtas sway and shake and shudder to the beat of ecstasy. They have been at it for close to a millennium and will continue to do so for eternity. There is no doubt that the Qalandar was a miracle worker—he is known to have taken to the skies when moved, known to have upended the village on the northern butte with his staff in anger—but the fact that he exerts such power over the fabric of our reality in this time is in itself miraculous.

Whilst the distance between the city and the countryside might be nominal—not more than an hour on these superhighways now, not more than a day on horseback then—and discourse might suggest

---

131. There is nothing there, save an unimpressive stone foundation of the Circular House (which did not appear particularly circular to me), the smooth chequered floor (of the first mosque in the Subcontinent) that recalls a discothèque, and broken ramparts overlooking a green lake in which wizened anglers lazily cast nets. If you like, you can search for ancient seashells and pieces of turquoise pottery, the odd lingam, amongst the rubble. If you have had something to smoke, however, you might be able to conjure the wrinkled lip & sneer of cold command.

that Currachee is integral to Scinde, technically, historically, or socio-politically, Currachee has been merely contiguous. It was only in 1795 that it was integrated into the local body politic. The Talpur rulers of Scinde had thrice besieged the entrepôt, and were thrice repelled. How the demonyms of Currachee managed to defy them beggars belief. The hardy populace relented only on the condition that the Beelooch mercenary force, a division of some twenty thousand, would remain outside town limits. Of course, we Currachee-wallahs even managed to expel the Britishers (rascals some if not rascals all) on several occasions before they managed a foothold, cannons blazing, thirty-odd years later.[132] Independence, then, is innate to the city.

Unlike the history of Currachee, the history of Scinde is fundamentally the history of the River Indus. Although the trajectory of the subsequent pages might be informed by my occasional meanderings over three quarters of a century through the province, I have travelled in my mind up and down the mighty Indus over the years & across millennia, from the Sapta Sindhu of the Vedic texts to the angular sun-baked streets of Mohenjo-Daro, the Singapore of yore:[133] one can surmise from the infrastructure that there was no spitting or paan-chewing permitted in the city-state run by the solemn priest-king. When the river shifted dramatically one fine day, however, order crumbled.[134] The great Chach rulers, ensconced downriver

---

132. They established a factory in 1800 only to be closed down in 1801. The Brits would conquer the province three decades later, slaughtering ten thousand souls with machine guns.

133. Most recently, I've read about a dig at the site of Chanhujo Daro in Sakrand, first conducted by R.C. Majumdar in the Thirties, and now by an attractive French lass and her serious-minded cohort. I can imagine walls emerging from the ground, pottery with patterns more elaborate than Art Deco. Why did Man require patterns five thousand years ago?

134. Science suggests that the sea level will inevitably rise one day to sweep that expertly administered island away.

at Debal, not to mention the citizens of my ancestral hometown of Thatta, would also suffer shifting tides and accompanying fortunes. The Indus has undoubtedly made & unmade civilizations, men: after navigating the length of the river for the first time in recorded history, Alexander the Greek was ultimately undone by it,[135] and that shifty spy Alexander Burnes, famously the toast of the colonials, paid for his betrayal of the river, of the land, in blood. This is why the Indus is both feared & revered.

I have pilgrimaged at the shrine of the River God, Odero Lal. You enter the unimposing whitewashed structure, ringing a bell before proceeding to either a dim, carpeted room that serves as a mosque, or a tomb surrounded by painted walls featuring frescoes of Dutch windmills, or a temple housing images of said deity riding the waves of the Indus on the back of a giant fish. At the annual celebrations, thousands converge. Tough dames sit on the low boundary walls in tight saris, sucking beedis. Inside, devotees chant bhajans to the tune of 'Mast Qalandar.' Uncannily, Musalmans also participate in the festivities. I have never come across anything like it in all my travels.

Of course, Scindee lore could easily fill all twenty-six volumes of the *Encyclopaedia Britannica*. Deities repose in rivers, djinns populate the trees,[136] and mermaids emerge from the lakes. When Ram, the slight caretaker of the Varun Dev temple on the Island of Manora, told me that he hosts the River God Odero Lal several times a year, I spent a night with him in the hope of an audience with the deity.

---

135. The second time it was navigated was in 1978 by Hamid & Naeem & KM—a distance of some three thousand kilometres.

136. Our friends in Mirpur invited us to commemorate Muharram once. One remembers the sweet scent of burning incense pervading the bungalow, though there were no incense sticks, and the distant thump of beating chests, though nobody was home save our host. One was told djinns gathered on the roof annually to mourn the Prophet's (PBUH) grandson.

We sat side by side on the beach, gazing into the swelling sea, heels dug into the damp sand. After we dined on whole fried mushka fish, one of the finest in the sea, Ram pointed towards the surf. 'He wades through the sea to the shore, not trailing a grain of sand. We talk all night. He always leaves before daybreak.' *What do you do the rest of the time?* I enquired. 'I wait.' Of course, He never showed that night (and Ram asked me if I could employ his son), but imagine—just imagine—if He had.

One of my formative childhood memories, however, involves a corporeal though no less magical marine creature. Accompanying Papa on a business trip to Sukkur, I was shown the famous blind dolphins at the Lloyd Barrage. 'Fishes,' he explained, 'swing their tails from side to side. But this is a mammal.' *A mammal,* I repeated. 'Mammals flap their tales up and down.' It was a revelation.

Whilst my father had close ties to the Interior, commercial and personal, from the Mir of Khayrpur (who hosted the biennial boar hunt) to the formidably moustachioed Rana of Amarkot (one of the most urbane gentlemen one has come across), the relationships have since lapsed (and the Indus has since been dammed), but Scinde continues to occupy a special place in my consciousness. My last trip to the province might just confirm it.

ON CONFRONTING MORTALITY (OR MAN AND MOSQUITO)

THE LANDSCAPE IS FLAT and still like a canvas. On either side of the dirt road, geometric plots brim with slender yellow-green stalks of sugarcane. We take in the air, bracing & fragrant with wet soil, as Jugnu expertly negotiates the winding track and Bosco breaks into verse: 'When streams of light pour down the golden west, / And on the balmy zephyrs tranquil rest / The silver clouds, far—far away to leave / All meaner thoughts, and take a sweet reprieve.' It is most unexpected and most apt, even if there are some fallow patches and, in the distance, an unsightly hedge of bramble. A couple of kilometres into the estate, after sighting a solitary banyan festooned with scarlet ribbons like a bride, we come across a boxy, whitewashed cement structure, bounded by a high wall. Once upon a time, it was possible to peer into the orchard inside, the branches sagging with ripening mangoes. Things have changed, but it doesn't matter; although feverish, I am at peace: I will be reunited with my boon companion soon.

I have been to Tony's twice, once when there was nothing save a sere expanse, and once after he settled in—for his fiftieth. I don't believe he has visited the Lodge more than twice or thrice since he abandoned it to pursue a Bachelor of Arts at a university in the United States of America, Tony being the first of our clan to venture to the New World. After graduating, he spent time in sin in the City of Sin, running a five-star enterprise known as Chucky Cheese. When he returned sporting jeans, velvety hippie locks and a cocky smile—a gay blade—dames, including the likes of Badbakht Begum, would say, *Your brother has bedroom eyes.* 'Ain't she darling,' he would drawl in the characteristic Yankee manner. But upon immigrating to the Interior, he traded his rakish ways for farm work, his faded jeans for starched shalwars. It's been donkey's years. It will be an event.

As we approach, however, an epic clamour rises from the compound, as if the very Hounds of Hell have been unleashed. Since the horn does not work, Jugnu hoots. Perceiving shadowy movement in the grilled port above the formidable iron gate, I proclaim: 'I am Abdullah of Currachee, son of Karimullah, brother of Fazlullah. I demand that you introduce yourself.' After a gravid pause, a tinny voice hollers, 'Sayien not here.'

'You call Sayien,' I shout. 'You call him now.'

The gate slides open after an eternity. A dark sinewy man with piercing kohl-rimmed eyes, shotgun slung over shoulder, ushers us into a short dark passage that leads to a horseshoe-shaped gravel driveway, demarcated by white bricks. Jugnu parks the Impala by the fountain featuring two interlocking fish spouting water through skyward mouths, a relic appropriated from the Olympus. Jugnu and Bosco help me out and up the steps into the anteroom. 'Good buoy,' Jugnu says in English, settling me on a settee.

'Good driving,' I say. She is a natural and knows it. After a fit & start, and driving for sixty kilometres at thirty kilometres per hour, Jugnu barrelled down the highway, horning, overtaking lorries and braking for the odd goat crossing the road. Of course, I did edify her on the fundamentals.[137] I disclosed one of my most effective

137. I could pen a manual entitled *Abdullah the Cossack's Rules of the Road*. Rule No. 1: Nobody has Right of Way. Rule No. 2: Everybody has Right of Way. Rule No. 3: The shortest distance between two points is not a straight line but a road free of traffic lights.

tricks: driving with the indicator on. When conventions are inverted, etiquette confounds.

AFTER TEA IS SERVED, there is rumbling outside, the crunch of gravel beneath tyres, the thump of heavy car doors, then the swish of starched cotton announces Tony. 'Thought I recognized that sweet jalopy!'

'Hands off, kid!'

'How the hell are you, Abdu,'[138] he says, embracing me, wafting cologne, dung and the sun, 'and the hell you doin' here?'

I could tell him that Comrade Bakaullah has returned from the desert, that I have arrived to rally support for the Lodge, that gangsters are out to jump Jugnu, and possibly me, that we escaped by the skin of our teeth from the city, but instead, broach a more pressing matter: 'I turned seventy and didn't even receive a dashed card!'

'I sent flowers!'

'The wreath? You sent the wreath? Wreaths are for the dead!'

Sweeping his salt & pepper locks back, Tony says, 'Sorry about that, Daddy-O, but my man organized it. I was dealing with all this shit—I'll tell you about it later—but first you gotta tell me what happened to you: you look like you've been in battle.'

My knees are soiled from the feline funeral, my bush-shirt blotched with sweat. 'Au contraire, mon frère,' I reply. 'I am preparing to wage war!'

'Who're your brothers-in-arms?'

'This is Bosco, grandson of one Felix Pinto, the Caliph of Cool'—the lad stands up but cannot enunciate because he has stuffed several stale crackers in his mouth—'and this is Jugnu, a near and dear friend of mine.'

---

138. For the record—always for the record—Tony's the only one on God's Green Earth permitted to call me Abdu.

Jugnu has lost the cap, loosened her hair, undone the buttons of her kurta at the chest, and looks like a dame again (and what a dame she is). 'Thank you for your hospitality,' she says.

Raising his thick eyebrows, Tony mutters, 'Mi casa, su casa.'

'Hear, hear!' I stumble.

Steadying me with a firm hand, Tony asks, 'What's wrong, Abdu?'

'Uric acid in the knees?'

'You're hot to the touch.'

'He has been running fever,' Jugnu says, grabbing my arm. 'He needs medicine and rest.'

'Come on,' Tony tugs, 'I'll show you to your room.'

Tony's large, lived-in suite wafts scented oils and marijuana and overlooks the orchard. It features modern amenities including a two-ton Korean air conditioner, a small refrigerator and one of those state-of-the-art television sets as wide as a blackboard, but the décor is decidedly rustic: a zebra skin lies across the floor and a pair of crossed Enfields are fixed on the wall (pilfered, if I recall correctly, from Papa) alongside lithographs depicting local vistas, a forgotten redbrick fortress, and the sombre grandeur of the necropolis of Makli. I would be pleased as punch to be interred in one of those solid tombs amongst the nestled cacti, but I am probably fated to waste away on the old four-post Burma-teak towards the far end of the room, draped with mosquito netting.

Surveying the premises, arms folded, Jugnu says, 'Chalay ga,' or *This will work*.

Winking at me, Tony says, 'Cool.'

'But what about Bosco?'

'Don't worry: there are other rooms, other—'

'Lie down,' Jugnu instructs, and I do as I am told. Then turning to my brother, she says, 'Take me to the kitchen.' Saluting, Tony leads her out, hand on the small of her back.

After ingesting a litre of water, a bowl of peppery chicken stock, and a pair of paracetamols—I don't have an appetite and feel like death—I lie across the bed in a borrowed cotton sarong ('It's the only thing that'll fit, Abdu,' Tony said) before lapsing into an uneasy sleep. I dream I am traversing a cavernous white-tiled room—it might be a hotel kitchen, a public loo, a morgue—when I am blinded by the savage swipe of a phantom feline. Presently, I notice an eyeball, my eyeball, rolling across the floor like a peeled cherry towards an open drain with the momentum of inevitability. The Cruel Logic of Nightmares dictates that I must trample it underfoot. It's a gruesome spectacle—fleshy juice everywhere.

I WAKE STARTLED AND shivering and squinting to check that my eyeballs are lodged in their respective sockets. I find Jugnu, unperturbed, lying snoring next to me. She does not lie like a lady; she lies with enviable abandon, rump exposed. I lie conjuring the moist, musty crevice of her buttocks, the whorl within, for I am known to be what is termed a Rump Man; I confess I stare at dames perched on the backs of motorcycles. At this juncture of history, however, Rump or Bust is neither here nor there; when one is depleted or dying, one requires companionship. Some find God. I have Jugnu. I have to hold on to her somehow; I must ask her for her hand. I sleep better after, and do not wake until white afternoon sunlight cuts through the mossy curtains.

Since the fever has not subsided and an alarming rash is spotted across my torso, a thermometer is produced and thrust into my maw. The mercury reads 40°C. I hear hushed discussion in the hall outside: *We need to get him to ... The nearest is ... He's in no state ... I'm calling ... He' ll be here within ...* I overhear Bosco rambling: 'You know, it could be some kind of erythema, which is fine, because it's usually caused by a drug reaction ... but then it could also be Scarlet Fever ...

meningitis … bubonic plague. My mother would know what to do … He can't die. Is he going to die?'

The doctor, a dark, distinguished, bovine-faced gentleman named Lal, calmly informs me that I am afflicted with the national epidemic known as Dengue. I want to ask him about the genesis of these new, fanciful, fearsome maladies in the headlines, viz., Swine Flu, Naegleria, Mad Cow Disease—and what of the classics: Rickets, Scurvy, Legionnaires'?—but the doctor repairs to the hall before I can articulate myself.[139] I can hear him fielding other questions. *Critical phase … low platelet count … six days, a week … Risks at his age … diabetes … fluid accumulation in the chest … Call immediately…*

There is no doubt about it: I am dying. And what a sorry way to die! A tragedy! A farce! I can imagine the inscription on my headstone:

HERE LIES ABDULLAH K. (THE COSSACK)
A MAN-MOUNTAIN FELLED BY A MOSQUITO

At some juncture, I crawl out from beneath the sheets, racked by a headache that permeates my ocular cavities, and notice Tony sitting bedside. Clasping his hand, I say, 'I want to be buried at the Lodge. They can't sell the place. Promise me you won't let that happen. Promise your dying brother.'

'I promise, Abdu, but you ain't dying: doc's prescribed aspirin, water and juice for God's sake!'

---

139. I have a sense that the changing pathogenic environment is informed by the chemicals we spew into the atmosphere, the chemicals we pump into our fauna, flora—the company that pioneered Agent Orange must be stopped—but we all also know that God, via John of Patmos, has threatened plagues at the End of Days. Although Nargis doesn't care, she might invoke 'Qiyamat ki nishanian,' viz., *The Signs of Armageddon*. At the very least, however, my end seems nigh.

'I bring you a pao of the best hashish this side of the Indus and you offer me juice?'

'Thanks a lot, Abdu—I'm really stoked—but you need to drink up.'

Between gulps (mercifully it's apple, not bitter gourd) I express the wish to divide a third of my assets amongst the Childoos, a third between Bosco and Jugnu, and the rest to Tony to do with as he wishes. 'Of course, there's nothing left … nothing left of me … I've wasted my life, Tony … Your brother's a failure.'

Running his fingers through my knotted hair, Tony insists, 'You made me who I am, Abdu.'

'Then why did you leave me?'

'It's got nothing to do with you! I split because of all the family shit. I needed something of my own…'

THE CAT CLAWS AT my conscience as I lapse in and out of consciousness: I find myself amongst mutilated felines twisting from the limp branches of the mango trees. Clouds of flies swarm the carcasses, crows swoop to pick at the offal, and there is the tangy stink of cat urine in the air. It is a wretched, revolting tableau, a forlorn corner of Hell. I do what has to be done: I find a scythe in the ramshackle shed at the far side of the orchard and hack each twine. I bury each carcass with blood-spattered hands before digging a ditch and crawling in. I shut my eyes and it's all over.

When I stir, I behold Bosco sitting perfectly still on a chair before me, hands flat on his thighs, like a chastened schoolboy. Taking my pulse, he asks, 'What will happen to me if you die?' When I stir again, Jugnu is lounging beside me, leafing through an old album. 'I'm dying,' I mumble.

'We are all dying,' she coos.

'Don't die before me. Everyone I love dies before me.'

Studying me with her keen obsidian gaze, she enquires, 'You love me?'

'I love you.'

Smiling widely, like a Dentonic-Once-A-Day-Everyday billboard, Jugnu kisses my blistered lips. 'You are my Rus Gullah!'

I cringe at the sobriquet but then reckon there is nothing wrong with being called a ball of cheese boiled in syrup. In any event, I want to ask if she reciprocates my sentiment, if she will marry me, but it is not an opportune moment—I cannot turn on my side, much less bend my knee.

I recall the doctor returning. I recall a rectal itch, the charnel balm of incense and roses and wet earth that sweeps graveyards at dusk. I recall Jugnu announcing, 'Your fever's broken. You're not dying tonight.'

ON THE GAMES WE PLAY
(OR HARDSCRABBLE)

WE INSTALL OURSELVES ON beach chairs in the orchard after the chirrup of parrots subsides, slicing ripe mangoes with sticky fingers. The sky is velvety at night and dusted with stars, the air thick with pyrethrum, hashish, nostalgia:

You remember Felix, the Caliph of Cool?
Rock star, that guy.
He got me snookered on my birthday.
Them Goans can drink anybody under the table!
Except me, chum.
Remember Uncle Ben?
That killer Cointreau!
You hear Mrs D'Abreo passed?
What a fine dame!
Do you keep in touch with anybody from school?
I barely keep in touch with family.

Whilst Tony is aloof when it comes to codes and conventions, he is an excellent host: if I require a cushion for my raw rectum, or Bosco expresses a desire for Pakola, or Jugnu mentions the gratification of sucking a beedi, the item materializes, courtesy of the gunmen-cum-bearers (or bearers-cum-gunmen). Tony might have apprenticed only briefly at the Olympus, in what is now called the Hospitality

Industry, but his sense of hospitality is innate; we are, I like to believe, fundamentally Mummy's boys. We have not spoken about her—if it were just the two of us, it might have been different—but she is always present. And because we are amongst company, I cannot find the opportunity to lobby for the Lodge. Instead, we palaver about this, that, the other—one evening, Jugnu asks Tony, 'What do you do here alone?'

'When I am not farming, I am making wine, breeding dogs, mastiffs mainly: Tosas, Neopolitans, Dogo Argentinos.'

'What's the name of that dog that was barking when we came, Uncle T.?' Bosco interrupts.

'I got two, brother-man: Hero and Daku.'

'Daku as in dacoit?' Bosco asks. Bosco keeps an eye on the boundary wall and asks when we are returning to the city.

'As soon as I have a serious chat with Uncle T.,' I assure him.

'And my pals show up every month,' Tony is saying, 'a couple landlords (cats who have studied abroad, you know), and this Communist pir from Sakrand, this retired colonel we call Flashman, and Hur—old Hawkeye—he drops in time to time. We smoke, drink, go fishing upriver or on the sea. There is a place called the Khadda three hours from the coast. It's like the border of the Continental Shelf. You find these massive marlin there, barracuda—kund, you know? In the winter, we hunt quail and partridge. It is a simple life.' Tony smiles. 'I am a simple man.'

'Haan haan,' Jugnu teases, *Sure sure*. 'You make tharra, kill animals.'

'Really small animals, Jugnu Begum.' Tony winks. 'I am a lover, not a fighter.'[140]

Jugnu persists, 'So you have a woman?'

---

140. Tony would repeat the adage ad nauseam when he returned from the US of A. At the time, one wondered, *Is it a mantra of Pragmatism? Transcendentalism?* but it just had to do with that Lazy Lester track.

'Well, yes, yes, I do,' he replies, 'but tell me, how did you and Abdu meet each other?'

'One afternoon,' Jugnu begins before I can get a word in, 'I was strolling in Garden when I stopped for corn on the cob.' I imagine Jugnu kerbside in a technicolour kurta, observing the gaggle of burqas, the street-side dentist, the laden donkey. She might have adjusted her bra, picked kernels from her teeth. But in the version she narrates, she neglects to mention that she had been trolling the streets since her lover was imprisoned down the road at the station. 'I saw a man,' she continues, 'who did not care for—how should I say?—social conventions. I thought: this is somebody I want to know. I pursued him, then he pursued me.'[141]

'You wanna elaborate?' Tony asks me.

'No,' I blurt, 'it's late.'

When conversations falter, or mosquitoes swarm, we play carom inside—Tony is the reigning champion—or Gin Rummy, which is Bosco's game. It's the only time he is in his element in the Interior. After beating everyone roundly, he explains, 'I used to play with Mum all the time. She taught me Scrabble also. Do you have a set, Uncle T.? We could place bets.'

'That's why I ain't gonna play with you, brother-man. You'll take all my money, my land, and leave me for dead.'

'Oh, come on!' Bosco pleads. 'What about you, Uncle Cossack?'

'I put ideas together, lad, not letters.'

To be entirely honest, late at night, I am eager to play other games, games adults play. The night after my recovery, I had shut the door behind me and lumbered towards Jugnu like a cheeky circus bear. Raising her arms like a ballerina, Jugnu allowed me to slide her kurta over her head & sample her dark, pubescent bosoms. 'Pasand aya?'

---

141. For the record, she employed the word 'rivaaj,' adding, 'Phir mainay iska peecha kiya aur isnay mera.'

or *Like it?* she asked, palming my head. They tasted tart, like green mangoes. 'Pasand aya,' I cooed with my mouth full.

We fell on the bed after, kissing and groping each other like children. But when she started unbuttoning my shirt—*tinker, tailor, soldier, sailor, rich man, poor man*—I childishly drew away. Whilst Jugnu has seen me shirtless, even pantless, it was as if I suddenly realized that I am a toothless, misshapen man who possesses breasts befitting an Italian matron and a briar of lint in the navel. 'The air conditioner,' I blurted, 'it's cold.' Unfastening my trousers instead, Jugnu appraised my member. I was afraid it would not respond but when she swallowed it whole like a moist seekh kebab, there was no doubt that all remained in working order.

Each time I attempted to negotiate her cummerbund, however, she swept my hand away. 'Not now, my Rus Gullah,' she whispered, 'not now.' What is it? Misplaced modesty? The dictates of the menstrual cycle? The clap? But what does it matter? We are lovers. We have time.

'WHEN THE HELL WILL you show me around?' I ask Tony over breakfast, in the hope we will finally be able to talk to each other, mano a mano. But Tony invites everybody for a jaunt across his estate. Jugnu announces she will drive. When Tony explains that the vehicle, a relic of the Second World War, does not feature power steering, she says, 'Chalay ga.' Bosco jumps up front, crying, 'Shotgun.'

'She doesn't drive like a woman,' Tony whispers as we lurch ahead on a dirt road,[142] dust billowing behind us. Tony is of the opinion that the most inept drivers in the country are dames and maulvis. I must concur.

---

142. Muddy aqueducts border the dirt road. 'No government in history paved these things,' Tony comments. 'Water wastage was 40 per cent. The dictator fixed it all in three years, but we hounded him out of the country.'

As we wend past women in colourful costumes squatting in the fields, clearing the land with dupattas slung around their backs, I say, 'You've become a regular feudal.'

'These women, they're tough cookies. They put food on the table. They wear the pants in the family. They share profits with me, fifty-fifty.'

'That's what they all say.'

'You're busting my balls but lemme tell you, I've set up a basic clinic and elementary school for the kids. I've even sent a couple for higher studies. You tell me who has done the same?'

When we pull up to a narrow sylvan chase by the canal bank—the border separating our land and the vast holdings of the neighbouring feudal—Tony says, 'I come here for shooting but I haven't in a while because things are dicey these days: the old man—you remember him, right, Dada's friend and protégé?—is on his deathbed and his sons are jackholes—'

'Jackholes?'

'Half jackass, half a-hole—know what I mean?—and they're itching for a fight. They got nothing else to do.'

When Jugnu points out a monitor lizard scrambling across a knoll to Bosco, I take Tony aside. 'Hidayatullah and Bakaullah are itching for a fight also. I have to ask you, Tony: Are you with me or against me?'

Leaning beside a tree, my brother sucks his teeth. 'Of course, I'm with you, Abdu—I'm always with you—but you gotta remember I also owe Bakaullah. He was there for me when things were rough in the US. He paid for my education. And, you know, we weren't always there for him.'

If Tony insists on dredging up the past, I could remind him that he is technically squatting: the land beneath our feet belongs to us all—no transfer certificate has ever been issued. Perhaps that is why he does not want to get involved. In the effort to save the Lodge, however, I am not in the mood to let it go: 'Let me remind you,' I say, 'I am the only one who went to him after the accident. I loved those children; I loved Bhabi. I did what I could do, but what could I do?'

'I know, Abdu, I know—'

'Bakaullah has principles, lofty principles, that are entirely his own.'

'Yeah, but you also live in your own world, Daddy-O. You see things the way you wanna see them, not the way they are.'

'This is about what's right: the Lodge is a monument, our monument.'

'If the Lodge had been declared a trust or something,' Tony philosophizes, 'there'd have been no discussion, no mess. Money creates and destroys families. That's why I left.'

'Yes, well, I have nowhere to go. I would have bought them out but I have no capital inflow. I can't even repair the generator. You're the ace in my sleeve.'

'Never been nobody's ace before—'

'You were always mine.'

'Lemme just think about it, okay?'

'Think quickly, kid. I had planned to be here for only three days. I need to leave tomorrow. For all I know, they have squatted on the property by now, sealed the doors.'

'Okay, but you gotta meet Devyani before you leave.'

'Who's Devyani?'

DEVYANI ARRIVES WHILST I am sipping cold, minty shikanjabeen in the orchard, Bosco is scouring the walls for dacoits and monitor lizards, and Jugnu is discussing the difference between wine and moonshine with Tony. 'You see the outhouse?' Tony is saying, with a wave of the hand. 'It houses my winery. I will give you a tour if you like.' But Devyani's advent defers the tour until daylight. We all stand to attention. We all stare.

Devyani is dusky and limber and what is known as Classically Beautiful in Our Swath of the World: big black eyes; small, straight, neat nose; pouty lips—a miniature come to life. Sporting one of those ankle-length Beloochi frocks, a lily in her oiled hair, and a winning smile, she says, 'Tony speaks about you all the time.'

'Well,' I begin, 'he might not speak about you as much as I would like but that's probably because he doesn't need to.' Quoting from Presley's canon, I elucidate, 'You're always on his mind.'

'That's very kind of you but I know he doesn't talk much about us. The arrangement's not very popular—'

'What arrangement?'

'The marriage, of course.'

'Of course, of course,' I repeat. I cast a glance at Tony fidgeting with the agate ring on his finger. Although I am hurt that my brother has not taken me into confidence, I declaim, 'I was delighted when I heard. You must come to the Lodge. We must celebrate properly.'

'We'll come whenever you'll have us, Abdullah Bhai.'

'How about tomorrow?'

'Dinner's served,' Tony announces.

The cook has prepared a feast: steamed king fish, biryani, sautéed lotus stem or, as the locals call it, bhey, and the bhey is exquisite. I had requested an authentic Scindee dinner, and Tony has delivered. Sitting cross-legged on a long mat inside, we silently devour supper, mopping our plates with greased chapattis. Jugnu belches in praise. Devyani belches in camaraderie.

'Where have you been for the last so many days?' I ask her.

'With my sister—she's had a baby.'

'Are you from here?'

'We are Bhaiband—we have always lived here.'[143]

'Where are your parents?'

'Her father,' Tony interjects, 'happens to be one of the biggest commodity traders in the province—we had a business relationship.'

'Then you must be close to him.'

As Tony runs his fingers through his mane, Devyani reveals, 'We eloped.'

I would have liked to pursue that trajectory but Jugnu asks, 'Where's Bosco?' The lad has slipped out of the room. I have to follow—the dogs could be out. I find him at the entrance, staring at the sky, hands stuffed into his pockets. 'What are we doing here, Uncle Cossack?'

I begin to hold forth on the Self as a Proxy for the Cosmos but Bosco stops me with an impatient gesture: 'What are we doing *here*?' he repeats, pointing to the ground.

'Oh. We had to get Jugnu out because of the trouble in the neighbourhood, and I needed to discuss some pressing matters with my brother—'

'I want to go home.'

'Aren't you having fun?'

'You nearly died, twice, and there are dacoits everywhere, monster dogs, monster lizards—'

'We haven't come across a single dacoit—'

'I want to play Scrabble with my mother.'

143. The Bhaiband community mostly populated the Interior whilst Amils mostly resided in the cities—recall the beautiful bungalows of Amil Colony in the heart of town. We knew Jethmal & Guli Jagtiani who ran the Laboratory Apparatus Supply Co. But I need not get into the various Hindoo traditions of the region here: Lohana, Sodha, Bheel, Kohli. That's work for a diligent doctoral student.

It's my fault: we ought to have played Scrabble. But the situation is presumably beyond Scrabble. 'We leave tomorrow if the coast is clear,' I promise, 'and I will call your grandfather as soon as we're back.'

The newlyweds are nowhere to be seen when we return. Whilst I would like to secure a commitment from Tony, I am distracted; I am plotting to get into Jugnu's shalwar. I tell myself that I will catch Tony in the morning. If not, the sojourn will have been for naught.

ON IN VINO VERITAS
(OR HOMEWARD BOUND)

BRUME SWEEPS THE COUNTRYSIDE on the last morning; one cannot see beyond the perimeter of the orchard. It is as if one is teetering at the edge of the world, the universe—a pleasing, bemusing sensation. I traipse through the cloud in my borrowed sarong, the grass wet under my soles, like a poet searching for inspiration, but then I descry ominous panting, the patter of paws in the background, and suddenly I am Red Riding Hood in the woods. But before Hero & Daku can make breakfast out of me—the Full English, no doubt: sausages, blood pudding & beans—the gunman materializes, wielding a rake. 'Hoosh,' he charges. 'Hoosh,' I mutter, gathering the folds of my sarong and scampering into the anteroom. The universe always reminds you how small, how silly, how vulnerable you are.

When the gunman ties up the dogs, I order him to, 'Call Sayien, call Sayien now!' It's time to get my head out of the clouds and get things done.

Tony saunters out in his own time, a joint wedged between his lips, clad in nothing but faded jeans sliding off his waist. He's an incarnation of his greyhound teenage self in the mist. 'What's up,' he says.

'I was nearly eaten alive by your dogs!'

'You know they're let loose at night—'

'I've been dodging death since I've been here!'

'It's a dog-eat-dog world, Daddy-O!'

'That's exactly what I need to talk about.'

'Step into my office.'

I follow him to the outhouse, a long, windowless, unremarkable concrete bunker on the other side of the orchard which houses an extraordinary operation: thick plastic curtains give way to a spic, span, fluorescent-lit, temperature-controlled, state-of-the-art laboratory. Pails, beakers, funnels and basins rest on parallel steel tables, and aluminium sinks run along the far end. Two large metal vats and several stacked wooden barrels rest next to a Frigidaire that could fit a bear. 'Would you care to sample some fresh wine, sir?' Tony asks, grabbing a bottle from the refrigerator.

'It's seven in the dashed morning!'

Tony flips the stopper, pours half a glass of white, and sips slowly, tantalizingly. 'Ah!'

'Give me that!' I say, swiping it from his hand.

'Santé!'

'That's the only French you know?'

'You know I was absent that day.'[144]

We sit side by side on a wooden bench, backs against the cool wall, savouring the concoction. 'Tell me,' I ask, considering the viscous streaks across the circumference of my glasses, 'how many grapes go into a bottle?'

'Something like six hundred.'[145]

---

144. Tony took French at St. Pat's, but his teacher, a Russian, rather, a White Russian, named Andrei Rachkovsky, who only wore shorts, would spend the class telling stories about escaping the revolution to Curachee via Ukraine and China.

145. I am no oenologist, but that seems excessive. I imagine ten, certainly not more than twenty go into a glass, and there are about five glasses in a bottle. If you double the number, or better yet, triple it, you still have three hundred unaccounted for grapes. I would wager Chambu would know—he knows everything.

'Remember those Gandhi Garden grapes, kid?'

'I dream about 'em!'

'You don't share your dreams with me anymore.'

'Oh c'mon, Daddy-O—it ain't like you told me about Jugnu!'

'What's there to tell?'

'You playing My Fair Lady with her?'

'She's self-styled, self-made, and not turning into a butterfly, but at this age, in this state, I'm just happy I have somebody who cares.'

'You've practically got a family, Abdu—Jugnu, Bosco and all.'

'Well—'

'It's about time you settled down, you incorrigible bachelor.'

'You seem to have figured it all out.'

'I'm sorry about the whole marriage thing, Abdu, but it was *a fraught time*, as you would say. You see, Devyani was married into some, like, aristocratic family, but her husband ditched her because she didn't produce any kids. Her father went apeshit when he found out about us. I'm sure he's behind those jackholes next door. You know, they keep stopping the water to my lands? I'm a small farmer. I can't take that sort of shit, and there's no—what do you call it—recourse here.'

'So what do you do?'

'It's a long story but I got some friends—Hawkeye for one—but he's retiring any day. I'm managing for now, but you never know when they'll strike again.'

'But you have gunmen.'

'Gunmen ain't good enough.' Turning his back towards me, he displays the gilded hilt of a pistol wedged in the waist of his jeans. 'This here is a .38 Snubnose Special. I'm locked and loaded!'

There is no doubt everyone is beset with their own particular, peculiar tribulations: some are born hobbled, some suddenly ail, and some happen to be in the wrong place at the wrong time. The threats to Tony are existential—it's every man for himself out here, anywhere. What can I do for him? What can he do for me? Whilst I would like to ask him if he has made a decision about the Lodge, to reiterate the odds—three to one without him—sitting thigh to thigh with my boon companion, I deign not to discuss the matter further; I have said what I have to say. Now it's up to him. Taking a final swig, I stand and proclaim, 'We're done here.'

As I march towards the house, Tony says, 'Keep the sarong, Abdu.'

'Gee thanks, kid.'

'It's time you retire Mummy's robe.'

WE BREAKFAST TOGETHER—'BREAKFAST of champions,' Tony proclaims: paratha, malai and lassi for me; paratha, omelette and sautéed potatoes for everybody else. I do not believe I suffer from cholesterol—what is it called now HDL? LDL?—but I suspect the spread is not particularly salutary for diabetics either. I do not know how the locals survive but this much is certain: Devyani thrives.

Sitting like a schoolgirl, legs folded behind her slender rump, she tucks in without remorse. And Jugnu, God bless her, has never been shy about seconds. The two seem to have developed a rapport but one never knows with women.

'What beautiful bangles,' Jugnu purrs.

'What strong wrists,' Devyani avers.

If they really are getting on, we might spend more time together—the four of us could visit each other over the weekends, in the city, the Interior—and who knows, we might even sojourn abroad en famille. That's what families do.

'I took Devyani to Colombo,' Tony is saying. 'I proposed to her there. You must go, Abdu—'

'We all should go together.'

'It's like the South Asian Caribbean. It's funny: they got the most brutal civil war in the region but you wouldn't know it—'

'Speaking of which,' I interrupt, 'have you heard anything about the situation in the city? There were dark clouds above Lyari when we left.'

'Out here, I don't know nothin' about Hyderabad, Daddy-O, and that's, like, down the road. Your city's a different world altogether. But lemme check in with Hawkeye. He'll know what's what.'

Pulling out his portable phone, he calls his old friend. 'Hur says trouble's passed for now. A dozen dead, and some Langra guy's on his way out.'

It's welcome news: the changing dispensation suggests that the threat to us is diminished. Bosco, however, seems nonplussed. The lad has been sitting alone, despondently spooning lassi as if it were melted ice cream. 'So the war is over?' he asks.

'For now.'

'I want to go home.'

'We're going, we're going.'

Before departing, before embraces and exchanges of promises, I call the Caliph of Cool. When I tell him I need to have a word, he says, 'I need a word with you too, man. Meet me at the Intercon at eight. I'm playing tonight.'

We leave for the city soon after. The trip back is mercifully eventless.

VOLUME IV

ON THE PROVERBIAL HEARTBREAK HOTEL (OR VIA CON ME)

WHEN THE CALIPH OF Cool plays the piano, he sprawls on the keys. From a distance then, from the sliding glass doors that open into the air-conditioned, chequerboard-floor lobby of the Intercon, it seems that the instrument is playing itself.[146] In another era, there might have been an audience, oohs, aahs, sibilant applause, but presently the only taker is a mop-haired fellow in a pine-green suit installed at the back of the coffee shop, portable phone glued to an ear. 'Hor ki al eh,' I hear him say, 'razi-bazi?'

As I arrange myself in a tiny wrought-iron chair before a tiny glass-top table, Felix prattles, 'Chopin, man! That cat was something else!'

Whenever he addresses Themes in Western Classical Music—the Caliph cannot help himself after a couple of bottles of feni—I find myself taken by the variety of heavy-liddedness that besets the best of us during the longueur of chemistry lessons. After all, there are more pressing matters in the world than hydrocarbons. There is, for instance, the matter of Bosco. When I deposited him outside the

---

146. The only other such pianist I have come across is one Paolo Conte. I must confess that I have entertained fantasies of being an old, smoky-voiced Italian, lounging on a balcony overlooking a *piazza*, ogling the dames in heels, crooning, '*Via, via, vieni via di qui / Niente più ti lega a questi luoghi / Neanche questi fiori azzurri...*'

Lodge less than an hour ago, he waved limply. The lad is losing his cool.

'What do you think?' Felix asks after completing the set.

'Bosco wants to go back home—'

'About Chopin's Number Two, man!'

'Oh. Right. It's better than Number One.'

'You big goof,' he laughs. 'You never learnt nothing. You just like those *dish-dish* numbers.' Thrusting a small plastic bottle of mineral water at me, Felix says, 'You want?' I take a swig and spit—I ought to have known better: it's feni, and feni is less than salutary without lime, without soda. 'You'll go blind drinking that hooch!'

'Then why're you the one with the cataract, my friend!'

'Why are you so spirited tonight?'

'I'm leaving, man, getting out.'

'What? Where?'

'The Australian asylum application came through. I'm taking Bosco and my daughter with me.'

'What asylum? What application? Why didn't you tell me, Goddamn it?'

'It was all on a need-to-know basis, and you didn't need to know.'

All of a sudden, I realize the bastard has been playing me like a banjo from the beginning. 'They'll have a chance to start a new life,' Felix is saying, 'no interference from the mafia, bloody nobody. You should be happy, man.'

'About what?'

'Your friend—'

'Abandoning me?'

'This is not about you.'

The image of Bosco skipping across the tarmac flits across my field of vision, polka-dot backpack slung over the shoulder, waving farewell. I feel suddenly bereft, broken. I feel like sobbing in the stalls of the men's room but before I can excuse myself, a turbaned bearer wearing an infelicitous smirk appears, tray in hand. 'Order?' he demands as if attending to a pair of fops.

'Sala, tameez nahin?' Felix growls, viz., *Don't you have manners, idiot?* I order a plate of marmalade shortbread biscuits and cold coffee.

'What do you think?' I ask.

'I'm fine with feni.'

'About immigrating, Pinto?'

'It's time, old friend.'

'You said Australia was a dashed penal colony, that nobody knows you there, that—'

'I've finally realized there's not much left here for my kind.'

We gaze sombrely at the traffic in the lobby. Several amateur art enthusiasts gawk at an exhibition on the opposite wall featuring Arcadian scenes rendered in watercolour: A Solitary Ox in a Field, A Smattering of Mud Huts, The Suggestion of a Storm in the Indigo Sky. The character in the green suit drifts by, portable phone still glued to ear, pursuing, it would seem, a pair of pale lasses wrapped in colourful scarves. A pack of children in matching ill-fitting jackets stomp into the hall that had housed the Nasreen Room. In the old days, air hostesses in stilettos and skirts and perfume would be milling in the lobby, sipping sundowners before a night out in town. The only excitement tonight is the promise of lukewarm kebabs and a bottle of pop. Sucking on the dregs of the cold coffee with a chewed-up straw, I ask, 'When are you going to take Bosco away from me?'

'A week or two—'

Pulling the last trumpeter by his bowtie towards me, I enjoin, 'Listen to me. I will make this right.'

'What the hell can you do? Take on the land mafia? You lost your mind, banjo?'

'I managed before, I can manage again.'

'You just manage yourself,' he says, 'that's more than enough.'

When the bearer reappears with the chit, Felix insists on paying. 'I called you,' I assert, 'so you're my guest,' but I realize I do not have currency on my person. Waving the bearer away—'Where are my biscuits?' I say—I ask Felix, 'Remember that night at the Excelsior?'

'My homecoming?'

'When you walked in, that bartender hollered, "You don't think I remember but I remember you: I remember that jaw, the trumpet. You have an obligation to this bar of six hundred and fifty-five rupees! And it's been outstanding for more than ten years!"'

'Ha!'

'Then I asked: "Do you know who this is? You know who you're talking to? This is the Caliph of Cool! You know this man composed the National Anthem? You know he knocked the Prime Minister to the ground? And now he's back from Down Under to preside over the City of Lights once again. You should give him another drink tonight and another drink after that. You should be grateful that this living legend is gracing this establishment with his presence!"'

'That was a different time, Cossack, we were different men.'

'It was like *The Gunfighter*.'

When the bearer returns, I tell him to put everything on my tab. 'In fact, feed the band as well. I want a three course Chinese meal—spring rolls and hot-and-sour soup, and Szechuan chicken and prawn fried rice, and that strange fried banana item with cream.'

'But I've already eaten,' Felix protests.

'You take it home.'

The bearer retreats hunched to the kitchen, adjusting his epaulettes, only to return with the manager, a middle-aged chap with dim eyes and a bright wide forehead. 'Is there a problem?' he asks.

'Since you ask, there are several issues that ought to be addressed: these chairs are too small, that art antiseptic, and the service should be attentive, not obtrusive. Mind you, these are not offhand comments—no, this constitutes a considered critique. You see, young man, I am

Abdullah the Cossack, the proprietor of the Olympus. You ought to know that I did not merely run a hotel; I ran an institution. I have had the honour of hosting nawabs, ambassadors, Stewart Granger.[147] Do you understand what I am talking about? Do you have any sense of history?'

'I know, sir, I know you.'

'Then you will be so kind as to put everything on my tab.'

'Yes, sir, no problem, sir, thank you, sir.'

'No,' I reply, 'thank *you*.'

The manager promptly delivers the dinner in brown paper bags himself, jumps to my aid when I attempt to extricate myself from the furniture, then presents me his card pressed between his thumbs. 'If you ever need anything, sir, anything at all, please do not hesitate to contact me.'

As Felix and I waddle out, two hapless old-timers, the staff salutes. There is no doubt that the Intercon remains civilized. The hotels around the corner, however, lack protocol, character. When the valet runs to fetch the Impala, Felix asks, 'Why don't you come along?'

'For a nightcap?'

'Australia, Cossack, Australia!'

The thought has never crossed my mind.

147. Granger actually never stayed at the Olympus. I just want to make a point. If I remember correctly, he stayed at the Metropole (and at Faletti's in Lahore).

ON THE ABJECT FAILURE OF THE LEGAL SYSTEM (OR A CLOUDY FORECAST)

UPON RETURNING FROM THE Intercon, I hear a howl from the balcony. It's Bosco, brandishing a cricket bat. *We've been burgled!* he squalls. As I hurry up, I reckon the lad would probably be safer at his place. But what is there left to steal, except, perhaps, the title deed?

The Lodge was burgled once before in the winter of '93, a troubled time in the history of the city: recall, the army had rolled in, the municipal machinery all but collapsed, and Babu wed Nargis. The day after the nuptials, four men in jeans, faces swathed in scarves, barged in. They were polite, professional, pointing pistols. The bride produced a couple of embroidered sacks full of envelopes. Although I would replenish some of the nazarana in time—Chambu had not yet taken me for a ride—I could not do much about the jewellery: bangles, earrings, filigreed gold sets. Nargis, poor girl, would suffer two miscarriages as a result—Trouble Breeds Trouble. We raised the walls after, and I personally supervised the application of jagged glass from discarded Roohafzah and Pakola bottles along the surface perimeter. What good did it do?

Whoever burgled the place this time around, however, did not scale walls or break the locks—it's as if a gale blew through. And like a farmer appraising damage to his crop, I flop to the ground, attempting to catalogue the loss—*Ramayana, Chachnama, Hamzanama, Baburnama, Akbarnama, Gandunama, Areopagitica, Encyclopaedia*

Britannica, Yahweh & Other Deities in Ancient Israel, Mushrooms and Other Fungi of Great Britain & Europe—but how do you catalogue a lifetime?

'Who did this?' Jugnu asks.

The finger of logic undoubtedly points towards what in police parlance is termed an Inside Job. 'You won't understand.'

'We're not safe here.'

There is no doubt about it: whilst others have guards nowadays, we only have the crows. At least I have Jugnu. 'I'm happy you're here with me,' I say.

The silence that follows would suggest indifference or worse, but I am too exasperated to pursue the matter. *Early to bed,* I recall, tucking Bosco in, *early to rise, makes one healthy, wealthy and wise.* If only I had adhered to the age-old adage, what a life I would have led! Slumping on my bed, I promise myself that I will sort things out once and for all in the morning.

BUT WHEN I HEAD out to meet my advocate bright and early, I find myself facing Chambu—the Swine's timing is uncanny—and wondering whether he had a hand in the burgled books. 'You know we are like brothers, family,' he begins, stroking his curly locks, 'and family always takes care of its own.'

'I don't have time for discussion today.'

'I am a simple man, Boss, but running this operation is not at all simple. Do you know that the closed jigger machine is at 29 per cent capacity? 29 per cent, sir! Can you imagine? We need to purchase new equipment—'

'Why can't we just fix it?

'If you finance some capital expenditure, Boss, you will make so much you will not know what to do with it. You could fix the roof—'

'How do you know about the roof?'

'You could even buy the property from your brothers—'

'You can stay here as long as you like,' I interject.

'I can wait.'

'I will arrange a cup of tea but it looks like the monsoon is upon us. If it rains, it will be difficult for you to get back to your hole.' And waving my parasol like an old dame caught in a downpour, I hail a rickshaw to Kapadia's office.

Nestled between a travel agency and an IT consultancy in the older cantons of McLeod Road, the congested financial mecca of the city, the building (and possibly the practice) has arguably become an anachronism. Trudging up the worn stone steps to the wooden boards that catalogue an ancient fraternity—CROMWELL BLACK LP, TOLANI ASSOCIATES, KAPADIA & KAPADIA—I am greeted by a smart, bird-boned Anglo who can type faster than anybody in the world. 'Good morning, Mr Abdullah. Good to see you. You've lost weight.'

'Why, thank you Ms White—you look no worse for the wear.'

'You'll have to wait if you don't have an appointment.'

Marching in, I proclaim, 'We'll be dead soon.'

Kapadia's lair recalls a monastery—slate walls, high ceilings and, save the whirr of the ceiling fans and ruffling paper, silence. Thousands of legal tomes & treatises fill tall shelves in a library spanning family, corporate and real estate law dating back to the Raj, and in the background, a grave portrait of Kapadia's forebear hangs beside three framed certificates. I do not possess even one, but then my scholarship is altogether of a qualitatively different order: the study of law is undoubtedly critical to the functioning of modern civilization—where would we be without Menes, Moses, Hammurabi?—but I have always felt that it is fundamentally not unlike the study of Betamax manuals. I must keep such sentiments to myself; I cannot afford to offend the mandarin.

As I seat myself before one of two identical bureaus piled high with a stack of blue files tethered by string, a voice enquires. 'Is that you, Abdullah?'

'You're a crack legal mind, sir.'

'I'm busy.'

'I can wait.'

'What is it, Abdullah?'

'My brothers are forcing me out of my house.'

'What do you want me to do?'

'Do what you do, damn it!

Kapadia's head emerges—round, shiny, dun-complexioned, floppy-eared and disembodied like the Childoos' Mister Potato Man Toy. Whilst temperamentally akin to the Gautama—Kapadia maintains his only vice is his evening tobacco pipe—he is a famously well-informed ascetic: the files in his head are arguably more extensive than the files in his office. 'Let me remind you,' he begins, 'that you have had a case pending against Bakaullah for two and a half decades and he has one against you. Do you really want to get into this mess? Why can't you talk about it amongst yourselves? You would be surprised, but tenderness can work.'

'Tenderness? As my legal advisor, you are advocating tenderness, sine qua non? You know that Bakaullah will keep pushing me—and I already have my back to the wall. I have come to lodge a case!'

'On what grounds?'

'Burglary.'

'What?'

'The man has stolen all my books! What sort of human being does that?'

'Do you have proof?'

'Do you believe that burglars are generally inclined towards literature?'

'Proof, young man, I need proof.'

'What about malfeasance, inter alia?'

Kapadia claps like a monarch. 'Abdullah Mian,' he begins, 'I have known your mother and father—God bestow Heaven on them—

and I have known your brothers. It is sad to me that it has come to this. I have considered the issue. I have had to consider these sorts of issues all my life. I believe it has to do with our laws of inheritance. This dynamic has defined our history. I cannot dispute that it's a just, equitable arrangement, unlike the arbitrary Western convention of primogeniture, but it has sown discord in every age. You see, man requires clear, iron laws to rein in his nature.'

'Right-O.'

'It has been a difficult year for me. I suffered a severe bout of pleurisy.'

'Are you contagious?'

'That's leprosy, Abdullah.'

'Oh.'

'They found my carotid is 90 per cent blocked. I'm told there's a certain activist Kashmiri doctor in America who specializes in stent technology, but how can I travel sixteen hours at my age? Just securing an interview for a visa is riddled by tribulation, not to mention the hassles at immigration. I don't have time—I'm working on cases that require immediate attention. And I'm the President of the Bar Association. The responsibilities are innumerable, especially these days—'

'I didn't know—'

'Ergo I would advise you to sit down and sort this matter out like men. We don't have the luxury of time. We're in our final innings.'

'But we're a team—'

'You know better than me that conflicts here are not merely man versus man but clan versus clan. And the fact is, Bakaullah's network is more extensive than yours. If you are unable to talk sense into that stubborn brother of yours, then you do not have much legal recourse.' Disappearing behind the skyline of files, he adds, 'Unless, of course, your mother gifted the Lodge to you before she passed. You would need the testimony of two adult witnesses.'

I sit in the august offices of Kapadia & Kapadia, probing an ear, mulling deception of Machiavellian magnitude. I might have had a colourful past, might have a number of outstanding loans that I may never reimburse, but I like to think that I am not a dishonourable man—my conscience is more exacting than any second-hand moral order. How on earth would I secure the talents of two witnesses anyway? Toto and Guddu? Barbarossa and the Djinn? Kapadia, for one, would wash his hands of the entire matter—and me. Gautama is undoubtedly testing me. There is nothing left to do but turn on my heel.

THE WIND WHISTLES PORTENTOUSLY outside, sweeping plastic bags into the air. Then there is a thunderclap and the heavens open up. Pedestrians dart beneath eaves, the odd tree; cobblers, paan-wallahs pack up shop. But the children don't mind: they emerge to celebrate in knickers, wading and splashing in the swelling pools and sumps. A poignant-faced girl chants 'Jeevay Pakistan' at the top of her lungs, rain cascading over her tresses—*What a glorious feeling, I'm happy again!*[148]

---

148. Not long ago, I bumped into an old schoolmate from Jufelhurst Days in the jelly & marmalade aisle at Agha's Supermarket. Tall, dark and bald, James, né Jamal, had returned from the United Kingdom after nearly half a century. Great Britain, he told me, was marvellous—he had become the Convenience Store King of Finchley—'but it rains there all the time, mate, in winter, spring, summer, autumn, every day, every year. It was bloody ridiculous. I always felt wet.' It was as if he had returned only to thaw. As we stood in the checkout line, he complained about aspects of modern Currachee, from the dramatically changed topography—'The city ends at Clifton Bridge'—to the electricity shortages—'I stub my toe every week'—but not about the weather. During the monsoon, he claimed, 'I enjoyed showers for the first time in a lifetime!' Indeed, rain might be considered cold and sinister in what is known in discourse as the West—who was it who said April is the cruellest month?—but in this city, Our Swath of the World,

But by the time I hail a rickshaw, perhaps the last available in the city, I am drenched in spite of my parasol—dawdling in the rain is an overrated pastime for us old-timers—and the driver demands double in accordance with the Natural Laws of Economics. As the gutters overflow, playgrounds transform into lakes, roads into rivers, it's like Dodgem Cars:[149] we avoid a Suzuki, a lurching lorry, but stall by the zoo. The driver shrugs. What to do?

Forging ahead on foot like a tightrope walker, afraid I will be electrocuted by wiring riven from poles, or fall into an open manhole, then get sucked into the muck and spit out into the sea, I imagine the headlines in the eveningers: Man Fished Out with Muck, or perhaps Muck Fished Out with Man.

Although I manage to survive the expedition somehow, trousers rolled up to the calves, shoes in hand, when I arrive at the Lodge, neither Bosco nor Jugnu are to be found. *That's it,* I tell myself. *They're gone, and they're not coming back.*

---

it undoubtedly heralds respite, heralds joy. Which is to say, one could pen a monograph on the Hegemony of Western Discourse on Meteorological Terminology.

149. Anthropologists ought to 'crunch the numbers': accidents occur during only two periods a year here, the Holy Month and the Monsoon.

ON THE CONSEQUENCES OF SOLITUDE (OR THE VISITORS)

SHIVERING, DISCONSOLATE, AND INDIFFERENT to the flying ants perched on my extremities, I languish in Tony's sarong, staring at the blurred blades of the ceiling fan. The clouds grumble, the light changes, then the call to prayer heralds the evening like a plaint—there's no escape from the Dungeon of Despair. There is no doubt that the problems that have vexed furrow-browed philosophers since time immemorial—Why Are We Here? Is Reason Sufficient? Is Reality Real? What is the Meaning of Meaning?[150]—pale in comparison to the disquiet, distress imposed by grinding, everyday loneliness. An article I came across in *Reader's Digest*, titled something like 'Loneliness is a Killer,' claimed the predicament has physical manifestations: it can hurt more than a twisted ankle, a bloody gash & untreated, can become infected like an open wound.

I do not require scientific studies, empirical data: my mouth is mealy, my eyes watery, and no matter how I position myself—lying

150. I must admit that I have not waded much into philosophical waters in the passing years, with the exception of Harry Frankfurt's *On Bullshit*, a critical volume in turn-of-the-century enquiry, which begins: 'One of the most salient features of our culture is that there is so much bullshit ... but we have no clear understanding of what bullshit is, why there is so much of it.' Frankfurt proposes developing 'tentative and exploratory philosophical analysis' concerning the matter. It's high on the Cossack's Must-Read List.

on my left, my right side, legs stretched, legs gathered, feet crossed, feet splayed—I feel my bones no longer support the heft of my flesh. There is no doubt that my ward would have diagnosed my maladies were he present, no doubt my lover would have run her long fingers through my curls to allay my anxieties. I should have bought her a ring from our jeweller a long time ago and promised her a stipend in perpetuity. She would not have left then. But perhaps it's time I escaped as well: I will look into booking a one-way ticket for Australia, and never look back.

AS I MARINATE IN solipsism, self-pity, humming *Oh dear, what can the matter be?*[151] I hear footsteps on the stairwell. Sitting up, I wish, I wonder: could it be Jugnu, Bosco, Barbarossa, Tony? The approaching patter, however, suggests a four-legged creature—an errant pye-dog perhaps, Pax Romana, Yorick—but to my delight, the Childoos arrive lockstep, hands tied behind bottoms. 'We are two ostrich!' announces Guddu.

'No,' Toto differs, 'kangaroo—'

'What fun!'

Opening his miniature hand to reveal a mauve ribbon and a couple of chipped marbles, Toto proclaims, 'We have somethings for you.'

'A ribbon! Two marbles! How thoughtful of you! I was just telling somebody the other day, *If only I had a ribbon and two marbles, I would be the happiest man in the world!*'

Pleased as punch, the two chant, 'Hip-hop-hooray!'

'Come here, boys,' I say, slapping the bed. 'What on earth have you been up to?'

151. For three quarters of a century, I've wondered on & off what kept Johnny. Did he find another girl, or was it something sinister: could he have been kidnapped, or died of sepsis, organ failure? It's not one of the enduring Mysteries of Our Times, but it is a matter informed by certain pathos.

'One day,' Toto informs me, settling beside me, 'it rained and rained again.'

'It was like pipi,' Guddu elucidates.

'I got wet in the garden and Ami pulled my ear.'

'Oh, the dreaded ear tug!'

'And one day,' Guddu adds, 'we sawed two racing donkeys on the road—'

'Yes but we went faster,' Toto interjects.

'Then what happened?'

'Nother Chacha was at Chacha Abu's house,' Toto replies. 'He was Baka Cha and sits in the wheelchair.'

'He gives us toffees,' chimes Guddu.

'One would hope his generosity's not limited to cordials,' I mutter.

'What?'

'Oh I was just saying that he never gave me any toffees.'

'Did you dos naughty pun?'

'I think Baka Cha is the naughtiest member of the family,' I mutter.

'No,' Toto exclaims, wiping his nose with his sleeve. 'I am!'

'Sing along!' Guddu insists.

'Ra-Ra-Rasputin?'

'Nother one.'

I scratch my head, clear my throat, and begin, 'Give me the ring on your finger / Let me see the lines on your hand / I can see me a tall dark stranger, giving you what you hadn't planned—'

As luck would have it, Nargis the Opossum walks in just then. I could wager that she has been standing on the steps for some time, listening to the prohibited Cliff Richard number, shaking her head and cradling her elbows, but as I brace for a rebuke, she greets me as if I have been crooning an Ode to the Almighty. 'How are you, Abdullah Bhai? How's your health?'

The query is so disarming that I do not even think to enquire about the burglary. Instead, I find myself saying, 'Thank you for asking, Nargis Bibi. All is well with me. Lot of rain this year.'

'Alhumdulillah. It's such a relief—it's been so hot. But the streets are in a mess: it took two hours for Babu to return home.'

'Oh my!'

'And more rain is expected tonight.'

'Winds must be blowing north from the Arabian Sea.'

But before I can make further meteorological small talk—'We should have a bumper crop this year,' or 'The rain in Spain stays mainly on the plain'—Nargis proclaims, 'Ninni time, bachon!' and leads the Childoos out. Oh, the cruel regime of Wee Willie Winkie, the bane of children and their uncles everywhere!

The terror of solitude is such that I consider inviting Nargis and Babu for a cup of tea and some Danish Butter Biscuits. We could all sit on the balcony like a family and watch the storm clouds—Cumulonimbus or Nicocolombus—sweeping across the sky. It would be grand!

To my surprise, Nargis returns at that instant as if she has read my mind. 'I forgot to mention Bakaullah Bhai phoned earlier,' she says. 'He's expecting you for dinner tonight.'

'Dinner with destiny!' I cry, as Nargis skips away. Then it begins raining in sheets.

CURSING THE RAIN, STARS, my brothers, sister-in-law, I pace up and down the balcony like a spider in a bottle until I am breathless and flush and feeble in the knees. Flopping on the cane chair on the balcony, I watch the trees trembling in the dramatic downpour, then ring the dinner bell to summon Barbarossa to make preparations for my journey: mackintosh, wellingtons, a boat, a lifebuoy. When I apprise him of the situation, he asks, 'What man allows his land to be taken from under his feet?'

'The Lodge belongs to the family.'

'Am I not family?' he asks, lucid as light.

'Go back to your village.'

'I will die here with my cock.'

'I might die tonight.'

Then there is a flash of lightning, and in the instant brilliance, I espy movement at the gate: Bosco in knickerbockers, wet and out of breath, and Jugnu, my Jugnu, glancing over her shoulder, a mangy alley cat tucked under her arm. Slamming the gate shut behind her, she bounds across the driveway. *I must ask her to marry me. I must ask her to marry me now.* But before I can get a word in, Jugnu pants, 'I think we were followed.'

'What?'

Soaked to the toes, Jugnu whispers, 'I think I recognized them, Langra's men.'

Langra might be on his way out but I can attest to the fact that desperate men do desperate things. 'Did you lose them?'

'I do not know.'

There is a crack then a hiss—the power line or circuit breaker. *What if they're here?* I wonder, *And what of the Childoos—those poor, innocent, defenceless Childoos!* 'This is my house,' I mutter in the dark, 'and they are my responsibility.' But as I roll up my sleeves to venture downstairs, something wet grazes against my leg and I squeal like the Proverbial Stuck Pig. 'What, Uncle Cossack, what?' Bosco cries.

Squinting, surveying the lay of the shadowlands, I realize it's the cat—what, what, indeed. 'Nothing,' I say, gaffling a rolling pin from the kitchen drawer. 'Nothing to be worried about.'

'Where are you going?'

'I just need to check on the generator.'

'I want to go home.'

'I'm coming,' Jugnu says.

'No,' I snap.

'You don't know them,' she whispers.

Pecking Jugnu on the cheek, I charge her to keep vigil—there is no doubt she can rule the roost—but on the way out, I pull Barbarossa aside, bidding him to follow if I do not return in ten minutes, and Barbarossa, foot-in-the-grave pensioner, grimaces and grunts like a plunderer raring to sack Delhi on horseback. There is no doubt in my mind that he will rescue me—if I do not kill myself first: it's pitch dark outside and raining sideways. I descend the spiral stairwell around the back tentatively, measuring each step with my toes.

Since the kitchen door does not budge—wood becomes swollen during the monsoon—I shove the rolling pin in the waist of the sarong and put my shoulder into the effort. 'Babu?' I call out, 'Nargis?' But it's as quiet as a graveyard. What if Langra's men are already here? What if they have bound and gagged my brother, his wife? Although I know my way around better than anybody else—I have negotiated the house blindfolded, playing hide-and-seek with Tony—I bang my knee against a chair and yell Bloody Murder.

'Who's there?' demands a voice.

'Me.'

A torch light shines in my eyes. 'Abdullah Bhai?'

'Everything all right, partner?'

Clad in a vest & knickers, Babu stands bowlegged, gaping at me. 'Is that a rolling pin in your sarong?'

'What? This? Yes. I was making chapattis when the lights went off. It's time you fixed the generator.'

'We've discussed it before, Abdullah Bhai: I bought it, so you should contribute to the repairs—'

'How are the Childoos?'

'They were startled by the storm but Nargis is with them.'

'So everything is fine?'

'Yes, yes. Why do you ask?'

'I want you to lock all the doors and check all the windows.'

'What's going on?'

'I, uh, hear there's trouble in the city.'

'I didn't hear anything about it on the news.'

'Trust me—'

All of a sudden, Babu yells, 'Behind you!'

Squeezing the hilt of the rolling pin, I prepare for the Moment of Truth—*I'll die with my boots on, a hero, a martyr*—but as I turn around in slow motion, a familiar silhouette materializes before me. 'Jugnu?'

Babu takes a step back, covering his crotch, more ashamed than scared. 'You know each other?'

'I don't believe you have formally been introduced,' I begin in a convivial tenor. 'Let me take this opportunity to introduce you: this is Jugnu, a dear friend and kindred soul who, I must add, is acquainted with the grand mysteries of life. And this is Babu,' I turn to say, 'my youngest brother, a renowned computer technician and expert table tennis player.'

'I am happy to meet you,' Babu squeaks, 'but is that a knife in her hand?'

'I told you, partner,' I ejaculate, 'we were preparing dinner.'

Folding the meat cleaver against her forearm, Jugnu plays along: 'I just cut up the chicken and wanted to ask what you want me to do with the head and feet.'

'The head, the feet,' I repeat, scratching my temple. 'We could use the feet bones for the stock—good collagen. In this weather, it's prudent to have stock on hand. Don't you agree?'

'But,' Babu interjects, 'I thought you had been invited to dinner by Bakaullah Bhai.'

'Oh, that reminds me: please tell Nargis to tell Bakaullah Bhai that I won't be able to make it in this downpour.'

'But I can arrange a Radio Cab. They're very professional. They could be here in ten—'

'In fact, I also want Nargis to tell Bakaullah that if *he* wants to meet *me* he can drop by the Lodge tomorrow, day after, or next week for that matter. As you know, I'm ordinarily free.' Offering an arm to Jugnu, I say, 'Don't we have a chicken to stuff?'

Slamming the kitchen door shut behind me, I grab Jugnu by the waist and spin her around in the rain. We remain locked in embrace—the flat of Jugnu's knife pressed against my flesh, my rolling pin wedged in my sarong—as the tempest rages about us. 'You need to get me out of these clothes,' Jugnu finally whispers. 'I'm wet.'

As I start to say *Marry me, marry me now!* I hear the gate creak open like a premonition and watch Jugnu dart into the gloom. Although the route is treacherous—ankle-deep water, invisible branches, the whiff of petroleum in the air—I follow, slashing invisible gangsters on the way like a Ninja Warrior. Rounding the corner, I spot her beyond the vegetable patch. I look at Jugnu, Jugnu looks at me. 'Did you shut the gate when you came in?' I whisper.

'I always shut it behind me.'

'Perhaps it is the wind?' I muse. Perhaps it's Bua, her husband—he is a locksmith, after all—but I suspect that it might be Langra's thugs.

This is no way to live, I think, *no way to die.*

ON CONFRONTING THE OTHER
(OR TIT FOR TAT)

CENTRAL JAIL IS DOWN the road from Garden, on the periphery of Hyderabad Colony—the shabby residential canton renowned for fair, feisty dames and pickled goods. Standing outside the compound of the turn-of-the-century sandstone structure, I sweat like a choice pickle. It's not just that the sun is criminal at midday; no, the storied prison has hosted independence fighters from the days of the Raj, Communists (including Comrade Bakaullah), venal parliamentarians and, since the theatrically inept Yankee operation in Afghanistan, terrorists weeded out by Tony's childhood pal Hur, a.k.a. Hawkeye. And now it will host me. A pair of knavish guards frisks me at the metal detector, muttering to themselves—I distinctly hear the words *khatay peetay*—but they have me all wrong; they do not know that I am a desperate man, and a desperate man is an impulsive man. I had been in bed a couple of hours earlier. I should have slept in, but had woken with a start.

The night was steamy, the roof dripped relentlessly, and I dreamt that I was an exiled head of state, compelled by circumstance to take employment as a maître d'hôtel at a restaurant in a faraway city. A small man with big teeth followed by four hooligans demanded a table. They ordered very dirty martinis, then roared, 'Now we want your head.' It left a bad taste in my mouth when I woke. 'This is no way to live,' I repeated to myself, 'no way to die.'

I called Tony, raspy-voiced. 'I need to talk to your policeman friend,' I said. 'Who?' he asked. 'Hur,' I replied. 'Why?' he enquired. 'Why do you care?' After obtaining the number, I dialled again: 'Hello? Hur? This is Tony's brother, Abdullah. I need to meet this Langra Dacoit. I need to meet him today.'

Jugnu sat up like a marionette when I put the receiver down. 'What was that?' she asked. Stumbling to the lavatory, straddling the commode, I tugged my numb member. 'I need to sort things out with your lover,' I replied. 'He's not my lover!' she cried, storming off. It was a wicked thing to say, but I was in a state: I had never visited the jail before, and if things did not go as planned, I would find myself on the bed of the Lyari River by dusk, rotting in a stew of raw sewage and industrial waste. When Hur called to inform me that I was expected within the hour, I vomited my breakfast: marmalade toast and tea.

A SHORT, CLEAN-SHAVEN, CLEFT-CHINNED, barrel-chested, uniformed man with a shock of white hair and a twinkle in his eye welcomes me inside the superintendent's office with a soft handshake. DIG Hur, the man known as Supercop in the papers, has not only put a lion's share of the inmate population behind bars, but has also negotiated decades of service with a reputation for integrity, a palmary achievement. Of course, I first met him when he wore knickers and licked candy floss. 'You've become famous since I knew you,' I say.

'Zindagi kay din pooray karnay hain,' he laughs, viz., *I'm biding my time until it's time to go.*

'So am I, but the city needs people like you.'

Offering me a seat and a cup of tepid tea, he says, 'The city can be sorted in six months—the per capita homicide ratio here was lower than Boston's a few years back—but they don't let us do our job. We operate under colonial laws instituted when the role of the police was to suppress the natives. The Police Reform Act was amended almost immediately after it was passed.[152] But I'm sure you haven't come here to discuss our problems.'

'I'm sorry to have bothered you, Hur—I know you have more important things to do.'

'You're like an elder brother, sir. And your request was a good excuse to stop by the jail. I had some work here I've been neglecting.'

'An interrogation perhaps?'

'You know I can't discuss such matters, but a word of advice since you are here: avoid public places in the near future. Our sources tell us miscreants are planning attacks in the city.'

'This is a savage age.'

'With all due respect, sir, why are you mixed up with the likes of Langra?'

'I'm not,' I reply, and feign bravado: 'I'm here to get mixed up with him—'

Just then a peon sheepishly enters the office and passes a chit to Hur. Scanning the note, he looks up and says, 'It was wonderful to see you. I'd press about your meeting but I have to get back to work.' Standing up, he adds. 'Let me know if I can be of any assistance. A car will escort you home.'

'There's no need—'

Fixing me with a look, he says, 'There probably will be.'

I am led through a series of gated corridors manned by wardens, through an enclosed open-air compound bordered by barbed wire, before being consigned to a windowless chamber with tawny peeling walls—undoubtedly the central interrogation cell of Central Jail. Settling on a steel chair, I am hot and bothered by a pair of hefty clegs,

---

152. Can you imagine that, for the first time since the aftermath of the First War of Independence in 1857, reforms were introduced in 2002, effectively insulating the police from political shenanigans? Can you imagine how many shenanigans occurred during the Era of Our Stiff Upper Lipped Overlords, not to mention after?

horseflies—a blur of green & red, intent on exploring my orifices. The logic that has led me to the dank womb of the prison seems foggy, foolhardy. I remind myself that both gangsters and the authorities are searching for Jugnu. Without witnesses, the police won't have a watertight case. And since Hawkeye is approaching superannuation, even if he were to look the other way for old time's sake, when it comes to said 'person of interest,' there could come a time when I would not only have to bear the wrath of Langra, but of the entire police force. 'You have to go it alone,' I tell myself.

AS I WORK THINGS through in my head, the iron door swings open and four men enter, ushering in a shackled character clad in purple exercise pants and a black kurta open to the navel. I would stand up, I should stand up, but am struck: although half my age, the fair, burly, chocolate-eyed, chinless fellow appears to be an earlier incarnation of myself. 'What is this?' Langra snarls, 'a joke?' Turning to me, teeth bared, he demands, 'How dare you disturb me?'

'I'm sorry—'

'You know who I am?'

Summoning every mote of courage in my being, I say, 'You, sir, are Langra Sardar, one of the most powerful men in this city, a legend. I am grateful that you have agreed to see me.'

'I have not agreed to anything!'

'Please allow me to introduce myself,' I continue. 'I am Abdullah of Garden East, the former proprietor of the Hotel Olympus. I am here to discuss Jugnu, I mean, Juggan.'

Sitting down like an emperor, elbows resting on the flimsy table that separates us, Langra commands, 'Dafa ho, ulloo kay pathon!' or *Leave us, bastards!* As the guards shuffle out like children, the gangster scratches his chin with the back of his hand, leans forward and says, 'Go on, fat man.'

Clearing my throat, I begin, 'After your incarceration, Langra Sahab, your, ah, friend Juggan had been wandering the streets around the police station in the hope of your release. As you know, she's devoted and dutiful but she's not God's goat—'

'God's cow—'

'It so happens she saved me from a group of Afghans in the Cloth Market, and since I owe her my life, I have been taking care of her in your absence.'

'You mean she's taking care of you.'

'Well—'

'Have you fucked her yet?'

'Sorry?'

'You haven't, have you—'

'I'm here to tell you that she's safe—from the streets, from the police.'

'Is that right?'

'I would like you to call off your men.'

'Is that right?'

'That's right.'

'What do you offer?'

'My word, sir.'

'And why should I trust you, fat man?'

'Because I like to think that like me, you are an honourable man.'

'An honourable man!'

'I understand you have to do what you have to do to survive.'

Banging his wrists on the table, Langra exclaims, 'I learnt to survive the instant I tumbled out from my mother's cunt! You think she raised me? She had four other mouths to feed, and my father, that son of a dog, came by once a year, high on hooch. He would beat her, fuck her, then leave. So when I was twelve, I smashed his face with a hammer when he was high, then distributed sweets in the neighbourhood. Do you think I would have turned out differently had my father loved me?'

'You made decisions.'

'I did what was required.'

'You were more decisive as a child than I am as an old man.'

'That's right, fat man!'

'I would like to bring to your attention that we are almost the same size.'

Langra grins, then grimaces, cocks his head to one side, then lunges at me. Toppling from my chair, I fall on my back like a sea turtle. 'Yes,' the gangster whoops, unfolding his strangler's hands to reveal a dead horsefly, 'but I am faster.'

As I peel myself off the ground, sore and wobbling like a zeppelin, the door swings open and the guards enter, braced for a fracas. It's an opportune moment to escape—Langra's hands might reveal my spleen next time—but before I turn on my heel and scurry into the harsh sunshine, tail tucked between legs, I tarry by the door a moment, hamstrung by the thought that nothing has been sorted, that the effort to secure the security of my lover, much like all my projects, has been inconclusive. *You had better do better than that, Cossack!* I tell myself. *You must do better than that!* 'With your permission, Langra Sahab,' I say, grasping the nettle, 'I would like to tell you a joke.'

'What?'

Taking a deep breath, like a conductor before a concert, I recite one of Pinto's gems: 'So when a horsefly begins bothering this chap, another chap says, *You know these things swarm around horse's arses.* The first chap protests: *But I am not a horse's arse.*'

Langra stares at me, poker-faced, leaning in as if he will lunge again if the punchline is not up to snuff. '*You can fool me,* came the reply, *but you can't fool the horsefly!*'

There is deafening silence, save gaseous gurgles in my gut, then Langra laughs riotously. 'Mota theek thak hai!' he hoots, or *You're okay, fat man!* When the guards join in like a Greek chorus, Langra roars, 'He's talking about you!'

Langra dismisses the guards for the second time and instructs me to sit down. 'I might be an honourable man,' he begins, 'but I cannot give you something for nothing.'

'What do you want?'

'You know, I have heard of your father—everybody knew who he was at one time—but nobody has heard of mine because he had nothing, he was nothing. Nobody would have known who I am, but I worked hard, worked with what I had: my fists and my wits. You think of me as a bad man, some beast, but ask anybody in Lyari about me. They will tell you I do work for them. You think the government does anything for us?'

'You are a social worker?'

'I solve problems: if there is injustice in my area or if somebody is in need of employment, accommodation, if there are issues with water connections or electricity—'

'I have electricity problems—'

'What have you done for anybody else?'

'I take care of my ward,' I reply, stoutly, erroneously, 'my brother's children—'

'I made something of myself, and here you are now, a nobody, performing for me like a monkey.'

'I am an intellectual!'

'What do you have now, fat man?'

Shifting in the seat of the chair, I mumble, 'I have my books, my work ... my garden ... my garment dyeing—'

And suddenly, I am Archimedes in the bathtub—suddenly, I realize I have something more tangible to offer than my thoughts. But if I do not make a cogent, compelling case, he will surely dispatch his goons after me for hello hi, salam dua. That's how it works, that's why Hawkeye suggested an escort. 'A thousand years ago,' I begin, pulse racing, 'the great Ibn Khaldun wrote that a civilization, like a family, has a life. The life of a civilization is about three generations, give or take a generation—'

'I do not need some dead Arab to tell me that.'

'I am at the end of a cycle, but you have your life in front of you—'

'That is right—'

'But you will always be known as a gangster—'

'Watch your words—'

'A thug—'

Slamming his fists on the table, he roars, 'Enough!'

'Forgive me, Langra Sardar—'

'I swear I will pull out your tongue and strangle you with it!'

'I am just trying to make a point—'

'What point?'

'What if you were to become a legitimate businessman?'

'What are you on about, fat man?'

'Allow me to explain: I own a garment-dyeing operation that spits out money every month, good money. I do not have much interest in it at this age, but I could sell it to you for a discount. I am proposing something for something: the business for Juggan.'

'But I can snatch it from you. I can snatch her, kill you, kill her.'

'You can kill whoever you like but we will all be dead soon, some faster than others. I am an old man. I will be gone soon. What good will I be to you then? Think about the future—you cannot fight forever. Think about your mother—what did she want for you?'

'Leave her out of this,' he mutters, but I can tell by the tilting of his helmet head, the tapping of his fingers, that Langra is listening.

Standing up, I declaim, 'If you are an honourable man, you will do the honourable thing.'

And leaving Langra considering the Trajectory of his Life, I stride through the musty corridors into the brilliant sunshine, having silenced one of the most powerful gangsters in the city.

ON THE BONA FIDES OF MANHOOD (OR RAZOR'S EDGE)

FELIS CATUS IS A singularly disagreeable species—haughty, lazy, capricious, ungrateful—most unsuited to human companionship. Whilst dogs guard the hearth, hunt game, tend sheep, lead the blind (and, as recent research in *Reader's Digest* suggests, sniff out cancer and other seismic events), cats spend the day licking their funky orifices, rubbing against animate & inanimate objects, and chasing the winged ants that appear after the rains. Only sovereigns as profligate as the Pharaohs could have been responsible for subjecting mankind to such wretched creatures. Jugnu's mangy cat bites the hand that feeds it. I have seen it myself, and that's not the worst of it.

One afternoon, I gift Papa's sterling silver mother-of-pearl shaving kit to Bosco, reckoning if he shaves regularly, twice a day, he can manage a nice even patch of growth to replace his trademark parentheses. *If you look like a man*, Papa once told me, *you might behave like one*. I demonstrate the proper technique as best I can, even if I only shave every blue moon, stropping the blade against a leather strap, dipping it into a mug of hot water & Dettol, then frosting the badger-bristle brush with cream. Bosco watches me like I would watch Papa, chin nestled in the crescent of his palms.

When I hand the razor to him, he exclaims. 'Boy, oh, boy!'

'Mano a mano,' I say.

'Like this, Uncle Cossack?' he asks.

'No, like this,' I reply: 'Hold it at a thirty-degree angle. Put two fingers on the tang—this is the tang. Yes, like that…'

As I observe his technique in the mirror, I glimpse an unholy spectacle: a triangular pile of excreta that recalls a slice of moist chocolate cake in the bathtub behind us. 'Jugnu!' I holler in horror. 'Jug-noo!' Arriving at the scene, she laughs.

'So?' she says.

'So!'

'You never flush after you piss.'

'Why should I waste water?'

'We all have bad habits—'

'I will no longer abide that infernal cat!'

'You need to atone for yourself,' she laughs again.

'I have been atoning for myself all my life!'

Marching out in a huff, I head to my refuge, the vegetable patch, barefoot, trousers rolled up to the ankles.

THE SOIL, RICH, WET and wormy, is pleasing to the sole, but the plot is in a pitiful state: the rains have swept the beds away and saplings lay strewn hither & thither. Only wild mushrooms sprout in the shade.[153] The first order of business, then, is to turn the soil, an exercise that demands stamina at the best of times, and the tap water is like tea today—I can fry an egg on my head. Mercifully, Bosco appears before I collapse, exchanging his parasol for my spade. Digging in, he says, 'Can I ask you something, Uncle Cossack?'

---

153. When I was seven, the sous-chef poisoned me, sautéing up wild mushrooms from the garden. Since I was too scared to tell Papa, I told Barbarossa, major-domo, who took me to Civil Hospital where my stomach was pumped. When we returned, Barbarossa threw the sous-chef out on the street. I've never had mushrooms since, but if I happen across the odd growth in the patch or, for that matter, the tinned variety at Agha's, I do wonder what happened to that poor, loutish sous-chef.

'Ask me anything, my boy.'

'Is it better to be like, I don't know, Socrates or Sam Spade?'

'There was a time when I would have been inclined to advocate the former, but I have been reconsidering the proposition. It's not a binary consideration: a thinking man who does not act is useless, and a man of action who does not think is no better than a thug.'

'I want to go home to help my mother.'

'You will soon,' I say, 'but you know you always have a home here at the Lodge.' The assertion is at least half true—I have been peddling half-truths all day: I told Jugnu earlier that I sorted matters with Langra, neglecting to mention that I proposed a business transaction to a gangster. Who is to say that he will not commandeer the property, settle the matter through the barrel of a gun?

'I want to become a man of action, Uncle Cossack.'

'Then let's make compost!'

We have not read together or taken our evening walks since our return from the Interior but, I reckon, at least we can tend to our roots. 'What do I have to do?' Bosco asks.

'I need you to collect cardboard, tea bags, eggshells, fruit, vegetable scraps and weeds, leaves, uprooted saplings, newspaper, chicken manure—'

'Chicken manure?'

'Cock droppings should do. Ask Barbarossa. Cat manure won't—that creature is absolutely useless.'

As soon as Bosco embarks on the scavenger hunt, mouthing the required items under his breath, I stretch across the deck chair in the shade of the eaves. And when I shut my eyes, penumbral flowers blossom before me—voluptuous geraniums, gardenias, moth orchids—and beyond, over the horizon, I can sense a golden sea. I could be anywhere in that moment—the South Pacific, San Remo, Ceylon—and anyone: a botanist, a sailor, a monarch (recall that after the occupation of the Great State of Hyderabad in '48, one of the mightiest leaders in the world set sail for Australia to till the land).[154] I might not be a king, but I could follow him Down Under.

Floating on the gentle wave of the reverie, I experience a tickling sensation—a spider web adrift, the wings of a butterfly—but as I lazily swat the air, my fingers graze against flesh, possibly, and rather unexpectedly, a bosom. Opening one eye, then the other, I find Badbakht Begum leaning over me in a floral kaftan, fragrant hennaed tresses unravelling over the ivory crest of her ample chest. 'I didn't realize you were so forward.'

'One reaches for low-hanging fruit.'

'There you go,' she says, popping a fleshy fruit the size of a ping-pong ball into my mouth.

'Prunus!' I choke, spitting out the pit.

'You've lost weight. You're looking good. How did you manage?'

'Dengue. You should try it. What are you doing here?'

Settling on the ground, she replies, 'I brought some fruit for the house.'

Whenever Mummy's cousins-in-law would turn up, Papa would mutter, *The cows have come to graze*, for Badbakht & Gulbadan have famous appetites, especially for exotic fruits. Since there was never much left over, I compensated with milky Bengali sweetmeats—ras malai, rus gullahs, sandesh[155]—undoubtedly contributing to my blood sugar. I have always suspected that Badbakht has been making amends since. Gulbadan, on the other hand, does not seem to care.

'We don't see your sister anymore,' I say.

---

154. The project would turn out to be a disaster of epic proportions. Tending to the earth requires innate talent, but 'the gods taught him neither to dig nor to plough, nor any other skill.' Nobody can say that about me.

155. For those who do not know, sandesh, essentially a curd, is so sumptuous that even the gods devoured it by the kilo—it figures prominently in the Ramayana. But mere mortals like me have oft enjoyed it, and then some.

'She plays bridge at the Gymkhana five nights a week with bachelors and widowers.'

'If she were to find a man at this age, it would surely augur Judgment Day.'

'Don't be mean, Abdullah.'

'Tell me, sweetheart, after all these years, the passing of the elders, the family's virtual dissolution, why do you still visit the Lodge?'

'I have a history with this place, Abdullah.'

'There's history elsewhere as well.'

'Your mother was the loveliest person I've known—her door was always open for us. And she told me before she passed to look after her youngest son.' Although I can appreciate the imperative, although I can imagine the scene—Mummy grasping Badbakht's hand on her deathbed—I wonder why I was excluded from the arrangement. I need looking after as well. 'Of course, I also love the children.'

'They're wonderful, those Childoos—'

'There's also another reason, one you should discern for yourself—'

'Why didn't you ever tell me all this before?'

'You're so busy with yourself, you never notice anything else.'

'You might have noticed that I might be homeless soon.'

'If you ask,' she says, standing up, brushing her ample rump, 'somebody might take you in.'

As she strolls off, buttocks swinging in the kaftan, I consider calling her back—*Listen!* I could say, *What do you mean?* or *Another plum please*—but Bosco returns, bearing two fetid plastic bags, announcing, 'This will be the best compost in horticultural history!'

'Well said!' Hoisting myself out of the chair like a cripple—my foot has fallen asleep—I stumble to inspect the contents. 'And a job well done!'

WE GO TO WORK—digging a shallow ditch (not unlike fashioning a grave for a cat), before carpeting the bed with straw and twigs and twine. Depositing the contents of one of the bags like treasure, I explain, 'You have to layer the wet and dry material alternately.'

'Like compost cake!'

'Exactly, Bosco, exactly!'

By the time the throaty azaan rings in the violet sky, the task is more or less complete, and there is always tomorrow. Lumbering barefoot towards the gate, sweaty, muddy, and reeking like cut onions, I spot the bhutta-wallah stationed across the street, blistering cobs over charcoal. When I cry 'Oye!' over the traffic, he runs over with a nice long specimen, brushed with lemon, clumpy salt and red chilli powder.

Biting the soft kernels, I feel right, feel whole—I reckon I can even toss the cob into the compost pit, the cherry on the cake so to speak—but just then, two wild-eyed bounders materialize beside me like Ateed and Raqeeb. Grabbing me by the arms, one snarls, 'If you do anything untoward, you will be sorry.' A white Suzuki with a cracked headlight pulls up kerbside and I am shoved in. The cob drops.

ON A CONSPIRACY OF THIEVES

(OR SAVING THE DAY)

SOME MIGHT RECALL THAT the potato-chip king was kidnapped for ransom from the vicinity of Cosmopolitan Society in '93. The family was told that if they involved the police, the victim would be shot. In any case, the police were not to be trusted then. A few years earlier, however, a retired justice (whom we all knew from Garden) and several stalwarts from the business fraternity founded what might be characterized as a Gentlemen's League of Crime Fighters. The man on the ground wore large spectacles and trousers across the stomach, but was sharp as a knife and hard as a hammer.[156] Within twenty-four hours, he retrieved the victim from a rented house in Metroville and, within a fortnight, the entire gang was hunted down and put away. By the turn of the century, the Gentlemen's League had contributed to dismantling the infrastructure of kidnapping in the city. The city would experience a renaissance thereafter—plays, concerts, art exhibitions, film festivals were advertised on the cramped poster board at Agha's Supermarket. But then the detritus from the Wars in the North—guns, germs,[157] goondas—began flowing downstream again. I am neck-deep in it.

156. Some compare him to the comic book character, Batman, and as with Batman, some allege vigilantism.

157. Few acknowledge that polio was eradicated in the city, in the entire country, until the brilliant Yankee plan to disguise spies as vaccinators. Meanwhile, Yankees claim vaccinations spread autism. Brilliant!

Wedged between two bounders smelling of cowhide, I am terrified—I do not want to spend my last days amongst the barbarians in a squalid quarter furnished with a mattress, prayer rug, and a pair of sponge slippers too small for my muddy feet. I want to die at the Lodge, on my bed, but not yet; there is much to be done: securing patrimony, matrimony, Bosco's security, The Mythopoetic Legacy of Abdullah Shah Ghazi (RA). I need to impart some choice wisdom about life to the Childoos: (1) Avoid toffees—we have sugar in the family; (2) Self-discovery is key to discovering the world around you; (3) Don't watch too much TV, especially the morally-dubious-if-not-bankrupt Tom & Jerry variety. I need to throw a going-away party with balloons and curlers and a big band, the Caliph of Cool strumming dudduddaada-da-da-da, duddud-daada-da-da-da.

As we hurtle through traffic, however, I wonder how long I have left: hours, days, a week? Who will save me—there are no gentlemen anymore—and who will pay the ransom? The Major? Comrade Bakaullah? Babu? Badbakht Begum? And where on earth is Tony? Those who can, will not, and those who will, cannot. When the announcement of my demise appears as a boxed advertisement in the paper—PRAYERS FOR ABDULLAH K. AFTER SUNDOWN—people will turn the page to read about the Bumper Cotton Harvest or the Demise of Field Hockey.

I am certain that the kidnappers are Langra's goons—he must have issued directives from the confines of Central Jail—but we do not seem to be headed into the narrow gullies of Lyari. As we skirt the grounds of Holy Trinity Church, past the moustachioed dwarf who sells balloons, I decide to speak up. What does it matter—if I am to die, I reckon, I die. When I ask, 'Where are you taking me?' the driver, a bald chap with a pinched face, glances at me in the rear-view with quick, slanted eyes and replies, 'To hell.'

Preparing for a long, bumpy ride, I rearrange my rump, but before I find an angle of repose, the Suzuki swings into the parking lot of a familiar block of flats off the thoroughfare to the airport—a curious turn of events. Taking in the Art Deco façade of Rimpa Skyline, defined in part by the stacked, magenta, rectangular balconies, I am reminded of my affair with Khaver decades ago. For all I know, the spectre of my lover haunts the paan-spattered stairwells; for all I know, she has conspired with the Cosmos to keep me captive for the remainder of my wretched life.

Pushed out like cargo and shoved up the stairs, I find myself standing in a vacant flat with freshly painted parrot-green walls, surveying the surroundings like a prospective tenant. There is a broom cupboard on my left, a fusty kitchenette to my right, and a creased tin of 'Luxury' emulsion paint lies next to a sunken ottoman: the only item of furniture in plain view. The windowpane at the opposite end is opaque with grime, and dust salts the cold floor under my feet. I expect Langra to appear any moment, snorting like a boar, pointing the barrel of a shotgun at my chest and demanding the dyeing business. But after quick, hushed discussion, I am thrown into the sarcophagus-sized broom cupboard by the kidnappers. I ought to bellow, bang on the door, but feel nauseous, faint. I see pink snowflakes float before me, then the paint fumes render me unconscious.

I CANNOT BE CERTAIN how long I remain trapped—minutes, hours, days—but when I come to, I find myself propped up on the ottoman, and as my head spins, the driver wheels in a wizened character with the mien of a marionette. When he glowers at me, head angled to the side, hands folded between the thighs, I realize that I have not been kidnapped at all—I have not been bound, blindfolded, held at gunpoint. No, I am hostage to a different but no less troubling situation. 'You are who?' he asks.

'Sir, sir-sir-sir-sir,' I stutter, standing up.

'Who is this?' he asks no one in particular.

'Abdullah, sir,' I reply, 'your brother, sir.'

The last time I met my brother must have been during the Chernenko Era, and like Comrade Bakaullah is now, Chernenko was famously frail, friable towards the end, wheeled to Politburo meetings, the lavatory. Like a dissident, I have eluded Comrade Bakaullah as long as I can, but now there is nowhere to go. 'You are a big mess,' he observes.

Scrutinizing my mud-caked toes, overgrown toenails, my paan-wallah attire, I ask, 'You are well, sir?'

'Do I look well to you?'

'No, sir.'

''Thou must be emptied of that wherewith thou art full...'

'*Sir?*'

'Sit down,' Comrade Bakaullah orders.

'I would rather stand, sir.'

'What?'

'I prefer to stand.'

'Speak up, man!'

'*I will stand!*'

'You will sit!' he commands. There is a dastardly conspiracy to seat me on low furniture—the Major, presumably absent on account of his spondylosis, must have something to do with it—but what to do? 'Your birth was difficult,' Comrade Bakaullah starts, 'you were born upside down. You do not know but you should now: your mother nearly died in delivery.'

The news hits me like an anvil: I've always believed that I emerged into the world like everybody else, feted with bouquets, fawned over by family; I imagine Mummy, ruddy, cradling me in her arms, gazing at me with wonder; but perhaps I am mistaken on all accounts; perhaps, I am fundamentally misconceived. I feel giddy, teary. And Comrade Bakaullah continues relentlessly: 'We hurt most those we love. You have hurt me, but I will not bear a grudge. I am an old man. I am dying. I want to settle my affairs.'

'I understand—'

'Seek not to understand what you believe, but believe that you may understand.'

'Sorry?'

'I am fair and forgive you: I am willing to drop all cases because I want the best for you, the best for us all.'

'Yes, sir—'

'We have collective obligations.'

'No doubt, sir.'

'Then you will leave the Lodge.'

'How can I, sir?'

'Speak up, man!'

'*Where will I go?*'

When Comrade Bakaullah gesticulates with matchstick fingers, the driver opens the door of the adjacent room. 'Your books are here,' Comrade says. 'They took care—they are professionals.' The kidnappers, I surmise, must be local employees of my brother's transportation & logistics business. 'They will bring the remainder of your possessions here, gratis,' he continues, 'and the place will be spic-span.'

'Spic-span,' I repeat.

'You will remember that I read widely once. I read until my vision blurred. I have read everything that is worth reading, but after the tragedy I found there was nothing in books but words. Words alone cannot sustain us. We have a higher calling. You will come to realize. You will do what is right.'

I would like to argue that notions of right and wrong are contingent, but feel weak and winded. It's not just the fumes or the inevitability of displacement but also the disclosure that I almost killed my mother. As Bakaullah prattles about Light & Darkness, the Universe & its Vastness, the room begins to spin again. 'In the end,' I hear the old man say, 'we must account for ourselves.' A document is handed to me titled Letter of Relinquishment. 'Everything must be written down. Give him a pen.'

As I sign my life away, however, I am blinded by coruscating Christmas lights—red, yellow, green—then darkness sweeps over me like the sea. Carried by molasses waves, further and further from the shore, a tree felled by a sudden squall, I flail, wail, call for help, but who can hear you on the open sea except the gulls? Gradually panic gives way to anxiety, anxiety to resignation, a certain equanimity. I find myself yearning to drift into the horizon. Before I know it, however, I am seized by invisible currents, an eddy and, in the end, yield to the inevitable: the frigid seabed, the open mouths of writhing hagfish—the fate of fodder.

WHEN I COME TO for the second time that evening, I am sprawled on the floor. 'Sit him up!' Comrade Bakaullah yells. 'Give him the Frooto! The straw, where's the straw?' I spit out the first gulp with my dentures and dignity—the cloying mango drink tastes like brine. 'Are you okay?' my brother asks. Dribbling juice from the side of my mouth, I nod, cognizant that my brother just saved my life—if not for the Frooto I would have undoubtedly lapsed into hypoglycaemia.

Just as I gather my wits, a brigand sporting a red knit-scarf bandage across the face barges in with a shotgun, shouting, *hands up-hands up*. It's the damnedest development. Is he, I wonder, one of Langra's goons? Corralling the movers against the wall, he surveys the room with piercing kohl-rimmed eyes, and I swear he winks at me.

'What is this?' Comrade Bakaullah thunders.

'Chup kar, buddhay!' gnarrs the gunman, or *Shut up, old man!*

Clutching the handles of his wheelchair, Comrade Bakaullah screeches, 'You dare talk to me like that! I will have you hung upside down!'

The brigand takes a menacing step towards my brother, but before any bloodshed can occur, Tony appears, swish-swishswish, followed by Bosco, trilby fixed on head, and Jugnu in flamingo pink. Darting to my side, she cries, 'What have they done to you?'

The mise en scène certainly suggests drama, violence: I lay slumped, shoeless, insensible, surrounded by brutes, my dentures in a puddle of spit on the floor. 'Why did you bring the boy?' I mumble.

'He followed the Suzuki in a rickshaw and I phoned Tony—'

'Who are you?' Comrade Bakaullah yells.

'His brother!' Tony proclaims.

'As am I!'

'Bakaullah Bhai?'

'Tony?' Raising an arm like a beggarman, he cries, 'My boy!'

Tony rushes to Comrade Bakaullah and kisses him on the head. 'It's been so long—'

'You have never thought to ask how I am all this time?'

'Sorry, sir—'

'What?

'I said, I'm very sorry, sir.'

'Speak up, man!'

'*How are you, sir?*'

'I cannot walk, I cannot wash myself. My body is useless.'

'That's very tragic—'

'Life has not been kind to me, but I had great plans for you. What are you doing with yourself?'

'I've become a farmer, sir.'

'Too bad,' Comrade Bakaullah says, shaking his head so vigorously that it seems it might roll right off.

'Oh, it ain't that bad—'

'Tell me: do all farmers have gunmen these days?'

'Sorry, sir,' Tony exclaims, ordering the gunman to leave the room. 'Forgive me, sir—Maggu meant no harm. But with all due respect, sir, this is an unusual situation.'

'What situation? There's no situation! Tell him Abdullah!' I try to reply but only manage a wheeze.

'He's lying,' Jugnu snaps. 'Abdullah was kidnapped. Bosco saw it. Tell them.'

The boy takes a step forward, solemnly, stoutly, doffing his trilby and pointing to the movers. 'I saw them take him away.'

Waving his arms, Comrade Bakaullah squawks, 'Who is this chokra?'

'I am Abdullah's lover,' Jugnu declares.

'Lover?' Bakaullah asks nobody in particular. 'How dare you come between family?'

'I know gangsters,' Jugnu retorts, 'and gangsters behave better than you.'

'I saved his life!' Comrade Bakaullah yells. 'Get him out of here!'

Grabbing Jugnu's wrist, I mutter, 'No.'

'Woe is me!' cries Comrade Bakaullah. 'You choose outsiders over family!' Turning to Tony, he pleads, 'Please do something. I am a dying man. I just want to talk, spend time with family, settle my affairs. Tell me, is it wrong? Is it a crime?'

As Tony considers the request, his portable telephone rings.[158] 'No, sir,' Tony replies, 'Excuse me, sir. I gotta take this call.'

'So let's talk over tea and patties, chicken patties—those flaky ones from Café Grand.[159] It will be a reunion,' he chirps, as Tony ambles to the stairhead, 'a proper homecoming, my treat!'

---

158. I believe his ringer sounded the theme music of the *Mission Impossible* serial—it's astonishing, modern technology. But then, I understand that portable phones broadcast films and play songs these days.

159. Unbeknownst to him, Grand has long closed. One fetches patties from the bakery at the Parsee Institute or Misquita Bakery. I don't have the stamina anymore or else every Easter I would queue outside for their famous Hot Cross Buns.

Swooning like a fakir on the floor—I hear Tony say, 'Yes, honey … no, honey … everything's all right, honey'—I notice the contract lying by the foot of the driver. 'Quick,' I whisper to Jugnu, 'grab it,' but she makes for my dentures instead. 'No,' I cry, 'the papers!' But it's too late: the movers seize her by the arms and pin her against the wall. 'It's over,' I mutter, 'we're done,' but then from the corner of my eye, I watch Bosco knuckle the driver in the sweetmeats, swipe the document with a single, sweeping gesture, and bound out the door like a stag. It's a command performance.

'Stop him,' cries Bakaullah.

As Ateed and Raqeeb scramble after Bosco, Jugnu pounces again, knocking them down like bowling pins. Turning to me, Comrade Bakaullah hisses, 'I forgave you, but what do you do? You forsake me! You forsook me when your sister-in-law died—'

Blood coursing, rectum trumpeting war, I cry: 'Where the hell were you when Papa couldn't feed or wash himself? Who was there with him in the end? Where were you when we needed you?'

'You blackleg,' he mutters, balls his veiny fists. 'You bastard.'

'I looked up to you once upon a time, Bakaullah Bhai—we all did—but you've changed: you might have become a good Musalman, but you have become a bad human being…'

At that instant, the contingent from the Interior troops back in, led fearlessly by Bosco. 'How did I do?' he whispers. 'A1,' I whisper in return, patting him on the back. The young man grins, rolls his shoulders: he knows he has saved the day.

Standing in the doorway, Tony quietly scrutinizes the stipulations of the document, shaking his head. 'It's a misunderstanding,' Comrade Bakaullah coos. 'To err is human; to forgive, divine.'

'No patties tonight,' I mumble.

'Tony, please. Please don't be like this. Don't leave me here alone.'

And turning our backs, we walk out—'This is not over,' yells Comrade Bakaullah—shoulder to shoulder.

VOLUME V

ON THE JOYS OF FAMILY LIFE
(OR LANDMARK DAY)

THERE IS A SENSE of occasion at the Lodge (even though the enemy has merely been thwarted) and the library has been restored (but much of my work is missing) for Devyani has accompanied her husband here for the first time. It's not quite the aura of a birth or birthday but everybody from the staff up is agog: Devyani is a bona fide beauty. Beholding her at the door, I kiss her on the forehead, proclaiming, 'Welcome, welcome!' like a ringmaster.

When Barbarossa returns with cake and patties, we sit in the parlour over tea in the finest crockery to discuss plans. Whilst our guests cannot be convinced to stay for a dinner party in their honour—Tony tells me that he must return to attend to matters of real estate—they agree to a family outing: I suggest a picnic and a proprietary tour of the city. 'Done and done,' Tony announces.

We all crowd into the Impala—Jugnu at the wheel, me beside, Bosco, Tony and Devyani in the back whilst Babu, Nargis, Maggu and the Childoos follow in Tony's Hilux—and head to Uncle Jinnah's Mausoleum. It's like old times: windows open, wind in the hair, hair in the wind, the smell of warm leather permeating our beings. The procession negotiates Britto Road to the sprawling hilly expanse of the mausoleum. Tiered, manicured lawns extend up the incline of the hillock to the white marble esplanade that supports the domed shrine.[160] One is always reminded that, in the epic clutter of the city, the compound offers rare vistas.

'There was nothing there but rocks when we were children,' I tell Devyani. Not long after Independence, we would stop to deliver food and blankets to the refugees with Papa, and later, Tony and I would cycle past—you could cycle anywhere in the city then—on our way to the Greenfields, our Jewish 'girlfriends,' observing the construction of the mausoleum. Upon its completion, I remember Papa remarking, 'A family gravitates around the father.' I didn't understand what he meant then.

I assume the mantle of Head of the Household at the picnic—a delicate act: I notice whenever Devyani or Jugnu beckons to the Childoos, winking, smiling, arms extended, Nargis, sitting angled from the spread, insists that they have more patties. As a result, they have enough patties to sustain them until winter. Although she circumscribes a circle with her finger—'We can play in this area only,' I hear her say—Toto manages to sneak over, negotiating tiffins and cutlery with great dexterity. 'You are whale,' he declaims, straddling my belly.

'Better be careful, child,' I say.

'Why careful?'

'The whale is a gentle creature—it only eats tiny planktons—but once in a while, the whale breaches.'

'What is breaches?'

'It leaps out of the water,' I say, 'like this!'

Whilst I attempt acrobatics on my back, Tony rhapsodizes about the joys of farming to Babu. I hope Babu develops an appreciation

160. The story goes that our founder's sister, Aunty Fatima, leaned on the government to nominate the Bombayite architect Yahya Merchant over a Brit. She always knew what she was doing. It's unfortunate, if not tragic, that the establishment marginalized her—our city, country might have been different had she been elected head-of-state. Imagine, just imagine.

for nature—the vegetable patch at least—though his variety is fundamentally incapable.[161] How do you put into words the sensation of grass tickling the sole?

Master Bosco, God bless him, knows all about it: stretching beside me, trilby tilted over forehead, hands clasped over chest, tan paws crossed, he takes in the afternoon like a gentleman. It occurs to me that I have never seen him sans socks, joggers; it occurs to me that I might not see his feet again. I want to tell him that I will miss him, sorely, but instead say, 'You're a brave young man.'

'The Lord helped me.'

'Providence has nothing to do with it—you believed in yourself, which is often more than I can say for—'

'What are you on about?' Jugnu interrupts.

Grabbing her hand, I sing that pop number that begins, 'Kinna sonna tainu Rab ne banaya'—*How beautiful has God made you.*

'You are very romantic, Abdullah Bhai,' Devyani laughs.

'We are but empty vessels without romance.'

'Hai, hai!' Devyani chirps. Turning to Tony, she asks, 'Now I know where you get it from.'

'I told you, I learnt everything I know from him,' Tony says.

'It's getting late,' Babu interrupts, uncomfortable with the banter. 'The children—'

'The children,' I insist, 'must pay their respects to the founder of our nation.'

Climbing up the steps, I cross the esplanade barefoot to the mausoleum, hand in hand with the Childoos. Our footsteps

161. Although the picnicking families, the merry gentry, appreciate the verdant lawns, they leave peels and crumpled Frooto boxes in their wake. There's no doubt that civic sense has to be inculcated, but who will do it & how? The Socratic Method? When I point out an errant plastic bag to a family of pink northerners, they stare as if I am mad, a farangi. Little do they know: I'm an original settler!

echo inside as if we are giants. When I raise my hands to recite a prayer under the enormous cut-glass chandelier,[162] my miniature cohort mimics the gesture. They insist on sitting in 'big blue car' with me after. There is no doubt about it: they are their uncle's nephews.

WITH THE PRETEXT OF passing by the sea, I lead the charge across town to the temple off Kothari Bandstand before Nargis can catch up—she is a staunch monotheist—but I am accosted by a stringy old man at the carved stone arch who declaims, 'Only Hindoos allowed.'

'Jeay Shankar,' Tony intervenes.

'Jeay Shankar.'

'Forgive him—he is not from these parts—but we are not visitors.' Wrapping an amicable arm around the old man, Tony discloses that his wife is Hindoo. 'Obviously, then, so am I,' he says. Pointing at his gunman, he says, 'And he is Hindoo as well.'

'What's his name?' the chap asks.

'Mohan. We call him Muggu.'

Gesturing towards me, he asks, 'And him?'

'Farangi,' Tony replies.

As he considers me, Guddu asks, 'What is frangy?'

'Franks,' I whisper.

'What is Franks?' he persists.

'Foreigner,' I whisper.[163]

---

162. It was, if memory serves me correctly, accorded by the Chinese. One hears, however, the Chinese are pushing another on us—one that is new and shiny, a necklace for a mistress.

163. Technically, 'farangi' is Persian for the Franks, a dashed scourge, like Walter the Penniless & Peter the Hermit—the Crusader Mendicant who slaughtered tens of thousands of Jews up and down the Rhine for the hell of it.

We are waved in after a brief recitation of the rules—'No shoes, no photo, no guns'—but just as we cross the threshold, Nargis catches up, calling the Childoos.

'My blood runs through them as well,' I say.

Turning to her husband, she exhorts, 'Do something,' but it's too late.

'Ta-ta,' Toto and Guddu wave like synchronized swimmers.

The steps lead down to a pristine chequered marble courtyard wafting incense. There is a giant green collection box in the middle, and a poster of the god of the Indus perched cross-legged on a giant yellow fish to the side. The children tug me towards the passage leading further into the cavern. 'Like the shrine of Abdullah Shah Ghazi a few hundred paces over,' I tell Devyani, 'Rateneshwar Mahadev is carved into a limestone cave said to open into the sea. Uncannily, the same infrastructure, the same mythology, informs the two sites.'

Except, of course, for the displays on either side—the fearsome Kali in her many-armed splendour, the depiction of Radha and Krishna's torrid tryst, not to mention the brass lingam inside the cavern, the statue of a certain Murti Baba lodged at far end. The Childoos, fascinated, keep asking questions: 'Why doesn't the sea come in, Chacha Jaan?'

'Magic, kid. It's magic.'

Tony sidles up to me as Devyani kneels in ritual prayer, flanked by Jugnu and a pair of squatting Childoos. 'You know, Abdu, this ain't over: Bakaullah will get the Major and the lawyers involved. You know the law's on his side, right?'

'I'm not worried—I have you now.'

'I got you out of that mess, Daddy-O, but this ain't a game you can win.'

'Why shouldn't your children play hide-and-seek in the garage like we did, climb the same trees, dig for worms in the same dirt?'

'Funny you say that: it so happens Devyani's pregnant.'

'*What?*'

'Shush,' he whispers, gesturing towards his prayerful wife.

Bowing my head, I pray as well—for Devyani, my niece- or nephew-to-be, for the Childoos, those crazy little Childoos, for our family: *picnics every Sunday please, or every other Sunday*—reckoning that if I pray with enthusiasm, somebody, somewhere, might just listen: Durga, Murti Baba, Abdullah Shah Ghazi (RA), or just my mortal relations.

THE SUN IS LARGE and red when we emerge, the sea glowing on the horizon like lava. Picnickers stretch across the rolling lawns of the park undulating below; children bob in a striped Jumping Castle at the end. I attempt ambling down with my nephews but Nargis leaps to their rescue, checking their extremities for cuts, bruises, signs of metaphysical trauma.

'Mama, mama,' Toto squeals, 'there are gods inside, and magic fish!'

Shooting a murderous glance my way, Nargis titters, 'Tauba-tauba,' as if the numina are Harbingers of Armageddon. 'Everything's a harbinger of Armageddon with her,' I whisper.

'Well,' Tony chuckles, taking me aside, 'I *have* taken up with a Hindoo, and you a transvestite.'

'What?' I exclaim, 'What did you say?'

Just then, Tony's portable telephone rings the *Mission Impossible* theme music. 'Bakaullah,' he announces, 'is dead.'

ON HOW TO CONDUCT A FUNERAL
(OR TIME TO SAY GOODBYE)

WE ALL HAVE EXPERIENCE with Death—mothers, fathers, wives, aunts, brothers-in-law, friends—but the death of a sibling is something like attending your own funeral. What is a brother if not a proxy for the self—a hamzaad? We wash the corpse for burial, a grim exercise made grimmer by discussion about the temperature of the water, speculation about the contents of the cadaver's stomach, this, that, the other. It has been an age since I have participated in the corporeal ritual, a procedure akin to preparing turkey for the roast, except the late Comrade's body is more quail than poulet: brittle bones bound in skin stretched and burnished by age. I sponge my brother's vacant, angular visage, quietly sob when he is dried and dispatched to the morgue, shrouded in a starched white sheet tied in large knots at either end.[164] I console myself like everyone consoles themselves—*he had a full life, he died peacefully, died in his sleep*—but cannot sleep well afterward. The roof continues to leak, that cat lurks in the darkness, and questions prick the conscience: *Did I deliver the coup de grâce? Did I kill my brother?*

---

164. The body was actually stowed at the Imambargah Khorasan. The procedure, all procedures really, is wonderfully efficient amongst our community. You don't have to think twice about any aspect.

The burial takes place the following afternoon, for it was too late for us dinosaurs to negotiate our ancestral graveyard the night before. There is further debate graveside concerning appropriate prayers, the positioning of the corpse, the contents of the pockets of those who place the body inside: when a contentious bespectacled uncle twice removed and twelve years my junior—we called him Uncle Sargum—raises the matter, I growl, 'It doesn't matter to me, it doesn't matter to him, so why the hell does it matter to you?'[165] Uncle Sargum happens to be in town from the United States of America, and these America Return Types believe they are evolved because they floss in the morning and use hand sanitizer before and after meals.

'Who are all these people?' Tony asks.

'Druids,' I reply, 'decoys.'

There are twenty, twenty-five souls—twenty, twenty-five more than will be present at my burial—including the movers. Bosco eyes my captors warily, but the bald driver who kidnapped me the other day falls on my chest, bawling. Who knows if he's swept by guilt or grief, but I reassure him with a pat on the back before handing him a bouquet of incense sticks to plant in the sodden earth that is shovelled atop the stone slabs. There is solace in ritual, the kabuki of last rites: you always know what to do. We wordlessly converge on Mummy's grave, scattering rose petals. We pray again, weep again, inhaling the balm of death.

When we totter back, the Major insists on hosting the soyem but I put my foot down: 'He was born at the Lodge,' I proclaim, 'and will be commemorated at the Lodge!'

'You denied him his right to the Lodge and now—'

'And now it's time to do him right.'

---

165. For the record, I do not, cannot descend into the grave—if I were to manage somehow, I would probably not make it out again—so Tony & Babu dutifully attend to the placement of the corpse.

AS SOON AS I return home, I phone my friend Zed, the editor of the biggest business daily, to place the announcement, then dial a reputable caterer, the son of one of the managers from the Olympus Days—'No problem, no problem,' he says as I delineate the inspired menu—and because I need to talk to somebody else, I phone the Caliph of Cool. After expressing his sincerest condolences, he asks, 'Aren't you relieved, man?'

'He had a tragic life, a tragic end.'

'You just worry about your end, banjo, but I tell you, I'm checking out next.'

'Australia?'

'Gonna rock and roll with the angels soon, play for my Maker!'

'You're not going anywhere without me!'

'You don't play nothing!'

'I clap—'

'Like a transvestite?'

'I think Tony told me that Jugnu's a transvestite.'

'Hoo-ha!' Pinto hoots. 'That's something else, man! You played patty cake with her?'

'She has cakes—'

'Cupcakes?'

'Small but—'

'Pastries, tarts?'

'Stop it!'

'There's only one way to find out!'

What to do? Discreetly explore the topography of her nether lands with my divining rod whilst she is asleep? What if I discover a bitter gourd in the brush? In any event, I have more immediate matters to attend to: the tent has to be pitched in the lawn, the chairs dusted, arranged in rows, the audio system set up for the presiding maulvi, and people keep dropping in on condolence calls. Cousin Gulbadan parks herself on the settee in the parlour, weeping as if she has lost her only son in battle. Badbakht's presence, on the other hand, reassures: whilst I sit sipping cup after cup of soapy tea, listening to my brother's praises by X, Y, and Z, she directs the tent-wallah quietly, efficiently—*yeh-nahin-woh, idhar-nahin-udhar*, viz., this not that, here not there—like the Lady of the Manor.

Clad in black, hair pulled back, Jugnu also plays her indeterminate part with certain élan. I watch her attend to an ancient matron who only speaks Gujarati and is blind in one eye. 'We come into the world without certainty,' Jugnu says, crossing her limber legs, 'and pass on without certainty.' I am particularly intrigued when I catch the Major's eldest son, that lothario, corner Jugnu in the kitchen. *She cannot be a transvestite*, I reckon—*the boy has a glad eye*. It doesn't really matter: no explanations are required, for nobody has asked about her and there is an unexpected crush.

Since Bakaullah had been an icon in Soorkha circles, a contingent of Communists show up in force, in flat hats and dark pants rolled up at the hem, reeking of warm smoke and exhaustion from protests against the state for a good half century.[166] Whilst I am of the belief that inequity has more to do with the Temperament of Man than the Momentum of History, it's not the time or place for forgotten contentions and I have to see to the larger contingent, the last of the Garden aristocracy: the retired justice, leaning on a cane, a mouse-voiced retired State Bank governor, the self-exiled hotelier. As the President and board of the Theosophical Society huddle in a corner, discussing the nature of reality with the Last Known Jew of Currachee,[167] an agile, bushy-browed octogenarian in a three-piece

166. The only one I recognize amongst them is the towering Sobo G.—ancient but unbent. Said Comrade once avowed, 'I am a three-headed monster: Communist, Hindoo & Scindee.'

167. Although known as such, he is not the last; those who remain exercise the Shia practice of dissimulation, viz., pose as Parsees, Christians. There were eight hundred registered Jews in the country when I checked last.

suit—'Life is all,' I hear somebody say, 'and all is life'[168]—Zed arrives with his subeditors, followed by the Brothers Ud-Din (Taqi, Fasi, Burhan), classmates, nemeses. They used to look up to us, literally and figuratively, and now as hard-nosed contractors, pioneers of nondescript residential blocks, look down at the entire city. I would wager that the carpet tycoon intent on the Lodge is their frontman. I would wager Hawkeye would know. I also want to ask him about the threat regarding public spaces, but the food is running out—*No problem, boss, no problem,* the caterer insists, shuttling the last of the canapés to the Sunshine Sweets people—and everybody keeps telling me that somebody called Rambo is looking for me. Who in God's name is Rambo, and why in God's name would he ask for me?

NARGIS AND HER ILK, aghast that the sexes have not been separated, lobby for zenana ad interim, and grouse about the presiding maulvi, a turbaned, teddy-bear-looking scholar with a doctorate in Comparative Religion from the University of North Carolina—a nonpareil, arguably as rare as hen's teeth. 'There are some fundamentals that are unchangeable,' he is saying, 'we all know what they are. But everything else should change and keep changing. Think of it as a spoke and wheel. Let us take the schools of law. How are the fifteen-hundred-year-old civil regulations of Baghdad, adapted to Islam by minds no different from yours or mine, pertinent here or now? We need laws for today, laws that govern technological research, emancipate women, but we fuss about the correctness of plucked eyebrows and the proximity of the commode to the sink! The great minds wrote treatises such as the *Fusus al-Hikam*, but what do we read now? *Bahishti Zevar*! Do you think the Prophet's (PBUH) wife,

168. I prefer the more elegant credo: 'There is no virtue greater than the Truth.'

Hazrat Khadija (RA), would have stood for such nonsense? We need an intellectual revolution, and we need it now.'

Just as I am about to sit—*If the Communists are listening,* I reckon, *everyone ought to*—a rough hand collars me from behind. It belongs to neither Communist nor Khoja, Gardener nor suburbanite, but a creature with streaked porcupine hair, face like a grenade, who growls, 'I am here for the dead.'

In a fit of panic—is he, I wonder, an incarnation of the Grim Reaper?—I offer him a passing tray of hors d'oeuvres. 'You must try the … the Bihari chicken satay.'

Popping one in his maw, he repeats, 'Dead do.'

'I don't understand,' I wince.

'Langra sends his condolences in return for the dead.'

'You mean the registry? The garment-dyeing business? But what of the municipal authority—'

'We've taken care of everything.'

Old Kapadia once told me that the principle of private land ownership is the Foundation of Capitalism, but Rambo does not seem to be interested in such vagaries—he is a man of concrete sensibilities. And I am a man who needs a garment-dyeing operation like I need a yo-yo. Scuttling up the stairs, heart pumping like a piston, I retrieve the file from my armoire, then scuttle back. 'What about the money?' I pant.

Snatching the papers, he snarls, 'What about it?'

Just then Tony materializes, minus Muggu.

'Where's a gunman when you need one?' I mutter.

'Aren't you the boxer?' Tony asks.

'Asia Cup, Gold Finalist—1997,' Rambo declaims.

'I knew it!'

'I was going to fight in the Olympics but they broke my foot.'

'You were very good.'

'The best!'

'Langra,' I interject, 'promised to pay and Langra's an honourable man, a man of his word.'

Raising his jersey before the biddies, the repo man bares his leathery belly to reveal a belt stuffed with tawny notes, reaches behind his waist, and hands it to me. 'One million.'

'But it's worth at least thirty—'

Pressing a dog-eared calling card in Tony's hand as if he has not heard me, he turns and leaves. 'Who the hell was that?' Tony asks.

'Thought you knew him.'

'Never came across him before in my life,' Tony smiles, 'but he's got a boxer's posture.'

'I'll wager that was Rambo.'

'You need to keep better company, Daddy-O—'

Just then a chap sporting a beret interrupts: 'Old men are like old cars: they need servicing.'

'You're a regular philosopher.'

'I am sorry about your loss,' says the mechanic—presumably, he has been watching, waiting—'but can you pay me?'

'Who else do you owe money to?' Tony asks.

'The toyshop, the bhutta-wallah, that swine—'

And on cue, Chambu materializes with his portmanteau. 'What a tragedy this,' he sniffles, 'what a giant he was!'

'You have a long life, Chambu—'[169]

'Verily, this has been a sign from the Almighty,' he continues as if he has not heard me. 'It is time we make decisions, Abdullah Seth, life and death decisions—'

---

169. It occurs to me that when one runs into somebody in Our Swath of the World after a casual if not causal mention, one says, 'You have a long life,' but abroad, one says, 'Speak of the devil.' In Chambu's case, obviously, the latter axiom applies, but one wonders why this disparity in discourse. And what about Rambo?

'I have made my decision, friend. You will be very pleased to hear that you have a new boss, a businessman of great stature. You might have heard of him: Langra of Lyari.' The disclosure renders Chambu speechless again. 'Good day, sir,' I mutter, 'and good riddance.' I am, as Tony would say, on a roll.

AS THE CANAPÉS DWINDLE, the crowd starts to thin. The Soorkhas, however, do not seem to be in a hurry. They continue debating the Right Way[170] and the legacy of Comrade Bakaullah, claiming, for instance, that had my brother not left the Left, he would have led them to 'victory after victory'—a tenuous assertion at best: the Left was long co-opted by that demagogue, so there was nothing left of the Left by the time it had to contend with the dictator. Nevertheless, I nod quietly, adhering to that age-old adage *De mortuis nil nisi bonum*, until a voice interrupts, enquiring, 'You going to drink tea all night?'

Turning, I find Felix Pinto standing, grinning. The Goans have arrived. Titus Gomes solemnly shakes my hand, followed by Bosco's mother in a teal blue blouse and skirt. 'I'm very sorry, Mister Cossack,' she says, kissing me on the cheek.

I too am sorry: I know she has come to take her son. 'God gives,' I mumble, 'God takes away.'

'I'm so grateful for what you have done for us, for Bosco. I don't know how we can ever repay you—'

'You can start by telling me your name.'

'Oh, I'm sorry,' she says, extending her hand. 'I'm Aline, Aline Braganza.'

'Then, Aline, you must invite me for dinner once a week, every week.'

---

170. In spite of our historic relationship with China—'As high as the mountains, as deep as the sea'—Trotskyites, for some reason, have always outnumbered Maoists.

'You must drop by!' Pot luck at the Braganzas! How marvellous! It would be like acquiring a new family! 'But you must know we've received our immigration papers.'

'Of course, of course,' I mutter. 'How can I be so forgetful?'

'I'm carrying my trumpet,' Felix interrupts.

I want to pin the old bastard against the wall, shake him like a rag doll, knock those dark glasses off his flat nose for the second time in his life, but instead proclaim, 'Then you must play.'

Repairing upstairs, Bosco, Jugnu, Tony, Devyani, Aline, Titus, the Soorkhas and I arrange ourselves on the veranda around the Caliph of Cool, who does not waste any time: whooping 'Hoo ha!' he snaps his fingers to kindle the beat for 'The Saints Go Marching In.' *Oh, when the fire begins to blaze, I want to be in that number…*

I try to cede to the Flow, as Tony would say, but the rip tide of anxiety keeps pulling me down: a few fenis into the night, I wrap an arm around Bosco's shoulders and whisper, 'You want to be a man of action? Become a doctor, son. You have excellent instincts in an emergency, a comforting bedside manner. Just don't become a writer—we're good for nothing!'

The young man gravely pinches his moustache in response. The growth still recalls the bristles of a frayed toothbrush but it will flourish in time. We, on the other hand, have run out of it. I want to tell Bosco that I love him, that he is the only son I have ever known, the only son I will ever know, but my tongue feels thick and I fear he will not reciprocate the sentiment; I want to stop him from immigrating, save him, do something, anything, but what to do? I produce his yo-yo. 'I believe this is yours.'

'I'm too old for this,' he says with a flick of the wrist. 'You keep it.'

Just then Badbakht, Barbarossa and the Childoos join in, following the music.[171] Guddu promptly hops into my lap, legs

171. I swear I can feel the djinn presence as well, a distant baritone humming, but perhaps it's Sobo or somebody else.

swinging, but Toto, a man of action, immediately starts mincing like a matador. Jugnu jumps in the ring and the dame can dance: Change-the-Lightbulb, Change-the-Lightbulb, Butcher's-Cut, Butcher's-Cut. Pulling Felix aside, I whisper, 'What do you think?'

'That child's a natural, man.'

'No! About her!'

'A bird in hand is worth two bushes.'

'What?'

'A bush in hand is worth two birds?'

'Are you drunk?'

'She don't have no Adam's Apple so you could be in the clear, but she could be hermaphrodite—'

Before the Caliph can expound other specious theories, the Major appears in spite of his spondylosis, *thak-a-thak-a-thak-a-thak*, ruddy-faced and raging, 'What's all this band baja?'

We all stop what we are doing—the hardened Soorkhas halt the Hopak Dance—anticipating drama, discord. Although I can wager that the Major put his brother up to the chicanery that ultimately led to his demise, I raise a glass and declare, 'We're holding a wake for our fallen comrade. Join us, sir.' Instead of bellowing *Nothing doing*, or *I'll sort you out*, as he is wont, the Major settles into a vacant chair and rests his cane. 'To Bakaullah,' I proclaim.

'To Bakaullah,' everybody cheers. 'Euoi, euoi!'

We are all together and it's all festal, but even after my last drink, I am acutely aware that I will be alone soon.

ON NOTIONS OF HONOUR
(OR THE BEGINNING OF THE END)

BEFORE MY BOON COMPANION and his wife depart for points north by northwest, before grand promises and red-eyed goodbyes, the dispatching of tiffins replete with our famous alloo bharay parathay and house pickles, before I am left to contemplate the world and my place in it, I ask Tony for Rambo's calling card, for I have hatched a Promethean plan in my head overnight. As my brother pats himself on the way out—keys, wallet, Snubnose Special—he slips the gangster's card to me which reads, MASTER FIXIT AC SALES & MAINTENANCE.'

"The hell you up to, Abdu?'

'Getting things fixed,' I reply, escorting him down.

'Yeah, well I got bigger eggs to fry.'

'Have some faith in your brother, brother.'

But when Rambo growls over the telephone, I feel pigeon-hearted. 'You know who I am?' he asks.

'Do you remember who I am?'

'You know what I can do to you?'

'Do you know what I can do for you?' I reply, girding my loins.

I hear him chewing on a toothpick. 'Meet me at Aat Chowk at eight.'

'How will I find you?'

'I will know when you are there.'

They say All Roads Lead to Rome but in Lyari all roads lead to Aat Chowk.[172] Statistically, only one in four rickshaw-wallahs venture into the warren of dim lanes after sundown. I sweat though the ride—the only establishment open for business is a hairdresser called New Balouch New Fashion—then sweat in a plastic orange chair on the pavement at a one-room roadside 'hotel' that only seems to serve clear tea with cardamom in miniature teacups. I scrutinize the five-storey ramshackle flats facing me, the clothes hanging on the balconies, the full moon above, in order to avoid the gazes of men with dangerous eyes. 'You lost, boss?' a voice enquires. Although a mere lad, stringy and not much older than Bosco, he sounds like a man to me.

'Just having a cup of tea.'

'He's here for the tea,' he laughs, addressing nobody in particular.

Whether he is bored, a born joker, a stool pigeon, I feel like I am at the schoolyard. Sometimes I suspect the problem is not the city; it's me. 'I'm meeting Rambo,' I ejaculate. 'Know him?'

Nobody accosts me after that—nobody, save Rambo. Pulling up an hour later in a charcoal Civic with tinted windows and a chassis that glows neon blue, he is accompanied by two Johnnies who do not appear to be air-conditioner technicians. One walks like a robot and sports wraparound sunglasses even though the sun has set, whilst the other wears a manicured beard and a shirt that reads, 'Peace,' across the chest, 'In the Middle East,' on the back. They sit down on either side of Rambo without exchanging pleasantries. 'So?' he gnarrs.

'I need a favour, Rambo Sahab.'

Leaning in, he says, 'Why would I grant you a favour?'

'I helped your boss, Langra—'

---

172. Tannery Road, Denso, Sheedi, Haji Pir, etcetera, etcetera, etcetera, etcetera. Italians might have called it Piazza Otto or Campo de Otto.

'I am running things now, and running out of patience. Do you want me to run out of patience?'

'Patience is a virtue,' I blurt.

'Stubborn, this one,' says Peace in the Middle East.

'He's like a balloon,' the other avers, 'and balloons pop.'

'I know you are a busy man, but I would just like to make you an offer of help before you pop me.' Rambo almost smiles. 'I have some friends who are being threatened by a bootlegger.'

'So?'

'I want you to put the fear of God in him.'

'You think I am a common thug for hire?'

'I think you can put the fear of God in people.'

'Have I put the fear of God in you?'

'I am an old man, Rambo Sahab—I am only scared of my conscience.'

'Stubborn, this one,' repeats Peace in the Middle East.

'Why should I help you?'

'After you met my brother at the Lodge he wouldn't stop talking about you and about the indifference we show to our athletes. Who remembers Bholu Pahalavan today?[173] You have raised the profile of this nation on the international stage but we are a nation that forgets: we lionize the dead but shrug at the living. My friend is the publisher of a very important newspaper, an English newspaper, and I am a writer, as you might know, of some renown. I am offering to write a fitting tribute to you: a full-page spread, an interview, with pictures. Do you have pictures?'

Rambo massages his nape. 'I have pictures.'

---

173. For those who do not remember, the great wrestler Bholu held the World Heavyweight Title, defeating Harbans Singh & Goldstein in the fifties and Henry Perry in '67.

'So you will help me?'

'I want to see the article first.'

'Done.'

WHEN I TURN UP at my editor friend Zed's office on Deepchand Road in the morning, he surveys me with owl eyes and says, 'You're crazy.' It is as if everybody has finally caught on. 'I run a business newspaper,' he adds. 'There *is* no sports section.'

I tell him that our families go back—they may not be amongst the original settlers but have become established Gardeners since—that we always allocated a portion of our advertising budget to their newspaper even though we had no need. All relationships have become fundamentally transactional, this for that, tit for tat. 'Moreover,' I continue, 'in these times, people like you and I need allies. Like this Rambo fellow. You understand? I don't know how you do it—publish a supplement, a tribute to our athletes, sponsored by tennis shoes—but do it.'

After a deep, soulful breath, he says, 'Affirmative.'

I interview Rambo on the telephone at home in the afternoon—he is pleasant and cogent like a radio broadcaster—and tell him to dispatch the photographs. Then I sit behind my typewriter and crack my stubby fingers, index, middle, ring, arrange and rearrange the papers on my desk—The Culinary Anthropology of the Subcontinent, The Abridged Timeline of Adjacent Metaphysical Epochs & Associated Environs, Notes on the Story of Man—devour a box of Blueberry Puffs, and smoke a wrinkled cigarette I find in the drawer. Although the formal journalistic mode of writing is not quite my cup of tea, Rambo's story gushes out like an open tap when I get down to it:

> Some men are born fighters. They fight to exit their mother's womb. They fight to make a place for themselves in the world. They fight because that's the only thing they know how to do.

Some men are forced to fight. They are teased, they are taunted by their peers. They are torn down and they build themselves again.

Rahim Balouch, a.k.a. Rambo, is one such man.[174]

I type through the evening, clack-clack, clackety clack-clack, ring—orchestral percussion!

When I'm done, I send Barbarossa to Zed with the copy, and drain a bottle of feni like a man who deserves every last foul drop, before passing out. When I wake, I call Rambo who tells me to meet him at his court at Aat Chowk. 'No,' I tell him. 'This time *you* need to see *me*. You come to Boast Basin. And don't keep me waiting.'

The street-side joint, adjacent to the Old Book Shop, is rudimentary—six carpeted charpoys arranged like boxcars—but offers barbequed udder, mint sheesha, and cold beer in stainless steel jugs from the wine shop around the corner. Since it's still early for dinner, the only customers present include a grandfather &

---

174. It continues:

He has been forgotten by us, by discourse, but let us remember that he represented our nation at the Asia Cup as a flyweight in 1997. He has been forgotten like our wrestling greats such as Gama & Bholu, our musical giants from Afzal Hussain Nagina Wala to Hamid Ali Bela, our writers, poets.

We are a forgetful nation. But if we don't understand our Past, we won't be able to negotiate the Future.

Rambo's future is not promising. He fixes air conditioners. Although more of a heavyweight now than a flyweight, he recalled his childhood to this scribe via telephonic interview. He was a slight sixth child born to a cobbler. 'There was no running water,' he said, 'and a drink of water was often dinner.' When harassed by bullies, he took refuge in a makeshift gymnasium near his home in the Ragiwara area of Lyari. 'What are you doing here?' asked a man named Jan Mohammed. 'I'm being hunted,' replied our hero. 'I can teach you to hunt if you like,' said his mentor-to-be. The rest, ladies and gentlemen, is history...

granddaughter quietly spooning chicken corn soup, and a couple of teenagers in jeans and T-shirts passing around a sheesha spout. Reclining on a tasselled pillow, I gaze at the sky, and the sky is like layer cake: pink on the horizon, violet in the middle and velvet blue above. The breeze carries the tincture of dead fish from the murky lagoon below, which the president once presumably planned to transform into a public dolphinarium.

When Rambo & the two Johnnies show up, the waiters stand to attention and other customers disappear—they must sense menace—but I parcel out copies of the published supplement like a monarch granting favours, farmans. The spread features a picture of Rambo as a gaunt nine-year-old in knickers, back against a brick wall; another, of his dramatic reincarnation as a welterweight, leaning into the camera bare-chested, brandishing gloves; and a recent passport picture with a pale blue background. As Rambo scans the material like a child with a new storybook, I ask, 'Do you want me to read it out?'

'You think we can't read?' Rambo asks. 'This one is matric-pass,' he says like a doting uncle.

On cue, Peace in the Middle East reads from the article out loud using his finger, translating as he goes along. Rambo leans in, head angled, brow furrowed, as if listening to a recitation from the Holy Book. They sit back after and nod to themselves. 'You understand,' Rambo announces. It's a grand compliment.

Snapping my fingers, I order four plates of kat-a-kat and a jug of local beer fut-a-fut. We pour ourselves tall tin glasses of the sharp amber brew and palaver like old friends about everything from the worsening municipal services to the imminent football World Cup: Langra, I learn, used to organize giant screens on the streets for the thousands of enthusiasts—one of his many magnanimous civic gestures—but now the responsibility falls on Rambo.

'You must come as our guest,' he says.

'You are too kind,' I reply. 'Please try some more of the kat-a-kat.'

'Brains,' one Johnnie remarks. 'Testicles,' says the other.

'Top notch,' Rambo chirps.

After wiping his tin plate clean with naan, Rambo dabs the sides of his mouth and passes around a thick hashish cigarette that tastes like bark and tickles my oesophagus. As my head swims in the fragrant smoke, he says, 'Let's go.'

'If there's space in the heart,' I chunter, 'there's space in the car.'

WE PILE INTO THE tinted Civic and pass quiet residential swaths, the police cooperative society, and a storefront advertising camel milk, before cutting from Belfast to Clarke Street. Disembarking outside the familiar, narrow, grey, four-storeyed edifice wedged between the surgical supplies store and abandoned lot I visited with Bosco, I raise my hand to beckon to an ice-cream-wallah, pushing his cart in slow motion—the tamarind flavour is divine—before remembering that this is not any Night Out with the Boys: Rambo & Co. retrieve weapons stashed in sideboards of the dicky and march in.

'What are you planning to do to him?' I slur.

'Fear of God is what you asked for,' Rambo whispers, flanking the door with the other two, 'Fear of God is what we will deliver.'

When I rap on the bolt-iron door of the third-floor flat, aware that I am participating in a crime, the hatch slides open and an eye materializes. 'A dozen,' I say, 'the usual.' As soon as the bottles slide out, Rambo shoves a pistol into the bootlegger's face and orders him to open the door. When he emerges—a hairy, gangly young man in a vest and jeans—Rambo strikes him in the face with the buttstock of a pistol. I watch the bootlegger cup his mouth, fall to his knees; I watch blood ooze out, teeth scatter like Chiclets on the worn concrete floor. As I turn away, Rambo hisses, 'You like throwing women, children out of their houses? What if I throw you down the stairs?' The man makes muffled, plaintive noises—*no-no, no-no, no, no, no, no*—and then there is a dull crack, a blood-curdling howl, and the door slams shut.

Clutching my watermelon head in a corner of the corridor, I tell myself, *It has to be done,* as mosquitoes drone relentlessly about, *there is no other way,* but I know I am no better than Langra, Rambo, the Johnnies: I do not have blood on my hands, but I have a blood-smeared conscience. Banging on the door, I plead, 'Don't kill him, don't kill him...'

When the door finally swings opens, Rambo stands in the frame, neck speckled with blood. 'We are professional,' he declares in English. 'We only broke his legs. He will never come back again.' As the Johnnies drag the limp body of the bootlegger by the arms, Rambo grabs a carton of feni. 'Help yourself,' he says, slapping me on the back. 'You look like you need a drink.'

As I shut my eyes like a child pretending to disappear, the only consolation in the penumbral darkness is the thought of facing Bosco and reminding him that he once said, 'If I can't put things right, if I can't do what I should do or must do, I'm no longer a good man.' But when I rap on the door of his flat, there is no response. Perhaps they are out, I reckon, or have retired for the evening. I rap again. I rap until my knuckles are sore.

It might be obvious to everybody but me: Bosco has left for good.

ON THEORIES PERTAINING TO THEODICY, ANTHROPODICY AND SUCH

THE HEADLINE IN AN evening standard the other day read: TREE KILLS BOY. Whilst the phrasing is maladroit, the incident tragic, it is an accident. Evil requires agency.

A man stranded on a desert island cannot do Evil. He can only be cruel to clams. Evil requires another.

The Capacity for Evil, like the Capacity for Good, is arguably innate: there are children who tear ladybird wings at age three[175] and those who let the creatures go after marvelling at them momentarily.

The most beastly of beasts—crocodiles, Komodo dragons, vampire bats, the great white—can be hungry, territorial, but not Evil. Only Man is. There was no Evil before him and won't be any after.

If there is a God then He might not be directly responsible for Evil (though dystheists would disagree), but there is no doubt that He is directly responsible for Man. One might ask, *Why did He fashion Man at all?* Why create a creature who possesses the capacity to wilfully inflict pain and misery on another?[176]

---

175. I've witnessed it myself: the Brothers Ud-Din, neighbours, nemeses, tortured insects willy-nilly.

176. A list of Bloody Swines in Modern Times must include the oft-forgotten Samuel M. Whitside, Marshall Bugeand, Mountbatten, David Shaltiel, Godse, Kissinger, Hassan Ngeze, Juvénal Habyarimana, Sankoh, Mullah Fazlullah.

Is Evil real, tangible, like a cat, or an idea, a concept, like infinity?

The Parsees might have been the first to acknowledge the relationship between Good and Evil: the supreme deity has to contend with Angra Mainyu, the Force of Darkness, but in the end Zoroaster has prophesized that Light will prevail. Wishful thinking?

Parsees ruled the Civilized World once upon a time but their numbers are down. It's too bad; save the adherents of Taoism, the majority of humankind does not really appreciate the Idea of Symbiotic Duality.[177]

Are notions of Good and Evil contingent? Is it wrong to kill one man to save one hundred?

If a murderous thug, thief, or paedophile resists his natural proclivity, is he nobler than somebody who is naturally kindly? The former makes choices. The latter simply follows his inclinations.

Is gangsterism fundamentally Evil or a natural function of the failure of the state?

Is Bosco Good? Langra, Rambo, Evil?

What about me?

---

177. Of the three monotheistic traditions, I believe only Islam's Malamati tradition does. As we all well know, the publicly pious are oft the most sinful amongst us. Malamatis, on the other hand, are oft publicly debauched. Said tradition emphasizes Man's piety as personal. I could not agree more.

ON THE PROVERBIAL DEVIL & DEEP BLUE SEA (OR THE LAST SAINT?)

SOMETIMES I FEEL JEALOUS of the cat. It's neither handsome nor particularly talented, adept only at severing lizard tails and catching the odd unhurried moth,[178] yet I feel a tightening in my chest when I happen upon Jugnu scooping the creature into her lap & stroking its furry jowls. I want to squeal when it shuts its eyes, purring extravagantly, an admittedly childish sentiment, one unbecoming of an intellectual, but one I cannot help—it's as if I am afraid that Jugnu has a discrete amount of affection, which if divided like a pecan pie or chocolate torte, will leave less for me. I swear that the feline is cognizant of the matter. Christened Sheikh Sahab by Jugnu for the white tuft under its chin, it's not particularly sage but is sentient: every now and then, it opens a turquoise eye to observe my pained smile, my nervous nod, and smirks.

There have been moments, occasions of levity rather than lenity, when I have found the cat crouched willy-nilly like a cheetah, stalking shadows, or sleeping on its back, head tucked in, paws folded over its chest. 'Admit it, Abdullah,' Jugnu has teased, 'you are becoming fond

178. So am I when pushed. If it could annihilate dengue mosquitoes or these insecticide-resistant cockroaches, become the proverbial Tees Maar Khan, that would be something—not enough, but something.

of the cat.' There is no doubt that Sheikh Sahab can strike fanciful poses but it also relieves itself in the tub once a week like clockwork. Consequently, I stridently deny any assertion that I am affected by the creature. Pulling Jugnu towards me, I kiss her on the eyes, neck, mouth, whispering, 'You're my only pussy.'

But only the cat has access to Jugnu's lap. Although I often attempt brushing across her nether region, especially at night when we lie on our sides in a cloud of beedi smoke, she inevitably turns or grabs my hand and kisses it before diverting my attention: 'How do you make perfect rice?' 'It's all about timing and proportion,' I reply like an ace chef. 'There is, you see, a science to steaming...'

Sometimes, I think, what does it matter? Love is Love, I tell myself—she is virginal, shy, traditional. (Besides, I have been suffering something like Athlete's foot of the groin.[179]) But each time I broach the matter of marriage, an undeniably traditional institution, she laughs or shrugs, expressing a gypsy sensibility: 'Mera kuch pata nahin?' viz., *Who knows about me?* or 'Mera koiee thikana nahin,' viz., *I have no station.*

Sometimes, I fall out of love. Sometimes we fight. One evening, whilst feasting on prawn masala and mutton ribs on the rooftop at BBQ Tonight, Jugnu shouts, 'Why do you blow hot and cold?'

'I don't feel like I know you.'

'Who knows anybody else?' she fires back. A dour, middle-aged couple at the adjacent table lean in. 'What are we but a series of impressions to each other?'

---

179. I suspect the condition is fungal, not just dry skin, causing me to scratch the folds of my crotch, but unlike cats, even fat cats, I can't simply bend to observe it. I suspect it has to do with the fact that I have stopped wearing knickers (the elastic bands have come undone). And since Bosco has gone—the lad could diagnose anything—I don't know what to do about it.

'I want to know, why have we not been intimate all this time?'

'You want me to strip now?'

The other diners must have complained because we are asked to leave soon after. I consider protesting—I know the proprietor, a scion of the Khans of Garden West—but it is time to leave: the ribs have turned to rubber. We laugh about it after, kiss, make up. Jugnu's shalwar remains tightly fastened throughout.

ANOTHER EVENING JUGNU INSISTS on the cinema. Although I might not care for Lollywood melodramas, one must necessarily defer to the demands of love. Sliding into a torn seat after the national anthem, I attempt to nap but it's chilly. I shouldn't have worn my Hawaiian shirt for the occasion—and Jugnu, keen on the lead, keeps digging into my side like an excited schoolgirl.[180] In an attempt to parry her elbow, I knock the popcorn into her lap. As I scoop the kernels, I can swear I brush against a fleshy bauble amongst the morsels.[181] Jugnu does not stir, but when the lights flood the hall at intermission she claims she has to buy beedis whilst I make for the washroom. Handling my member, I wonder, *Who is Jugnu? What is Jugnu? Firefly? Phantom?* before drifting out.

Since the fumes from the lorries on Bandar Road turn my stomach, I slip into the old Parsee Colony (past old Ankelsaria Lodge, Vareen Villa) and settle on a bench in the tidy park in the centre. Once upon a time, I celebrated animate spring festivities in the secret canton like a pagan, but spring has long passed—the dry, dusty wind from Quetta stirs—and the locals have long retired. I survey the sky,

180. One must concede that that squinty-eyed, mole-cheeked star, son of Christian silver-screen siren Neelo, is a man's man.

181. In passing, I must invoke that cryptic verse that goes, 'Materterae si testiculi essent, ea avunculus esset?'

hoping for a meteor or eclipse, some celestial event, a sign, but am left connecting the dots.

When the neighbourhood security patrol accosts me—Katrak Park, I am told, shuts at dusk—I scrape back to the cinema, but the show is over: the villain has been vanquished and the hero and heroine are presumably in bed. If only my story were so tidy. I dawdle amongst the motley cinephiles streaming out of the gate. I wait for Jugnu until the gates shut, then catch a rickshaw to the Lodge.

Barbarossa is waiting for me at home, smoking a hookah in the shadows. 'The cat killed my cock,' he announces. 'That rooster will crow no more.'

'The chickens have come home to roost,' I mumble. 'Where is Jugnu?'

'When she came, I told her you would be at the shrine.'

'Why would you say that?'

'Tonight is the Urs, my son,' he says.

Slapping my head, I exclaim, 'Then I must go!'

SINCE THERE IS EPIC traffic on the dual carriage between BBQ Tonight & Kothari Bandstand, I park in the lot adjacent to that mall, then set off on foot following the faithful seeking protection from oblivion. I consider stopping by a roadside fortune-teller to have cards picked by a green parrot but, I figure, what is fated is fated and I am on a mission: purchasing a plastic bag brimming with rose petals from the florists at the gate, I approach the boxy, blue-and-white striped structure, draped in beaded lights befitting the occasion.

A concourse of pilgrims stretch across the esplanade, picnicking & palavering, whilst the orthodox lean into strident hymns under a marquee set up on the western end. Surveying the crowd, I shed my slippers at the shoe station and head up the damp carpeted stairwell. The balm of sweat and incense pervades under the glittering dome—

the aperture in the back offers only momentary respite. I glance at the ever-moving spheres of heaven above, the Cimmerian sea below, then make my way to the gilded tomb to spread the petals and utter a prayer: 'Grant me peace, Jugnu.'

When I cross into the zenana, a custodian screeches, 'You are not permitted!'

'Who does not permit it?' I ask.

'*Sarkar!*' he declaims.

'My lord is God,' I cry, breaking free, 'my Lord is Ali (AS). Who are you to stop me?'

The women do not seem to mind me: heavyset matriarchs and maidens with bleached, bangled arms, and bonny girls with bows fixed in their hair all amicably make way. But Jugnu is nowhere to be seen. Before I can plot my next move, a familiar, flirtatious troupe of sari-clad transvestites hook arms to the courtyard around the back. 'You have forgotten us, Laddoo Mian,' they chirp.

'How can anybody forget you?' I twitter.

There is the smell of hashish in the air, and past the cave the chords of harmoniums stir the heart: the qawwals chant that modern masterpiece we all know: 'Sakht mushkil mein hain.' I sing along, 'gham se haaray huay,' viz., *We are in trouble, Lordy, defeated by despondency.*[182]

'You can join us,' the swarthier of two remarks, 'but you will only be allowed to clap.'

'Ladies,' I say, taking my friends into confidence. 'I need to find somebody in the zenana.'

182. There was a time when one would bump into Purnam Allahabadi at the shrine, professional chemist & the finest lyricist of our age—we all know that he penned 'Bhar do jholi.' Few know that he invited me to Lahore to discuss poetry & metaphysics every time we met, but I never made it and then he died. We all have regrets. We will all be dead soon.

'Come with us, Laddoo Mian,' they beckon. 'We'll take care of you if you take care of us.' When they help me up the steep steps to the roof, I scrutinize the darkened faces and call my lover. A small transvestite stands up, swinging tresses as if emerging from the sea, and purrs, 'I can be Juggan.'

'Take your pick,' another says.

'Come,' I beckon. 'I will fill the lot of you.'

And climbing down to the far corner of the courtyard, I purchase a cauldron brimming with biryani, as I have on occasion, then ladle the fragrant coloured rice onto tin plates for the gay troupe. 'Grant me peace,' I repeat each time I distribute the steaming alms, 'grant me Jugnu,' though I am not certain if the prayers of the delinquent, the dishonourable, are honoured in Our Causal Universe.

When I head back to the shoe station, however, I spot a silhouette in a tangerine costume loitering by the entrance. 'It worked,' I cry, 'it worked!' Jugnu flies towards me like a silver-screen heroine—hair open, lips pursed for a bright kiss. I hear violins and flamenco guitars over the drums thumping in my heart, but when she reaches me, she grabs me by the collar as if to shake me by my foundations. 'Why,' she demands, 'did you leave?'

'You are not the woman I thought you were.'

'You are not the man I thought you were!'

'I am not a saint!'

'I was not looking for a saint!'

'Come with me.'

'Dafa ho,' she exclaims, or *Go to hell*.

And as she turns away, there is a thunderclap like the Bang at the Beginning, the Clanging at the End—oh, it strikes, it strikes! What's that old ditty, *Merrily, merrily, life's a waking dream*? I find myself lying on the stairs groaning, 'I am fine, fine ... this happens all the time ... just need Frooto.' When I crane my neck to survey the surroundings,

I descry petals amongst shattered glass, twisted slippers amongst rubble, bodies strewn hither thither. *There will be a bed of fire,* I recall, *and blankets of fire over them.*

I am alive and want to live, but find myself negotiating the dead.

AFTERWORD

I KNOW HOW ENDS end. I read many books once. But as I wind up this volume, on life, death, and everything in between, I don't quite know how to go about doing it myself. As Uncle Cossack said, there's a difference between knowing and doing. Maybe nothing more needs to be said, nothing more needs to be done. After all, this isn't my work. I've played editor, but I'm no wordsmith.

They say that words can change the world. I don't know if Uncle Cossack's words will change the world, but they changed me. I was displaced as a teenager, and floundering. Uncle Cossack took me under his wing and guided me as best he could. It's rare in this 'savage, insensible, distracted age' for somebody to just care.

It's not that I didn't or don't. I tried getting in touch with him when I received the package but failed. It was difficult to go about it from Australia (although I did manage to trace Mr Kapadia). I was doubly determined after I completed the project, even if I knew I'd be setting myself up for disappointment.

During the holidays, I booked tickets to the city of my birth. I hadn't been back since I left, and my wife, Mary Anne, and the boys, my childoos, had never been at all. We stayed in a hotel near Rimpa. I hired a car and driver. I wanted to postpone the inevitable, so I worked backwards: I took the children to the temple first, then the mausoleum. As they ran around the lawns, I recalled picnicking there with Uncle Cossack. I was on top of the world then. I felt like somebody for the first time in my life.

One day, I took my childoos to the beach, another, to the zoo. The neighbourhood had changed. Walking from the zoo in the direction of the Lodge, I got lost. There were new apartment blocks everywhere. Just as the boys were getting antsy, I chanced upon the old roadside dentist, who pointed to a yellow high-rise with clothes hanging from the balconies. The Lodge had long been knocked down.

I was in a bit of a daze for the rest of the stay. Mary Anne suggested I see a doctor but what would a Panadol do? On Easter, she insisted we attend mass at St. Patrick's. There were thousands of parishioners, but I felt alone. I prayed and wept out of guilt.

After leaving the Lodge, I realized that Uncle Cossack had done so much for me, but I'd not be able to do anything for him. And the thought that we had been lying to him all along gnawed at me. What would I say if I were to meet him?

'The first year was difficult for us, Uncle Cossack. We lived pay cheque to pay cheque. Mum didn't readily find a stable job, and Grandpa played some gigs in bars but nothing came of it. His health deteriorated, and the year I went to university, he died of cardiac arrest. He lived a full, long life but...'

I found Mr Kapadia's obituary on the internet. I tried and tried but couldn't locate Uncle T. Maybe he finally left for Colombo. But before returning to Australia, I visited the shrine by the sea. It had completely transformed, resembling one of these new malls. Drifting around, I came across a hunched man in the back, smoking hashish. His eyes were bloodshot. He grabbed me by the arm and said, 'He comes sometimes at night, and we sit together and we laugh.' I kept asking him who, and he kept grinning. I waited by the entrance nevertheless. I waited until the wee hours. Nobody came.

Uncle Cossack once said, 'I don't have a head for science, but I understand that the world's made and unmade every moment each time you blink. It's all quantum. It baffles the mind but quickens the pulse: imagine a cataclysm, an earthquake or volcano spewing lava one minute, and the next it's as if nothing happened. Who says the dead can't be resurrected? Who says the city will nary be the same?'

There is such possibility in the thought. But such things are philosophical. I just wish I'd said goodbye.

—BB

A SOCIOCULTURAL GENEALOGICAL TABLE

Issac (PBUH)
s/o Abraham
(PBUH)

Sher Shah Suri
of Bihar
Ablest Pathan in history & ruler of the Subcontinent
(b. 1486 d. 1545)

Anees of Calcutta
(Mummy)
Legendary beauty & housewife
(b. 1906 d. 1971)

Ismail (PBUH)
s/o Abraham
(PBUH)

Ahl-e-Bayt
Family of the Prophet (PBUH)
(mostly d. 10 Oct., 680)

Abdullah Shah Ghazi (RA)
Patron Saint of Currachee
(d. ca. 800)

Lava/Lau (PBUH)
s/o Lord Ram

The K.'s of Thatta
Lohana clan that venerates Pir Sadr-ud-Din
(ca. 900)

Karimullah K. of Currachee
(Papa)
Business tycoon & proprietor of the Olympus
(b. 1895 d. 1978)

Hidayatullah
(a.k.a The Major)
Retd. Major turned real estate baron & President of the Rotary Club
(b. 1929)

Many wives, many children

Abdullah
(a.k.a. The Cossack)
Vice President, Olympus Hotel, turned gardener & intellectual
(b. 1940)

Sporadic, informal arrangements, at best

Rahimullah
(a.k.a. Babu)
Sullen boy turned IT professional at a Shariah-compliant leasing firm
(b.1951)

Guddu & Toto
(with Nargis the Opossum)

Bakaullah
(a.k.a. Comrade)
Communist turned founder of a logistics & transport LLP in the Bedouin Hinterland
(b. 1935)

Wife, progeny died in accident

Fazlullah
(a.k.a. Tony)
Ladies' man turned agriculturalist & outdoorsman in Scinde
(b. 1945)

Regular trysts with a number of ladies

GLOSSARY OF TERMS FOR THOSE ENGLISH-SPEAKING PEOPLES WHO ARE UNFAMILIAR WITH OUR IDIOMS

AS A translated Arabic acronym, *an honorific employed in service of the family of the Prophet (PBUH)*, but I don't speak Arabic.

bacha *A child, a kid.* I am, for starters, not a bacha any longer.

baithak Many houses in the Subcontinent traditionally featured a *sitting area*, sometimes covered, sometimes open, usually in the middle of the structure. One dined there, dallied, debated, dozed. The Lodge doesn't feature a baithak. The aesthetic that defines the Lodge was modern a hundred years ago.

bakwas *Bavardage, bovine faeces.* What else needs to be said?

balti A Brit visiting the city once was found pacing outside the loo by his host. When asked what was the matter, he neighed, 'There doesn't seem to be any water in the taps for a proper bath.' The host immediately organized a bucket of warm water and deposited it in the tub. The fellow paced some more. 'Thank you,' he averred, 'but that seems much too small for me.' When the water pressure is weak in the pipes, then one is compelled to take a balti, or *bucket*, bath. Note: In some parts of the country, you will also find *balti gosht*, or bucket-cooked meat.

band baja 'Band' is band—some usage is universal—but 'baja' can basically be applied to any musical instrument that is not a drum: a horn, a guitar, even an electronic synthesizer. Coupled, 'band baja' might be translated as *song and dance.*

beedi *A cheap cigarette, the shape and size of a slight lady's finger, wrapped in a leaf of* B. racemosum *and string.* It tastes like goat.

bhabi *Sister-in-law.* Sisters-in-law & brothers-in-law traditionally get along (whilst mothers-in-law & daughters-in-law do not) but this is not the case in my case (except for the instances of the late wife of Comrade Bakaullah and, recently, Devyani).

biryani *Saffron rice, typically with chicken or mutton and a potato or two*—a legacy of the Persian culinary sensibility of the Mughals, though flavoured rice is popular the world over: paella in Spain, risotto in Italy.

bowarchi *A cook, or chef,* though the idea of a chef is a foreign concept. Note: It can have derogatory connotations, as in, 'Do you want your son to grow up to be a bowarchi?'

burqa The Holy Book urges women to cover their adornments. Adornment can only mean bosoms because men are exempt from the injunction. In Arabia, however, they believe women ought to be locked up and not allowed to drive. Since this sensibility has permeated parts of the Subcontinent, women who hail from the urban middle class don *the ghostly, ghastly black shroud.* They are socialized to believe ears are adornments. But in the rural hinterlands of Scinde, and even in the Poonjab, you will find women with their bosoms hanging out, tilling the fields.

carom Carom might be described as *billiards without cues or balls.* The framed plywood board measures two arm's lengths and is oft powdered with boric acid to facilitate movement. The strikers are wooden disks that are flicked by the thumb and forefinger. I wrote a letter to the Olympic Committee in '83 to request the inclusion of the game but have not heard back yet.

Chalo, chalain, bachon *Let's go, kids,* a phrase that never fails to upset if not upend doting uncles.

channas *Chickpeas,* a ubiquitous street food on the roads of our city and many cities of the region, often served with tamarind chutney, fresh cut onions and peppers. I would have plate upon plate of the concoction as a child but now I refrain because everything is tainted.

chokri *Lass*. Yes, lass explains it.

chota chota *Small small*. Sometimes coupled idiomatically with mota mota (*fat fat*).

chukandar *Beta vulgaris*, or *beets*. Can be used to denote colour.

chutiya You could translate it as *asshole*—figuratively, it has the same resonance—but technically, it has to do with another orifice.

dehria Literally, a materialist, but in our sociocultural context, connotes *an atheist*. Whilst atheism is associated with sixteenth-century Europe, few acknowledge contributions of Musalman thinkers including Al-Razi, Al-Rawandi, Al-Ma'ari. Note: I've sometimes wondered, Are lazy atheists agnostics?

dhaba *Roadside eatery*, usually specializing in a particular dish. There's a place in Cantt that only serves up omelettes, for example, and Al-Kabab in Bahararbad only serves barbequed udders. There's nothing like some good barbequed udder.

fatiha *A short prayer recited for the dead*.

foon fan *Pomp, circumstance*, or, if you like, *hoopla*.

fut-a-fut *An alliterative phrase that connotes speed*. For example, I need to relieve myself fut-a-fut. When I need to go, I need to go.

ghazal If you have forgotten my exposition on the form, it is basically *a love poem*.

God's cow *An innocent*.

hakim In Our Swath of the World, there are three categories of medicine: hakimi, homeopathic and allopathic. A hakim is a *traditional, viz., herbal doctor*, who might prescribe the broth of a beard of corn for sundry kidney ailments, a curious, questionable, though generally benign, remedy. I am not certain that said broth works, but when I once fell and sprained my wrist, Barbarossa made me plunge my trembling hand in a broth of sheeshum leaves before bandaging it in honeyed dough. It worked wonders. Homeopathy, however, can kill you. It's a pseudoscience.

haleem *Thick lentil stew*, often prepared with chunks of beef, mutton or chicken, that is served during holy months.

haramzada *Son of a bastard.* Also see Shehzada.

Hor ki al eh Poonjabi for *What's up? What else, eh?*

Imambargah *A community centre and place of worship for the followers of Ali (RA).*

Irshad *Recite, please,* as in, 'I just recalled a verse of Wordsworth.' Irshad.

keekar *A ubiquitous, thorny, dark-barked variety of tree featuring yellow flowers,* first described in some Greek botanist's treatise circa 40 BCE. Everything seems to be attributed to the Greeks, from a pot-to-piss-in to phenomenology.

khatay peetay *Eating, drinking.* Although we all eat & drink (even insects and tree bark in some parts of the world), the term connotes class, wealth, prosperity. Somebody hailing from a khatay peetay household, for example, doesn't merely eat & drink but eats & drinks well.

kurta *A baggy shirt with buttons down the chest and slits on either side, that extends to the crotch, knee or ankle, depending on the wearer's sex, the season, or the dictates of fashion.*

Lava / Lau *s/o Lord Ram (PBUH).* Founded Lahore, a noteworthy achievement, but his brother got Kasur, which is something like Remus getting Siena. I like Siena. I have seen pictures. I would like to go before I pass.

loadshedding *Planned or unplanned power outage.* Although an infrastructural issue, it might be explained by One of the Fundamental Laws of Economics (and the only such law that one is cognizant of): When demand is greater than supply, things sour.

Lucknavi *A demonym of Lucknow,* a famed city in what has become the United Provinces but was once the state of Oudh. Lucknavis will maintain that the cultural apogee of their city is unique in the history of man. But neither the French nor the Poonjabis would agree.

lambu Slang for *a tall man.* Also, khamba.

lunghi *A wrap for men,* one of several that can be found across the Subcontinent—dhoti, lehcha, the most well-known being a sarong. Lunghis, unlike sarongs, are unstitched.

majnun *A mythological lovelorn lover*, the subject of a poem by the medieval Persian poet, Nizami.

mashallah *God bless you*, a banal exclamation—why should God bless you when you sneeze?—which might suggest that there is no causal relationship between intent and action, action and result, because only God is the Great Mover.

matric-pass Matric is class ten so matric-pass is short for *somebody who has passed matric*.

maulvi / mullah *Musalman clergy*. The maulvi or mullah has traditionally been ridiculed in Musalman lore because he is an oaf, but in the last century he has earned great currency.

Muharram More than thirteen hundred years ago, the Prophet's (PBUH) grandson, Husayn (RA), and his friends and family were slaughtered by the governor of Syria during this *lunar month*.

nanga-patanga *Naked, nude*. Note: a female nude would be nangi-patangi.

naswar *An awfully pungent chewing tobacco* that's stuffed between the gum & cheek, and periodically spat. Catherine de' Medici's son reportedly used it. In these parts, however, Renaissance Men avoid it.

nazarana *Monies bestowed upon a married couple*, a tradition at Pakistani & Italian weddings.

nazir *Court-appointed land appraiser*. Never met one, never want to meet one.

paan-wallah *Purveyor of paan*—a wonderfully refreshing digestif or narcotic wrapped in beetle leaf. Also see *radi-wallah* & *tun-tun-wallah*. Note: no entries for *ice-cream-wallah* as the import is obvious.

Pakola *Traditional Pakistani bottled ice cream soda*. Pakola doesn't need advertising but I like the jingle, 'Dil Bola, Pakola,' or 'the Heart Says, Pakola.' It sounds like one of Rumi's verses.

palla *A big yellow bony fish*. I don't eat enough fish.

pao *A unit of dry measure in the Subcontinent that was made obsolete by the colonial apparatus*. Although a pao is 233 grams in our neck of the woods, it's less in Nepal and considerably more in Kabul, which actually explains a lot of things.

paratha *Fried flatbread.* Good with sweet or savoury dishes. One was weaned on paratha and clotted cream, sprinkled with sugar.

PBUH An acronym that connotes the awkwardly phrased benediction, *Peace Be Upon Him.* I understand some Christian evangelicals employ the even stranger 'Angel Upon You,' or AUY. One wouldn't want angels swarming about oneself; one passes gas when one is upset.

qawwali *Musalman spiritual music* that is known because Bollywood keeps appropriating it. Traditionally a qawwal troupe features two primary singers on the harmonium, two backup singers, a percussionist and a couple of clappers. I've always wanted to be a clapper.

qeema *Minced meat, usually beef.* Although we throw in all sorts of vegetables—peas, beans, green peppers—I am wild about qeema with potatoes.

qiyas Arabic for *analogy*—a tricky tool employed by certain scholars to interpret the Holy Book.

RA A translated Arabic acronym, *a necessary honorific for saints* but I don't speak Arabic.

radi-wallah *Purveyor of radi, or junk material*: yesterday's newspapers, tin cans, cardboard, empty plastic bottles. Indeed, radi-wallahs provide a mobile recycling service.

razi-bazi I am no expert, but I believe the Poonjabi phrase might translate to *All good?*

sajjhi *Salted, barbequed meat,* a culinary specialty of Beeloochistan. In Curachee, there were a number of sajjhi joints in and around Hassan Square once upon a time, but Hassan Square is no more.

salam Literally, *peace*, but practically, *hello*. You reply walikum-us-salam.

salam dua 'Salam' translates to *peace*, 'dua' to *prayer*. In Yankee vernacular, I believe, 'salam dua' is *meet & greet*.

sarkar *Boss*, and could also connote The Boss—viz., God, not that crooner.

sayien *Sir, in the Scindee language.* Everybody's a dashed sayien.

seth *Baron, technically, or boss; sir.* Businesses run by seths are usually run into the ground.

shalwar All articles in the foreign press describe our national dress as *loose, baggy trousers*. They call it salwar for some reason across the border.

shehzada(y) *Son of a king, a prince.* Charles of Wales is a shehzada, and probably will remain one.

shikanjabeen *Traditional minty lemonade* seasoned with salt & white or black pepper. Can be mixed with vodka to fashion a local gimlet.

single-pasli Biblical lore suggests that Eve was carved out of Adam's pasli, or *rib*. I don't understand. Why not the femur? After all, it's the longest and strongest bone in the body.

soyem The rituals associated with our funerals are usually completed on *the third day after a death*.

Sunnah *The Way of the Prophet.* Some maintain that wearing trousers or shalwars above the ankle, for example, is Sunnah. During the Prophet's (PBUH) time, however, they wore no shalwars or trousers.

tauba-tauba I don't say it myself but it has *something to do with repentance*. It brings to mind the following verse: 'Come, fill the Cup in the Fire of Spring / The Winter Garment of Repentance Fling / The Bird of Time has but a little way / To fly—the Bird is on the Wing.'

tharra *Local moonshine.* Recipes vary from lower to upper Scinde to the Poonjab. In Hunza, they call their proprietary fruit liqueur Hunza Water because it is as plentiful as water.

toofan *Tempest.* Abdullah Shah Ghazi (RA) protects Currachee from storms, typhoons, tsunamis and other inclement weather.

tun-tun-wallah *Purveyor of sweets* (though technically speaking, 'tun-tun' dervies from tintinnabulation, or ringing of bells). Tony loved those faux cigarettes that came in miniature cigarette boxes but were actually peppermint sticks.

Urs *The death anniversary of a saint,* but might be best described as the Marriage of Man with his Maker.

zenana *An enclosure for women* characteristic of both Hindoo and Musalman households of a certain socioeconomic status in Our Swath of the World—the working class do not have such a luxury.

ACKNOWLEDGMENTS

FOR STARTERS, I SHOULD thank the good folks at Roadside, the IWP residency at the University of Iowa, and LUMS who have nurtured this project by furnishing me with time, space and money over the life of *The Selected Works of Abdullah the Cossack*.

I am also thankful to the old denizens of Garden who opened their doors and delved into the past to help me reify the present, particularly Parvez Iqbal Makhdumi, Zahid Alvi, Habib Fida Ali, Furrukh Iqbal. I have also had several dozen conversations with others about the city over the years from the sage Jamshed Cowasjee and storied Freddy Nazareth to the lovely Ishaq Balouch and legendary Arit Hassan. While they are too many to mention on this page, I am grateful to each.

I would also like to thank the readers of early drafts of the opus, masters of the craft one, masters of the craft all: Abdullah Hussain, Zulfikar Ghose and, always, Lee Siegel, ensconced too far away on a postcard beach in Hawaii.

I must mention those who have always lent me support, succour through this project and others: my parents, brothers, Doc Kazmi, Irfan Javed, Sadia Shephard, Heidi Ewing, Abbas Raza, Afshan Hussain, Maya Ismail, Marina Fareed and, of course, Shahrbano Iqbal.

I must especially thank John Freeman, an early supporter and force of nature, Ayesha Pande, for finding the opus a home with Grove, and Margaret Halton, one of the most thoughtful, patient, generous and dedicated agents around. Indeed, without Margaret, there might not have been no Abdullah, no nothing.

And lastly, and perhaps most importantly, I must thank Aliya, without whom, I would not have been incarnated as a novelist.